Grass Roof, Tin Roof

DAO STROM

Grass Roof, Tin Roof

A Mariner Original

Houghton Mifflin Company

Boston | New York

2003

For information about permission to reproduce selections
from this book, write to Permissions, Houghton Mifflin Company,
215 Park Avenue South, New York, New York 10003.

Visit our Web site: www.houghtonmifflinbooks.com.

Library of Congress Cataloging-in-Publication Data is available.

ISBN 0-618-14559-1

Book design by Melissa Lotfy

Printed in the United States of America

QUM 10 9 8 7 6 5 4 3 2 1

A portion of this novel was published previously, in slightly
different form, in *Still Wild* (edited by Larry McMurtry, 2000),
Watermark: Vietnamese Poetry and Prose (1998), *Vietnam
Forum* (1997), and *The Southern Anthology* (1996).

ACKNOWLEDGMENTS

The following is a work of fiction. The characters, events, and locations in this book are not meant in any way to represent any actual persons, events, and locations. Though I've used some historical circumstances and actual place names, the depictions of places, people, and events are entirely fictional. Still, this book would not have been possible without the influence of certain persons and places whose stories have touched me, and for whom I would like here to express deepest respect and gratitude: my aunt and cousins in Saigon; my aunts, uncles, and cousins in California; my birth father, Vũ Quốc Châu, and his family; too many Hangtown friends and mentors to name; my sister, Nina, my brother, Tony, and, most especially, my mother, Thai, and my father, Palle. My thanks also, of course, to Dave and Lincoln.

I am grateful to my mother also for her help with many, many research details, and to Ta Quang Khôi for his translation of the verse in "Passenger."

For their generous support and/or guidance along the way, I would like to acknowledge the Patricia Roberts Harris Fellowship in Fine Arts Program, the James Michener–Paul Engle Fellowship Program, the Texas League of Writers, the Money for Women/Barbara Deming Memorial Fund, the University of Iowa Writers' Workshop, James McPherson, Marilynne Robinson, Kyung Cho, and Heidi Pitlor.

Grass Roof, Tin Roof

1

FIRE HAZARDS

My mother collected newspapers. Mostly Vietnamese publications sent to her by old friends now living in San Jose or Los Angeles. She clipped articles and stowed them in binders and envelopes, supposedly to be organized into some form of record at some later date. My mother was apt to get lost in a task, so enamored was she by the possibilities — the wealth — of information, and so reluctant, too, to reach any end that might force her to admit unrequited ambitions. Who is to say if she would actually need to look again at any of these papers? Yet she could not throw them away. My father, who had also thrown away a past — his by choice, however — criticized my mother for refusing to let go of pain. He called her selfish.

"Your mother," our father would say, not unfacetiously, "your mother is a fire hazard."

And I would take this in. Certainly he meant her papers, but in my young mind it was she I saw going up in flames, up into black curling smoke. It was her hair I saw shriveling to ashes and rising, her flesh melting; it was her eyeglasses I saw exploding from the heat and then — as in the movies — only the frames that survived and landed, with a dramatic thunk, at the edge of a circle of ashes. It would be the end of a scene, the glasses in the foreground of a low-angle closeup shot in which smoke and a few glowing embers of orange were a blur in the background. My mother would be gone from me; I feared this constantly. She was vulnerable and a little afraid of the world and smaller than average. She sat on a pillow

when she drove and wore high heels everywhere, even at home.
Whenever she went alone to a movie or to run an errand, I prayed
for her safe return. I worried she might be kidnapped by a strange
man as she crossed a parking lot, and we would be left to live with
just our father.

It is true my mother almost burned to death once in her child-
hood. She was playing in the kitchen with her older brothers when
they turned on the stove and accidentally set her on fire. It was a
gas stove; the flames jumped, or my mother was standing too close.
If it had not been for an aunt passing unexpectedly by the house
that afternoon, that might have been the end of my mother, then
and there. But the aunt threw a blanket over her and saved her. My
mother was six years old. She later told me this story as a kind of
justification: it was the reason she never taught us how to cook. As
for my mother's collection of newspapers — these have since been
thrown away, too.

PAPIER

I

It was a grand story with many events and an inconclusive ending, and it left her with an ache in her brain and heart, a feeling
akin to wanting. Wanting tinged with amazement and understanding — the ending would always be inconclusive — and this
was why the story worked as well as it did; this was why it was so
affecting and rending and lingering. For many nights afterward,
she went to sleep wishing she could live this story and picturing
herself after the experience a wiser, sadder, nobler person. Or she
liked to imagine meeting a man who had lived through such
an experience, a humble, beaten man whose integrity only she
would recognize, and she would be his friend. She wouldn't ask
for more than that.

She had been introduced to the story by a man whom she
knew only by his first name, Gabriel. He was a French war correspondent living intermittently in her country and his own.

2

When she met him in 1969, she was twenty-four years old, unwed with one son, then a toddler, from a previous relationship, and she was taking French and English literature and language classes at Saigon University, where Gabriel often came to visit the teachers, many of whom worked on the side as interpreters. She had aspirations of being a writer or artist; she hadn't decided yet which kind. On her first date with Gabriel they saw an American movie about the life of Vincent Van Gogh, starring Kirk Douglas. The theater was mostly full of American GIs and foreign news correspondents and their Vietnamese dates or associates, English-speaking, local advocates of democracy — writers, teachers, print and broadcast news reporters and employees, students, businessmen, travel guides, and ambitious prostitutes. Tran did not align herself with this latter group, and trusted Gabriel did not either, though she knew it would look suspect, a local woman on the arm of a foreign man. Her foreign man, the Frenchman, however, was obviously not a soldier; for her sake, he wore his press jacket (she had insisted on this, wanting the distinction to be clear, but had told him it was because she liked him better in the jacket). His build was also too slight and reserved for a soldier, and he was older, with a long face and faintly smiling, thin lips. Tran thought Gabriel's deep-set eyes — with their yellowish hazel color, behind wire-framed glasses — held an intellectual, disenchanted cast.

The movie was maudlin and heroic, this in a time when such sentiment in the movies was still cathartic — though it is likely any movie featuring the likes of Kirk Douglas would have been cathartic at that time, at that outpost. Already a sense of hopelessness and consternation pervaded the streets, though people seemed to be laughing, selling, buying, venting opinions, and eating and drinking with all the usual fervor; it was this fervor, in fact, that seemed now volatile and dangerously indifferent. Tran felt watchful in public places. And though she would in all sensible mind claim not to admire any military, she looked with a naive respect, even a deferent longing, toward the American military men, for the very details of their dress and physicality (the size and stoutness of their bodies, the muted colors and fitted cut of their clothes, their sweat-rings that seemed evidence to her of their formidability rather than — as it seemed with the local militiamen, whose uniforms always sagged — their inability to cope) had in her mind aligned themselves with a concept of order.

Tran was wiping her eyes when the lights came up at the end of the film, and when Gabriel asked why, she replied in her cautious French, "I understand very well the melancholy of the life of an artist." She had actually meant to use the word *l'angoisse*, but when *la mélancholie* slipped out of her lips she realized this was more right: a more subdued, less violent — more poetic, even — portrayal of the pain she had meant. Suddenly the small theater trembled in a great ground-shudder and there was a muffled boom and the noise of commotion outside. Inside, people began to panic and run for the exits. Gabriel took hold of Tran by both shoulders, pushed her into a corner against the stage. She felt the rough efficiency of his body pressed suddenly, unsexually, against hers — she felt more conscious of this than of the rumbling walls, to which she had already surrendered her fate in the first instant. With intensity Gabriel was watching the crowd, craning his neck. His body blocked Tran's view and she found herself staring at the fine brown hairs of his chest, visible through the folds of fabric between his shirt buttons. She closed her eyes. Then the shaking stopped. They made their way toward an exit, and when they came out onto the street they saw the throng of people gathered in front of the bookstore and mail depot, its front now blown open and billowing black smoke. Three Vietnamese civilians writhed on the sidewalk in front of the mess, crying in pain; a few local policemen and Americans were running toward them. Gabriel directed Tran to wait at the back of the crowd. "I have to work," he said. Then he took his camera out of the small canvas satchel he wore slung over his shoulder. Tran watched his back (his shirt half untucked, the seat of his pants rumpled) pushing through the crowd.

Later, much later, they would define the bombing as fate — not necessarily to say that their relationship was doomed, but that this omen was representative of what was to come, or the nature of how things were to open between them.

The novel he had recommended to her was an American classic, *Gone With the Wind.* They read passages together ("If you want to learn English you must read this story," he'd said; "there is not much good about the English language except this story"). It was Gabriel's favorite American novel for a couple of reasons: one, he saw it as a great depiction of "the American insistence upon naivete"; and two, he liked those literary classics by authors who had never intended to be authors, who said all they needed to in one book alone. There was something more honest, more respectable, this way, he theorized, as if the book, the story itself, had forced its way out of the reluctant author, rather than the other method, where the story became tangled up in an author's ego. This author was a woman (which appealed to Tran) in the 1930s, and the novel had a good dose of everything: the rise and fall of vanities and societies, births and deaths, unrequited loves, illegitimate children, an irrepressible heroine, a scandalous hero. And at the center of it, a civil war between North and South, something relevant. Occasionally Tran and Gabriel would discuss the parallels between life and literature and politics and cultures, which spanned years and seas.

Tran did not always understand Gabriel's theories but was drawn in by his wry spirit, the nonchalance with which he delivered his well-informed and devastating perceptions about current politics, the same politics that only distressed Tran's Vietnamese colleagues and sometimes confused Tran; she could easily find merit in every point of view. In fact she somewhat admired Gabriel, his aloofness, his sense of comedy, which was almost cruel and thus took on another quality — acerbic, tragic, self-denying. How did one become like this, she wondered, so intellectual and so resigned yet *not* resigned, by sheer virtue of a commitment to that very attitude? The more time she spent with him, though, the more she began to see cracks in his mask. When they practiced reading in her language, his accent was slow and clumsy and almost embarrassingly earnest. The way he would point to objects on the street (phone booth, gutter pipe, spokes of a bicycle wheel) or a part of her body, and ask her the words that named these places, these appendages. His candor and his deep, eager, fumbling voice repeating after her at first surprised her; she saw a man who desired to be someone other than he was, whose knowledge and wit encumbered rather than enlightened him. She understood then the grace, the simplicity, he saw in her — and the lack of which he despised in himself. Thus did clumsiness and a hidden vulnerability become the characteristics she associated with *white*. His white body, covered in dark curling patches of hair, was long and awkward and remorseful when they made love. His white linen shirts, wrinkled and sweat-stained. His white skin that seemed so thin and unsuitable a cover, especially under the tropical sun, and made nudity look unnatural (she soon developed the impression that white people were meant always to be clothed, that it was their more natural state). Yet he was her vessel and gateway both, to a strange vision of power and regret, to so much of the outside world she didn't know how else she would ever reach. Though she did not think she loved him, at times she felt sympathy for him.

Then she began to experiment with trickery.

Things like: when once he pointed to the arch of her foot, she gave him the word for the palm of her hand, and told him the palm was the arch of the foot. How often would he need these words anyway, she would think, as she swapped other words and objects. Doing this caused her to realize how arbitrary and tenuous the association between an object and its linguistic representation could be, in some cases absurd, even. She did not know why she tricked him like this. It was a joke that paid off only much further down the line, to another audience, and she, the initiator, would never witness or know of its end. The only satisfaction she received was in knowing she was effectively deceiving someone. And these were not outrageous untruths, just pointlessly misdirected facts. Language, she saw, was a thing that relied on faith.

When Gabriel's assignment in Saigon ended in 1971, he returned to France; someone else had always been there waiting for him. Tran was not mournful and told him confidently that she wished him well and would not miss him, that theirs had been what it was for the time it was — an intimacy enabled yet limited by the temporal circumstances of war, a situation wherein people like him (more than her) could for a period disinhabit the more regulated life to which they must eventually return. Tran was not an impractical woman; back in 1966, when the man who was her son's father had denied any involvement with her, she had learned her first lesson about the potential disappointments of love. In short, she had learned not to count on reciprocation. He had been a slightly older man, an established schoolteacher in their community, and he had introduced her to much about philosophy and the creative life. For the first few months after discovering she was pregnant with his child she had pursued him, demanding either money or that he marry her, and he had laughed her off, claiming that her relationship with him was merely a schoolgirl fantasy. Where the live proof came from, he had said, he would leave to speculation. Tran had felt crushed, indignant, humiliated. She went to a fortuneteller who informed her she should not try to marry before the age of thirty, as all her lovers would either die or leave her. And a man from far off would come for her one day. "I tell this to many women, it is true, to keep their hearts awake, their hopes up, but to you I mean it," the fortuneteller had said. And for the first time in her life Tran had experienced the resolve of *knowing*. Yes, she would have the child, but she did not want or need the father. Her own father was shamed and her mother heartbroken when Tran announced her decision. But they could hardly deny the presence of new life when it arrived.

Tran would not know until many years later that in 1975, not long after she left for America, Gabriel had returned to Saigon looking for her, had gone knocking on doors of old friends asking after her. In the end she would never know for certain if the man from far off she finally reached was even the correct one.

◦ ◦ ◦

It is said love can move any mountain is how she began her version of the story, *and love comes to us when we are not looking, when we have turned our backs on its very possibility, have resigned ourselves to the longing. Yet when it comes, we know it from the first moment the would-be object of our affection appears. We know love by both the dread and excitement in our hearts, by the resistance our minds raise against what our hearts are straining toward; we know it by the fact that we cannot stop it once it starts to happen and suddenly the world is full of a sense of great and imminent change just ahead: the most minute detail overflows our senses now with the indescribable pleasures of hope.*

It was heavy-handed and sentimental and she recognized this, but it was the best she could do on a first try. She also believed that what came out first was rawest and truest, and should not be revised, to uphold its integrity. She had no diligence for backtracking. She was a young writer. Eager to expel her words.

Her story was commissioned to appear as a daily serial novel in one of the city's independent newspapers. A writer friend had secured the assignment for Tran, and it was to be her first citywide publication. A big step, for she had previously published only a few articles and short stories in reviews and smaller papers. "This editor, you have heard of him, he can help you," her writer friend assured her, "as he has helped many like us."

The man her friend spoke of was the paper's chief founder and editor, but because of his notoriety in politics, he and others had decided his affiliation would be best maintained as an unofficial relationship. Only his close colleagues knew his role. He filtered decisions through a young, posing editor in chief, and any actual writing he did he credited to other writers (some of whom existed, some of whom did not). His physical presence in the office was explained as visits to friends or consultations as a technical adviser. He shared a semiprivate office with the senior reporters, and entered and exited the same way most of the staff did, through a back-alley entrance. For the most part, he was not recognized and went about inconspicuously under his assumed name. He had assumed names at least five other times in the past fifteen years, and had still been jailed four times for what the ever shifting government had labeled "the creation and advocation of slander and/or immorality." He had been dubbed a "gadfly." But he took no side wholeheartedly when it came to the subject of the war — not the Communist, not the American, not the South Vietnamese — for he believed each to be a flawed system. Rather, he believed the true source of all troubles between humans ran someplace far deeper than politics.

It was under his latest name, Le Hoang Giang — a nom de plume alluding to the evanescent quality of autumn, translated literally from the Chinese as "yellow river" — that Tran met him.

He was thirty-four years old, an unassuming presence, slender, with kind eyes, a long, gentle face, and a warm smile. His hair was black, his skin very brown. A hint of knowing and humor lingered about the edges of all his expressions, as if he were continually assessing but withholding judgment. In a crowd, he was likely to retreat, to stand against a wall or leave without warning or good-bye.

"Tell me your idea," he said brusquely the first time she sat down before him. As she began to speak, he rested one hand on his cheek and fixed his lucid gaze upon her.

"I want to write a love story based on the American novel *Gone With the Wind* — you have probably heard of it," she told him, suddenly unnerved by his attention. "I want to set it in our country, but follow the same story line as the original. At least in essence I want to follow it."

He smiled as he leaned back in his chair and looked out the window. On the opposite side of the street below was a sidewalk café that was a popular hangout for the paper's writers and supporters; it occurred to Tran he could have been staring out the window minutes ago and seen her seated at a table down there, awaiting her appointment with him. It was raining, and the sound of water beating on the tin roofs was like nails in a metal can. Rain dripped in heavy streams from the eaves outside the open window.

"I read that book a long time ago," said Giang. "I found it moving. And so thorough. You must've been just as moved by it as I was."

It didn't seem necessary to respond, but out of respect Tran said, "Yes, Uncle." She felt she must address him formally, as her elder.

He looked at her again. "What will happen in your version of the story?"

She told him: instead of Atlanta at the crumbling of the Southern Confederacy, it would be the northern port town of Haiphong at the climax of French rule. The heroine would be from a rice farm in a small northern village, and her family devout French-influenced Catholics. The family would be forced to flee south at the advance of the Viet Minh, and the story would follow that passage, which would bring the heroine to Haiphong.

"But mostly I want it to be a love story," explained Tran. "The heroine is torn, you see, because she is in love with a childhood friend who has gone off to fight for the Viet Minh. Then there will be a second man, who is committed to neither the French nor the Viet Minh — he just wants his own personal freedom — and he falls in love with the heroine and pursues her though she tries to deny him. She herself is apolitical. She doesn't want to go any farther south simply because she is waiting for her childhood love to find her again. Maybe my story will reflect some contemporary issues. The heroine might find herself suddenly on opposing sides from the man she loves and once could trust, but mostly, to be honest, I'd like for my story to focus on the personal, emotional lives of its characters. When it comes to literature, that's what I'm truly interested in, you see."

"Yes," said Giang, seeming bemused, "life is never interesting unless one is in love with another who is in love with something or somebody else." He was looking at her now, but Tran felt as if he were speaking more to the space behind her than to her directly. "Where is your family from?"

"I was born in Van Dinh in the north and in 1954 we fled south. My family — my mother, most of all — is Catholic."

"And where does your desire to be a writer come from, then?"

"Ever since I was a child I have sought comfort in books, in stories," Tran said. "My family was poor and my father could not pay for me to get a proper education, yet I insisted. I read every book I could get my hands on, I begged my brothers — who did get to go to school — to share their lessons with me. I had many disagreements with my father until finally he allowed me to take a class here and there. Then I worked hard and paid my own way through university."

Giang gazed at her placidly. Then he nodded. "It is no new thing, you know," he said, "this story of men going off to war and women waiting in anguish for them to return. Every continent in the world knows this story."

Tran didn't speak, unsure if he meant to belittle her ideas.

He sat forward, laying his forearms on the desktop, his back slightly bowed as if he were about to stand. He turned his face toward the window for a moment. She could hear the hum of activity on the floor below, voices and typewriters and drawers slamming and laughter and footsteps. Finally Giang spoke: "I want you to write whatever you wish, and I will see that it gets published. Do you know, little sister, that is all I want to do myself? I am starting to think the only reprieve we will ever get from this war is when we are able to create — and it won't lie in our hands, but in our minds alone." He smiled sadly. "Every day I am more tired. Last night we were up very late, working. As usual." He laid his hands flat upon the desk. She noticed they were large, his fingers long and tapered.

"Thank you, Uncle," she said finally, understanding it was time for her to go.

Giang would tell her months later (when all formality between them had truly dissolved) that he'd witnessed his fate in life sealed one morning in 1955 in Hanoi. He had been eighteen years old.

He'd written his first political essay criticizing the disunity of their nation (though he'd been cautious and also frankly undecided enough to cast no direct blame on either North or South government), and it had found its way into the dissident literary

11

and intellectual scene that was forming at that time in the North. The essay was not a spectacular piece of writing; it was naive and spirited but had at its heart a certain lament — a sincere sadness over what was being lost at the partition of their population. An elderly established writer Giang respected called and wanted to meet him; Giang agreed to travel from Pleiku, where he had been studying, to Hanoi to meet the writer that weekend at the south end of Hoan Kiem Lake. But Cuong Phong (the name Giang wrote under at that time; not as subtly poetic in meaning, it translated awkwardly as "strong wind") never made it to the café: a flu inexplicably gripped him the night before and he stayed in his hotel room, sweating with fever. He neglected even to send a message. On his way out of the hotel the next morning, he learned that several bistros near the lake had been bombed the previous evening, and the man whom Cuong Phong was to meet with had been killed.

The then–Cuong Phong walked out of the hotel and up the street seeing everything with intensified exactness. So that he stared, and the world of hearing left him. The unfamiliar city's gray streets and rusting metal gates and thin, dull silver-and-black bicycle tires and brown wood sidings and brown faces struck him; even the gray stripe of sky between two houses seemed solid and throbbing. He kept his head down as he walked but felt the heat and the stirred air around each body he passed. He crossed a street and stepped onto an ornate footbridge spanning a portion of the lake. From the north end of the lake, he could see the south end — the row of storefronts, the new cavernous holes in two of them, the surrounding storefronts with their awnings and curved balustrades intact. He turned his eyes toward the water and rested his arms on the rail of the bridge. For several minutes he stared at the dark surface of the water. He did not notice the elderly woman who had stopped beside him, put her hand on the rail, and leaned forward to peer into his face. She was asking if he was ill.

"No, no," he said, trying to shake himself out of his fog. "I'm fine. Please let me be."

The woman glared at him and said nothing for a moment.

Then she declared, "That is what is wrong with you young people these days. You are all trying to do everything on your own. You forget you were born tied to your mothers."

He didn't know how to respond. He frowned, confused.

"Where has respect gone these days?" continued the woman, her voice rising. "You young people are all ill."

He put his head in his hands. "*Ba*," he said, using the proper address for a young man speaking to an elderly woman, "I am sorry. Forgive me." He repeated this several times, deeply frustrated, as the old woman continued to regard him with her stoical expression. Finally, though he knew it was the rudest gesture he could make, he turned his back and walked away without excusing himself.

And years later, the moment still resounded in Giang's mind. He heard himself repeating those words and felt how they continued to fall short, words so impotent, he told Tran, "and me repeating them again and again with an excruciating yearning." They were lying together in a borrowed bed in some other colleague's apartment (arrangements like this were necessary, as Giang was married and they were hesitant to go to Tran's apartment for fear her neighbors would talk), as he told her his story. "You ask, so I tell you. *That* is why I write," he said, "because I've not forgotten the feeling of being on the bridge that morning with the old lady. I've still found no satisfaction with it. None."

Phuong-Li did not care for politics. To her it was a futile way to expend one's energies, and she did not understand the tension it stirred among people, the long heavy silences and sharp looks and charged nonchalance that passed now among her peers who held varying views. Phuong-Li merely wanted to play with old friends as they had when they were children, chasing each other about in the rice fields or laughing at something simple like the nickname Snake she had given one boy because he could not pronounce his words correctly and he spit when he talked fast.

"Why do you call me that?" the boy asked her once.

"That is my secret," Phuong-Li teased him, and her other friends giggled.

The boy, because he was fond of her, was flattered by her attention, no matter what the reason, so he answered to the name Snake.

Phuong-Li liked to recall these small, clever childhood games; they gave her a sense of importance, of secret control. Years later she saw the boy she had called Snake. He was now nineteen years old and had been away at school. What kind of school she did not know exactly, for she'd never asked. School was school, that vague process a few children, usually boys, went through. And when they returned, people bowed with deeper respect to these sons, and mothers blushed with adulation if it was their own sons returning in such style, for to parents, schooling meant potential wealth. To Phuong-Li, it meant very little.

He came to her family's house with another neighborhood friend, and when Phuong-Li's little brothers opened the door, the friend asked for her. Snake hung back, his hands in his pockets, and looked at his feet. When Phuong-Li came to the door, he waited to see if she would recognize him before he spoke. She did, and jumped forward to embrace him. Time and what she considered to be maturity had made her magnanimous toward all past acquaintances, close or not. He raised his face and smiled, showing warmth and something else, a certain light at seeing her again. It was in her eyes as well, though she did not realize it.

"You've grown up to be so pretty," he exclaimed.

"And you've learned how to speak properly!" she teased him.

"I've learned many things" was his demure response. "Yes, I've learned lots of awful and good things." The stiltedness in his tone almost bothered her, but she dismissed it as some new style of speech; she was too caught up noticing how good he looked after these years away, the way he now held himself, the confident tilt of his head, the lazy sureness in his smile and in his calm, smart eyes.

Later, he smoked cigarettes with her older brothers while discussing politics and life in the city. She did not listen to their words, did not recognize that they were secretly probing one another with statements meant to provoke responses that would reveal their true allegiances. She did notice a tension in the air, although it only made her lament to herself: Why could they not all get along like

old friends, like they used to, instead of indulging in all this tire-
some talk? She admired the way Snake spoke, though, his easy
mannerisms, the fierceness that lay beneath his composed veneer,
showing itself only in small movements — the quick, forceful lift of
his chin at a sound in the kitchen, the brusqueness with which he
struck his matches. She thought he must be saying important, intel-
ligent things, even if she did not understand them.

No, she cared nothing for politics. After that day, all she cared
about was love.

In the spring of 1972, Tran was in her seventh week of writing
daily installments. She woke early in the morning and brewed
herself a cup of coffee in the apartment where she now lived with
her six-year-old son. They lived alone, the two of them, because
Tran had felt her sisters and religious mother could not understand the life of a writer, especially when it was a woman who
sought such a life.

Tran stood over the small stove in the far corner of the first-
floor room, gazing each morning at the wall as she fried an egg
for her son, her thoughts drifting to another world, of horses
and hoop dresses and colored silks, of idle, well-educated, well-
mannered women, servants announcing visitors in doorways of
parlors. Tall, handsome, white-skinned men in waistcoats. They
bowed and kissed the ladies' hands. And from this place her
thoughts would then drift into the world of Vietnam. But she
was unable to conjure any images of a parallel world here, only a
vague sense of longing. The world of Vietnam was too visceral
and incongruent next to the polished drama of the America in
her mind. Even her imagined version of Vietnam — the bustling
port town of Haiphong in 1954, the setting of her story — was
humid and overcrowded and raw. (It resembled present-day Saigon, the only experience of a city from which she had to draw.)
There were no equivalents here to the panoramic views of rolling
green hills outside windows of estate houses, as existed in that
other land. Even the war here was not so noble and deeply felt a
calamity as it seemed to be there. Here the war was bogged down
by the clearly unromantic facts of industry and contradicting

chains of command, and it often stretched on for months without incident. And when an incident did occur it was always outside the city limits, far enough away to seem almost — though not entirely — irrelevant. As for the views outside Tran's windows, they were of the stucco walls of neighboring buildings. The inner walls of her own apartment (which she would stare at for hours each morning as she typed) were pale blue and cracked. The only decorative architectural elements were the concrete blocks with rough-edged patterns of ellipses and curved diamonds cut into them, which fitted into the windows as screens. When the sunlight came through, it cast these patterns in shadow on the concrete floor.

Tran slid the egg she had cooked into a bowl and set it before her son, Thien. While Thien ate, she combed his hair. Sometimes she would tell him a tidbit of what she was working on in her head. "Maybe today is the day Phuong-Li will encounter her old Uncle Minh in the market," she would say. (Writing a serial novel was as much an adventure as reading one, she had found. She turned in her installments daily or weekly without much revision or forethought, and the pieces were published immediately, taken out of her hands, cemented in ink that quickly. It made plot seem to her a live, unpredictable factor she was stumbling blindly after, trying to keep up with it.)

Thien would respond appropriately, because he had been following along; all the names of persons his mother spoke of he accepted in the same way, whether they were fictional or real. "Will Uncle Minh punish her for how she ran away last week?"

"But she knows Uncle Minh's secret, that he married his wife for her money, because she has met Uncle Minh's other daughter, remember? The one no one is supposed to know about."

"Uncle Minh is a bad man," Thien might say, and often Tran was proud of his astute judgments.

After breakfast each morning she walked her son to the end of the alley where it met an avenue. There he joined several other boys, and Tran watched as they raced across the avenue and through the gates to their school. Then she walked — smiling but not speaking to anyone she passed — back to the apartment. And once inside, she would sit down to write.

II

They came to her apartment in the middle of the night and woke her. With Giang were two men, young reporters she had seen around the newspaper office. One waited, smoking, behind the wheel of Giang's car while the other stood outside her door. Giang waited halfway down the alley, pacing in the predawn light.

"He says you must come with us. He's heard a rumor. It's important we investigate this," said the man at her door.

Tran did not hesitate to wake her son and take him over to the woman next door. Tran had been asked before to accompany reporters on their outings — they knew she would be interested in the outings as research, or sometimes they just wanted an extra eye along — but this was the first time Giang (whom she knew by reputation to be one of the more esteemed senior reporters) had singled her out. The woman next door, herself a mother of five and familiar with Tran's erratic schedule, welcomed Thien.

Tran fumbled for her camera and notebooks and left with the men.

The road out of the city was narrow and bumpy. As it was still the dry season, dust rose in their wake. Once, they stopped and the two younger men got out of the car to urinate by the side of the road, their cigarettes still poking from their lips, while Giang and Tran waited. The unwoken world outside the car's dirty windows was cool and blue and silent, and this made Tran aware of the silence between her and Giang. But she did not think much of it. She told herself he was just treating her as one of the men and there was no need between men to fill silences. Secretly she felt flattered; she felt her inclusion in this excursion to be significant. Proof that her insights or opinions had been heard by him and others, and noted. Especially in this time when men disregarded women's minds. She had done all she could not to appear a typical woman: she wore her hair short and spoke casually about sex, passionately about existentialism. She wanted to show them her mind was sharp. She could handle as much as they could.

The men got back in the car and they resumed driving. The city disappeared behind them into a crooked, cramped, hazy line on the horizon. Clumps of listing, bamboo-roofed shacks appeared at intervals alongside the road. The men were talking about the latest Communist incursions into the northern and central parts of the countryside. Now they were making inroads in the far south — where they were headed — as well. The government controlled barely more than Saigon, and that only through an excessive amount of corruption.

"But I must believe in peace," said one of the young men, "because I have just squandered two hundred U.S. dollars on stock options for the new Vietnam Coca-Cola!" He laughed.

The other reporter slapped Giang on the shoulder. "Where are we going, huh? I hope there's a bigger story this time than the last time you woke us up at this hour," he remarked cheerfully. To Tran he said, "Last time we waited for six hours in the cold behind the garbage bins in back of the house of the supposed mistress of General Lo Minh, to catch him accepting a bribe, but all we caught were four cats and a dozen hungry rats."

Giang shook his head, smiling slightly, but didn't reply, and the men didn't seem to expect him to.

Tran looked out the window. The spaces between shacks widened, the sky brightened. They drove past swamps and groves of tall, reedy trees and a few early travelers on the road toting straw baskets of rice or produce or prodding along their pigs and cows. The reporters arrived near the village of Ha-Kan just after dawn, where they stopped at the edge of a rice field. Giang cut the car's engine and they listened to the rustling of the rice stalks, the twittering of birds, the whirring of crickets.

"This hamlet was raided last night by the VC. Some of the village children fled to the jungle, where they happened upon a sight certain members of the South Vietnamese army wanted to protect, so they chased the children out of the jungle and shot them where they were hiding in a herd of water buffalo. The children will probably end up tallied among the VC dead, my source tells me. But I want to record some evidence of the truth before then. Do you have your cameras ready?" Giang turned to the young reporters.

They went on foot by a path through the trees, across a narrow arm of the river. The sky's faint colors changed and deepened above them like the images in a photograph developing, slowly. The fog uncurled from where it lay, low, around their knees; it seemed sentient, damaged, angry even, as if it did not want them to walk through. Then something solid came into the morning. They began to see purple water buffalo carcasses on the road, matching the pale purple swath of sky still lingering above the wet fields like a bruise.

Once there, the four walked among the bloated purple-black bellies that were like mounds of dark earth, Tran and the two reporters wondering why they had been brought to look at dead animals and daring not to express disappointment for fear of appearing callous to the cause. Brown-black blood ran out of each wide nostril. The animals' coats were mangy and smelled faintly like iron. Tran knelt to look more closely at a hoof. The last time she had stood this close to a water buffalo was as a child — when her family still lived in the far northern countryside where the air was so crisp it woke your skin in the morning. Tran found herself looking at the buffalo now with affection. Yet she knew it was not the death of animals they were here to mourn.

When she glanced up, Giang was watching her (his mouth slightly open, he seemed to be searching for something), and in that fleeting look she recognized something, if for only a flash. The depth with which he was watching her watch the dead buffalo — it was as if their faint understanding of whatever this incident might mean was profoundly the same. She saw it surprised him, but it did not surprise her. She knew then that some form of a romance would occur between them.

However: Love was not roses or white towers or any such nonsense. Rather, it was a call from some darker well of the heart possessing no regard for the rules of life, for the ideals of human sacra-

ments, even. What love required of its participants would occur heedless of violence and happiness alike (she would write this into her story somehow later).

Breaking the spell, Giang said, with what seemed like a levity both concentrated and painful, "It must be the season for children to turn into buffalo."

What they found was a house.

They came upon it after an hour of wading through marshy fields and swooping vines. Hidden in the jungle as it was, it rose out of the foliage like a lost palace, and they felt as if they had discovered something — a sense of mission. They crept stealthily around its perimeter. They took pictures of its mishmash of new and ancient styles of architecture; the bluntly geometric shapes of its walls and windows; its few jutting towers or chimneys (they couldn't tell which); its ornate portico; its red door, vivid and oversize; the guardian-dragon screens on either side; the gleaming tile floors they spied through its diamond-shaped windows; the courtyard with its marble benches and white stone fountain in the center; the textured clay shingles of its roof. They made out the house's breadth and height. They trekked back through the jungle and photographed the house from a distance as it had first appeared to them, from a low, wide angle, for dramatic effect. They took notes fervently. It was an incongruity in this jungle, making the jungle itself seem suddenly an alien landscape to them. They shook their heads and communicated to each other that they were reviled. They were seething, full of a sense of themselves as justly embittered beings. When they spotted the guards (armed men not in recognizable uniform), the four lay low in the foliage and felt it encompass them. With satisfaction they let the vines scratch their skin, the mud soak their feet. And in their minds they equated comfort with corruption, with power, with envy.

That evening, she followed him at a distance as he walked into the city's quarter of poorhouses, a place she had never been before and knew no virtuous woman should go, and soon her curiosity turned to ire. "What kind of man is he? For what unspeakable intention can he be skulking about among such dwellings?" Her thoughts churned viciously. "Who is she? What does she have that I don't have?" He was leading her down an alley with foul-smelling gutters. She lifted her skirts, remembering herself in front of the mirror that very morning, turning this way and that, trying on dress after dress in anticipation of seeing him and thinking desperately, "It will not do, it will not do."

Now she thought, "This is what I have dressed for."

She followed him into a narrow alley behind a row of houses, and when he stopped at a door, she hid, flattening herself against the cool stone wall. He rapped three times on the door, paused, then rapped three times more in a deliberate rhythm.

The door opened, a shaft of yellow light fell on his face — he was so handsome still! — and he stepped inside, and the door closed. She did not see the face of the person who had admitted him.

How long would she wait? And for what, should she find out? Would the truth about him only disgust her and force her to see plainly that he inhabited worlds in which she had no place? She wished that she were older, her life less sheltered — she wished she'd known more hardship. Maybe then she would have acquired some of that roughness, that bitterness, that would have made her a woman for whom he would risk shame. Anything, she thought, anything but to be the one spying and desperate and lonely — oh so! — in the shadows of real life.

And there was a fire (later she thought of it often): the village was ablaze when they came out of the jungle. Like ghost-witnesses, the four had slunk through the tall grass. Men, women, and children were running, scattering into the trees and nearby rice fields, their black peasant rags and conical straw hats flapping. Grass roofs shriveled. (Later the military-issued report would claim that the villagers were spies and that the village had housed propaganda, tools, and provisions for the guerrilla enemy forces.) In the grass, Giang touched Tran's arm and nodded toward the fire and said without pretense, "Take heed. No love story is complete without one."

They drove back to the city with their notes and film, and once home set about writing what they believed to be the truth about the secret house in the jungle and the general who they believed had pilfered government funds in order to build it. During a discussion in Giang's office, Tran tried to interject some of her own ideas, but in their eagerness the reporters talked over her. After making a few attempts she retreated, consoling herself in her head: You don't even care about politics. You're a fiction writer. You're writing a love story, more valuable in its own way.

Once, Giang gave her a small, patient smile; he had caught her eyes wandering. She was no longer confident about why she'd been invited to come along on the investigation in the first place.

The next day the story ran. When Tran arrived at the newspaper offices in the afternoon as usual to turn in her daily installment, which she had spent the morning writing, she was surprised at being greeted with nods and cheers from other staff members. She — it appeared — had written the story, with the field help of the two young reporters; there was no mention of Giang. Photographs of the extravagant structure in the jungle and the raided, burning hamlet nearby ran next to an exposé on the accused general's career and crimes. Beneath his photograph ran a long list of names — other government and military officials and their illegal activities. Bewildered, Tran read the story and stared at her name in print above it. When she asked, no one knew where the two young reporters were.

"In and out as usual, those boys," said one clerk.

"I underestimated you," said another, coming forward to shake her hand.

This was how it began. In the following months, Tran's popularity grew — her notoriety, in fact — as more articles were printed under her name. Articles of a slyly observant, condemnatory, apolitical bent — never siding with any of the official parties, only pointing out their contradictions. Colleagues said about

Tran's pen name (which she had chosen rather naively at the beginning of her work for the paper, as she'd noticed most writers used pen names) that now it made sense. "Trung Trinh, master of the woman's style of attack," they said, joking that they'd previously not understood why a romance fiction writer would choose a pen name that made reference to the Trung sisters — Vietnam's legendary women-warriors who had risen up in rebellion against their Chinese overlords in the first century A.D.

Tran was surprised to find that even when she said little or nothing, her character was meritoriously assessed: people took her silence as knowing. They deferred to her in discussion, even when she made only vague comments. Giang had explained she need only nod and say she was "still thinking about it" if anyone asked a question she couldn't answer; in private, he briefed her on the subjects of the articles. Gradually, she felt her confidence grow, her own writing develop irony. She learned how to absorb necessary information quickly; she appropriated gumption. Though she saw herself becoming somewhat a pawn in this game of his, she also couldn't deny her new freedom. Her wit was sharper, as she now knew the inner workings of the paper. Sentiments, false hopes, the old *yens* of her former romanticism, could no longer sway her. And though she knew her new skepticism threatened to desensitize her to the actual issues about which they were writing, she could not fathom going back. Her previous position seemed now unconnected and vulnerable and embarrassingly innocent.

They worked late many nights. They worked with their heads bent over documents or photographs, and Tran slowly became more knowledgeable about — and even on occasion contributed to — these stories attributed to her. Giang made it clear she was doing him a favor — he was grateful, solicitous, charismatic. They were great friends, he would say, each helping the other by doing the very thing each wished to do most, and was this not the philosophy of self-fulfillment unfolding as ideally as it should? Was this not Equality, that beautiful, modern, Western thought? He wrote his stories, she wrote hers. The romantic nature of her fiction protected him — the censors were slow to examine political articles written by a woman romance writer. And yet the people knew.

(The reason he had chosen her was simple: he had to choose someone he wouldn't mind divulging his secrets to, and it was always, he said later, better to choose a person he thought might be a potential lover.)

It began in the midst of those late nights, the pressure, the exhilaration of secrecy shared, emotions fueled not only by personal but also worldly concerns. She knew he already had a wife and children, but she didn't worry about this or feel guilty. She didn't hope he would leave his family, either. According to Tran's own Buddhist-Existentialist-derived concept of Truthful Living, it was the circumstances in which one lost all sense of time and consequence and reason that revealed when one was living one's true destiny. And so she reveled in the immediacy of their suspended moments, in which she thought neither of futures or pasts, nor of fantasies or realities. She became *shell, cavern, empty well:* she became replete. A sensation of sheer life, of Meaningful Living (how else could she put it?) loomed over her like a great umbrella. As a lover he was gentle, compassionate, and warm, appropriately woeful at the could-have-beens of their situation.

She liked the way men looked at her during this time: with energy, with challenges, with a curiosity that was intellectual and spirited — and liked how they would joke with her and tell her frank things about other women she knew they'd never shared with a woman. They trusted, even feared her; for here was one woman who couldn't be and didn't need to be fooled or wooed. Concerning love, she told herself she was practicing the Buddhist paradox of "living simultaneously": immersion and non-attachment together.

She kept busy. She was tenacious and vigilant at her work. During this period her writing sprang from her without her prescience: her fiction became more violent — sometimes this surprised her — as the calamities of war caused her characters to act out undue passions.

■ ■ ■

"School is more important than God." One morning Tran found herself saying this to her son.

Thien had been contesting her and asking questions she couldn't answer with tact. Questions concerning the rituals they did or did not perform, as Catholics, that might put them out of favor with God. It was his grandmother's — Tran's mother's — influence; Thien had been spending his afternoons at his grandmother's house while Tran was at the newspaper office. That morning, Thien wanted to practice his penmanship by copying out prayers, instead of doing his French vocabulary homework. Tran was at the stove fixing his breakfast.

"You won't do well in school just because you believe in God, God is not your teacher." This was the best way Tran could think of to emphasize the importance of keeping education and religion separate — in her mind, the former was crucial while the latter was optional. "You need to do well in school if you don't want to end up like the kids on the street or in the countryside who can't even spell their own names!" Thien bowed his head, and Tran asked him a question in French: "*Ou est le gâteau?*" She meant "cake," but he heard "boat."

"*Le bateau est à l'ocean,*" replied Thien, glumly.

She tried to smile, teasing. "*Et est-ce que tu aimes manger le bateau?*"

He looked at her and frowned. Then he walked to the corner of the kitchen and sat on the floor, pulling his knees into his chest and burying his face in his arms. He yelled, "*J'ai pas faim!*"

She set his breakfast on the floor before him. "Let it get cold, then," she snapped in Vietnamese.

Tran had scheduled her son's days to be full; she wanted him to become cultured. This meant art lessons, music, English, French, literature, drama — even soccer (it was the European sport of choice, as Tran understood). How could she explain to Thien that it was in *these* activities that he would find salvation, not in his grandmother's sad, persistent prayers? She saw her mother as a victim of submission; her husband, Tran's father, was a philanderer (as so many Vietnamese men were), while God constantly required her to be on her knees. She had spoiled her sons, too, and two were now dead from drink and war; the richest one was a gambler and ruthlessly selfish; and the other two were lost to her, having "died" into lives of vice. *Saigon has become like Babylon,* she lamented. Now the old woman lived an ascetic existence of cooking, cleaning, and performing other duties with her unmarried daughters and their illegitimate children (Tran was the only one who'd acquired the means or drive to move out on her own). A houseful of unweddable women and a wayward husband. Neighbors looked on them with pity. Tran had grown up terrified of becoming like her mother or older sisters. She saved her allowances for months just to buy a book; she lied about running errands in the marketplace in order to attend forums on French literature.

"You're only a half-woman, that's what I hear people say," said her son, after he had begrudgingly begun to eat the food on his plate.

Tran was at her desk, sipping her coffee. "Who says this?"

"The other ladies, when they come to Grandma's house. Because you're never with me, and you don't know how to cook or clean properly. They say you walk like a rooster and smoke cigarettes and drink beer like the men, and that's why no man wants to marry you. What man wants to marry a woman who's like a man?"

"I walk like a rooster?" Tran was appalled and amused by this, thinking Thien must be misrepeating what he had heard.

"Yes, a rooster," said Thien emphatically. Then he stood and demonstrated, with his hands on his hips and his elbows sticking out. From what Tran could gather, it had to do with her chest — the women were claiming she pushed it forward when she walked — and the bold uncouthness of her high-heeled boots that made her gait stiff and unfeminine and her footsteps loud, as if she meant to always announce her presence well ahead of her arrival.

"They are just jealous," said Tran. She felt miffed but slightly triumphant, too.

That afternoon she took Thien to his grandmother's house. She was thinking she would hire a maid soon, to lessen his visits to his grandmother. Tran and her mother did not converse in either a friendly or a strained manner; they nodded and gave each other perfunctory information. Tran's mother brought a plastic bag out of the bedroom and immediately set items on the floor around Thien. Wooden cars, a toy helicopter, green plastic soldiers, some items that were not toys but appeared still to hold interest for him — an empty tin can with a colorful label, an assortment of mismatched chopsticks. As she was leaving, Tran saw her mother moving toward Thien with a plate of rice cakes.

Her colleagues greeted her jovially as she entered the office. Shaking that morning's issue, one reporter (whom Tran sensed fancied her) exclaimed, "And how does the beautiful, mysterious Trung Trinh find time to be both subversive and romantic? What a remarkable woman!"

"Ah, but does it not take one to have the other? Does each simply not lead to the other?" teased another colleague. He was the same age as Tran, a photojournalist who kept mostly to himself and exhibited a carefree nature no matter the severity of his subject matter.

"Quan the philosopher," said the first reporter, not without admiration.

"Quan the skeptic," said Tran coyly; then reticently, coolly, removed her jacket and seated herself at her typewriter. She had her own desk now and composed her daily installments in the office, often finishing minutes before the deadline.

Quan nodded and smiled. He shouldered his camera bag and walked away.

"So," shouted a woman from a desk nearby. "What are the lovers up to today, Miss Tran?"

Tran glanced across the large room toward the stairs leading to the upstairs office where Giang worked. "Today I think I will put them on a boat," she said grimly, "with a cake."

The boy was four now, and sometimes she saw too much of his father in him. She had only married the man because it had been expected of her, as it had been expected of her true beloved to marry his arranged bride. The general's daughter. Now they worked side

27

by side, caring equally for each other's sons. All the men were gone. What did it matter anymore, the old rivalries among women? They all had love at stake now. Talk of fleeing was circulating in whispers in wash circles. The general's daughter was secretly packing, weeping as she sorted memorabilia and made wrenching, frivolous decisions over items of sentimental value. Passions passed, Phuong-Li had learned, but true love was lasting. It did not need reciprocation, it did not require consummation, it knew nothing of time. It knew nothing of safety.

Today was the boy's birthday, and she would take him down to the water to watch the fishing boats. The boy loved boats. He was always asking her to "watch, watch" as he did one trick or another. Phuong-Li was not particularly patient with children and tired quickly of his enthusiasm. She sat in the sand and touched her ribs. It had been four years ago — oh, how she had hated being pregnant! She remembered. Too well. She drew circles in the sand. No, it could not be happening again, not so soon, could it? Out on the water fishermen's nets arched through the air and landed, imprinting their grids on the shifting surfaces of the waves and catching sunlight in tiny squares of silver — fleeting seconds at a time — before sinking down into the warm darkness below.

"We're great friends, are we not?" said Giang that night. "I feel I can tell you anything." They were working late as usual, drinking coffee and wine. Outside it was raining in thick, dank curtains of water. From a window across the way came the voice of a singer, wafting unharmonically against the drum of the rain in a pitiful, extended wail. This singer, whoever she was, was always singing melancholy songs late at night.

"Sometimes I feel I live in a vaccuum, so isolated from the rest of society even when I'm in the midst of everything," said Giang, "but I also feel this is the truest existence one can live. It is something about the forlornness, the *sharpness* of the forlornness — do you know what I mean?" He was sucking on his cigarette, one eye squinted, one hand poised above the typewriter keys. "I feel as if there is something happening, something vital. I think you must feel it, too. There are no accidents, you know. Though it may seem many things are against us in our work, in our personal situation, too. Still, I know I am *right* with the world. I'm doing what I can, what I should." Then he shook his head and smiled gently, in a self-effacing way. "Look at me. I will type myself into oblivion."

She was sitting cross-legged on a chair on the other side of the desk, facing him. "Do you think we are losing our war?" she asked.

"It's inevitable," he said, holding her gaze.

A team of government police barraged the office the following morning. Rumors had been circulating of such police action against other newspapers. Semantics of certain ordinances were being interpreted now in stricter fashion and enforced, in order to tighten censorship rules. The police stopped at Tran's desk and ordered her to come with them. She protested, demanding to know why, and the men stood in indignation around her — the reporter who fancied her tried to lie that he was in fact Trung Trinh, a man writing under a female alias; Quan the photojournalist yelled uncharacteristic (for him) curses; other reporters said, "Take us instead. Are you so cowardly you must pick on our women staff members alone?" Only Giang kept his face down, melted into the background, left by the back door.

The police held her for interrogation. As they laid before her all the pages of the past episodes of her serial novel, they asked her to explain details of fashion and etiquette and dialogue between characters; they demanded to know what subversive messages each of these items encoded. She denied having encoded anything, but they insisted again that she "explain the codes." In the end, they pushed her to her knees and lashed her hands with a bamboo cane, a symbolic gesture, they assured her, not meant to cripple literally (they knew it was more important to break spirit than body). Maybe next time she lifted her pen she would hesitate.

Tran sobbed into her welted hands. The baby inside her kicked.

▪ ▪ ▪

Later that night, she did not consider where the smoke would go, or that it would have to rise. Her son was coughing when he crawled down the ladder of their sleeping loft and peeked in at her on her knees before the small metal pail in the middle of her papers on the floor. She had been burning the original manuscript pages of all her serial episodes, although she knew this, in fact, erased nothing.

"Mama? What are you doing?"

"It is only me," said Tran, glancing up at the blur of her son through her heat-fogged eyeglasses.

Tran found a maid in the week following the police interrogation. She did not want to rely anymore on her mother, did not want to face her patient but scrutinizing eyes on those nights (which seemed now to be increasing) she stumbled in at past midnight to retrieve her sleeping son.

The maid was a charming girl, but simple. She loved children. She had come to the city from a southern coastal hamlet because her family needed the money. In truth the city terrified her — she said it was the ugliest, most exciting place she'd ever seen — and she was baffled by the impatient city folk and the women who ruined their God-given female beauty with strange, modern styles that cut and squared and blocked energy rather than letting it flow in the natural way. She declared to Tran with sincere concern: "Mrs. Trinh, you should never wear your hair like that. Hair is much more beautiful if you *don't* cut it!" Tran was amused by the girl's perceptions, her naivete and lack of intellectual preoccupations. She was sure her son would be cared for wholeheartedly.

The maid's name was Muoi Bon — "Number Fourteen." This had been her place in the birth order of fifteen, only eight of whom were still alive. This kind of naming was standard in the countryside, where parents often didn't count on all their children surviving; it was testament, too, to the parents' humility — they expected nothing different for their children or themselves. (Tran had to credit the maid's parents for including even the dead children in their numbering system — she had thought most peasant families would be purely practical, not sentimental, about their losses.) Muoi Bon was nineteen years old, with fluid black hair and dark, clear skin. By city standards she was not beautiful, and this seemed as apparent to her as the shape of her feet, which were soft and oblong and chubby around the ankles. Her whole appearance was soft — slope-shouldered, flat-bodied, wide-faced, neither fat nor thin — and she seemed to have accepted being defined by her ordinariness. It connected somehow, Tran thought, to her willingness to work. (Tran saw something of the skewed power of Communism in this. How were these people to know any better or different, ever?) Though at the same time, Muoi Bon was eager to recognize beauty in other women and girls.

The maid saw Tran as beautiful, or as a former beauty at least. In the maid's eyes (Tran knew) she also appeared well-off and eccentric and probably selfish — living in her own apartment with her son but no husband and voluntarily away from her own mother.

"You could be still very pretty, but now you are getting a little old," the maid told Tran. "Don't you want to be married?"

And Tran would graciously try to explain some of the concepts of feminism. She would explain that the work she did, all this handling of paper, was in fact her "labor of love." *I make stories, little sister,* she told the girl affectionately. But she could see the maid was confused. Weren't stories well enough told through one's grandmother's lips? And what did paper have to do with love?

For the maid, who had never learned to read, it was impossible to fathom the connection between strange symbols on a piece of paper and, say, the tree in her family's backyard, or the brown riverbank she loved to roam. Reading in her world was akin to the act of listening to insects chatter in order to ascertain the weather.

"Language is what can preserve your memories about experiences, you see," Tran tried to say simply, "so that we don't forget, and so that we understand those experiences better."

But Number Fourteen did not understand the meaning of the

word *preserve,* nor could she understand the need to "understand better." What did that mean? She was of the sort of mind that didn't question what seemed readily apparent: she knew where she had come from and that she would go back, always. For her, there was no need for records or questions; home would always be the center of her world, and the rest was not so important. Language for her was no more than what people said or did. She never doubted words — she only doubted people. A lie was a lie if the teller was a liar.

"And what is all this talk, talk, talk of troubles everywhere today? I hear people say 'life is so bad in our country, we are doomed.' I don't know why they're saying that," said the maid. "I think our country is beautiful, only the city is ugly. But the city is not our whole country, is it?"

Tran smiled, knowing she could feel free to leave her work lying about, certain the maid wouldn't be able to make any sense of it.

But occasionally on the evenings when Tran brought home a friend or two (usually men), she would notice a slight difference in the maid's attitude. The girl would not look Tran in the eye and treated her deferentially, as she would any male guest, yet there was more to it than that. The girl's deference, Tran thought, was not entirely submissive nor was it uncomprehending. Rather Muoi Bon seemed to be treating her now as a traitor. Sitting at the table with the men and laughing at their jokes, Tran would begin to have a feeling almost of shame, but also of lonely, indignant satisfaction. And though she felt her behavior — smoking, drinking, speaking her mind — affirmed her atypicalness, her eccentricity in the girl's eyes, she also felt an absence, a question: was this — the men's table — what she had partitioned herself off to? She was sure she appeared confident in her unorthodox ways, but she didn't always feel natural or entirely truthful in exhibiting them, and she sensed the maid saw this.

While the men did not.

Some days the maid and Tran walked to the big Ben Thanh market. The maid clutched her small satchel, money and belongings inside, as they pushed through the thick, loud crowds of bartering women and shopkeepers. Tran observed how timidly the girl made her small purchases, and how she shook her head wordlessly at abrasive vendors who shouted to her. This market was ten times larger than any she had previously known, she told Tran in polite awe. It was interesting and deceptive, Tran thought, and yet entirely honest — this girl's careful approach to new things. (Tran suspected the girl was tougher and more adaptable than she appeared; timidity was just the face she had been raised to present to others.) All she wanted to find here, the maid told Tran, were a few small gifts to take home to her family when she returned for her monthly visit.

III

Then she saw, through the window, out in the distance across the field a swaying light that could have been a handheld lantern. Could it be he? They had all fled south, but she had remained. She had even given her son over to the other neighbor-women's care — or mercy, whichever it was — and let them fear her lost, she didn't mind, for she had a greater concern. When it came closer, she heard the lantern's clank and the whistle of someone's tired breathing.

He was walking gently on the stones outside — they turned and crunched beneath his tread. Oh, how she loved him! Oh, how she envied the stones their contact with his feet! She had to close her eyes for a moment and steady her breathing. This house and all the neighbors' houses were empty; the two of them would be the only ones left to walk through the abandoned familiar streets and lament the losses, nothing to divide them now, nothing to save or comfort them but each other. He came now and pushed upon the door.

But something was not right, something was different about him. His face showed no surprise at finding her, and he was not alone. His companion stepped forward and prodded her with his rifle. "Who are you? What are you waiting for? Who called you here? Why are you hiding? What are you hiding? Speak! Speak now!"

His face stony, he refused to recognize her. He was turning his back on her pleas for recognition. "You are mistaken, Comrade,"

*he said. And then he added, almost sympathetically, "You should
never trust a snake."*

She awoke in a prison, a hole in the ground . . .

IV

In her eighth month of pregnancy, Tran was facing a trial, the
newspaper was facing shutdown, and neighbors and many other
people she encountered daily were either denying or praying in
the face of coming changes in the political climate. In the countryside, entire families were lynched, their heads strung from
tree limbs, mouths agape. This, among a long list of horrors the
approaching Communist takeover was likely to bring. At the
National Cemetery, mass graves had been dug and filled as bodies were shipped in by the truckload, with no time or means
for proper identification. Reporters took gruesome snapshots of
bloodied bodies and bulging eyes — the dead looked stunned.
Suicide in the cities increased.

Tran moved cumbersomely through these months, continu-
ing to believe only in the newspaper's single-minded rebellion,
the artists' cause of freedom of speech, which aligned itself with
neither the approaching forces nor the failing and corrupt current government. She had spoken to no one of her pregnancy
until it had made itself plainly visible and other women had begun — without acknowledging the pregnancy directly — to bring
her extra food and pull out chairs for her to sit on during meetings. Giang was the only person she had told before this point,
and he had shaken his head. As if it were the bearing of his *own*
feelings about the situation — and not the bearing of the child,
exactly — that would be most taxing. This had been enough to
tell Tran he had no intention of supporting her. (Only Muoi Bon
met Tran's news with enthusiasm, and with genuine new vigor
took to the household duties.) But Tran had been through this
once before, and this time she figured it was best not to raise a
fight or ask for compensation or even acknowledgment. She
knew Giang's reputation was more important to him than anything else. Nothing was personal that was not political here.

They passed each other in the halls now with lowered eyes. Hers was not the only alias he used anymore; he had begun using it less ever since the first few visits from the police. And no one was interested in or entertained by her serial lately, either. For some reason it was not the same — with the writer so regrettably, unmentionably pregnant. Everyone, it seemed, shared a sense of chagrin and karma.

Giang's wife began to visit the newspaper offices regularly to bring him meals. She dressed tastefully, her hair done up immaculately. (Tran would not look up from her desk or would look up only briefly as the other women called out greetings to Giang's wife.) She was an attractive but vain woman who Tran knew from hearsay fancied herself a poet, but her poems had been published only because of her husband's influence, and she had never shed her true desire for wealth despite her husband's unflagging idealism. Tran also knew from hearsay that though the wife was aware of her, they did not speak of the other woman. At least he has granted us this much, Tran thought. But she wasn't sure whom he was really protecting.

In the end, she went to the courtroom alone.

What have we done wrong? I would ask God, if I believed in Him. Oh, these sad, sad days. You want to understand that the world works justly, and that war with all its atrocity and catastrophe is simply part of the greater Order, the yin to the yang of prosperity and peace we had for x number of years, et cetera. You want to believe in the story of the man who lost his donkey but won a horse. You want to believe in Philosophy. But my children, my unborn and my son, there is much that is unfair and I cannot explain why to you, though I bring you into this world to face it. I feel it crucial to tell you (should I not return or be able for whatever reason to say it to you in person): I am sorry.

"This is it?" said the managing editor. "This is your installment?"

Tran nodded. The page he held in his hand was more than half blank, more than half white.

▪ ▪ ▪

"We have before us a rather amoral and rash character. She follows her heart — to the detriment and neglect of all her relationships, even her maternal one. What kind of woman is this? She is a *selfish* woman. A *revolting* force. She is oblivious to the facts of the world, caught up in fantasy and ideas. She is also a subversive, *conniving* woman — secretly in love with a different man than the one she is married to. What are we to make of a writer such as Miss Trung Trinh, a.k.a Trinh Anh Tran, who creates a character so morally deprived and presents her as a heroine?"

"But I must point out here the prosecution has no imagination, or compassion. For who of us has never known the passions, the obsessions, of love? I must also add: this is a *story* we are speaking about, this is *fiction*. Miss Trinh Anh Tran is merely a talented writer who has created a world and characters that've garnered a reaction of controversy. If anything, I think this controversy serves simply as testament to her talents."

At one end of a long table, in the square green room with the small windows high along only one wall, Tran sat next to her defense attorney, a young man who was a friend of the newspaper. At the other end of the table sat the prosecutor's team. The presiding judge was a man whom Tran knew to be also a local Catholic priest; in her opinion he was narrow-minded and prideful, exactly the type who would not be on her side. In the middle of the table was a tall stack of newspapers — all the printed episodes of her serial novel — and her hardcover copy of *Gone With the Wind*, which the police had confiscated from her apartment. (The book was a gift from an American correspondent, a woman journalist, and though Tran considered herself a nonmaterialist, she cherished it. It was the 107th edition, and as she understood it, the more numerous the printings of a book, the more valuable it must be, for it was only the classics, the works of lasting merit that could possibly sell widely enough to be printed over and over.)

Tran was only half listening. At eight months, she had begun to mostly ignore the outside world. She was awaiting the baby not with joy but rather a certain numbness, a helpless acceptance of the fact that soon she would be going through the agony and upheaval — the wrenching unpredictability — of labor. And on the other side of that, more unknowns that she did not have the energy to ponder.

She heard herself reply to a question. "I just used history as a backdrop. I admit I did little research. Accuracy about the war was not my point."

The prosecutor proceeded to read from a newspaper folded open before him: "*And in the shadows he would find her; she had fallen asleep at her vigil. Such a long vigil it was! And she was tired and excited with worry, with longing, with a whole turmoil of longing she wished so to express. I can't keep it in any longer! she thought*... How can we in this political climate not construe this as dangerous literature, alluding to insurgent action, so unfamiliar and yet exciting to our little heroine? The character who comes to *find* her, to waken her and remind her of her *vigil* in this scene, is in fact an agent of the soon-to-be Communist Party! Need we say more?"

"But the defense would like to point out, if we are to give even slightly serious consideration to this interpretation of the author's story, what happens to the heroine later in the story regarding her affair with this so-called insurgent Communist character. He *betrays* her. And we as readers are steered not to like him at all after that point."

Tran began to think of fires: the village at the edge of the jungle, the smoke that had woken her son that evening several months ago. She had had in mind a plan for another fire — at the heroine's village, set alight by soldiers. The heroine would make a narrow escape (from the underground prison where Tran had left her) into the night as the fields raged about her; perhaps a second man would appear, unaffiliated with either side — a roguish man. Not unlike that famous scene in that book — though they had horses in that land. It was much more dramatic with horses, thought Tran.

The true intent of the trial was to be presented to her in another room.

Tran sat in a chair before the judge at his desk, and a woman (it was not clear what this woman's role was) stood at the judge's shoulder. She was matronly and austere of face and more frightening to Tran than any of the men. She was dressed in a black military skirt, with fringed red epaulettes on her shoulders.

"Who is the father of your unborn child?" she asked.

Tran had answered this question a number of times in recent months. "A friend who is dead now. He had an accident."

"A friend? Your moral character becomes more and more reprehensible, little sister. It would not be hard to believe you are a writer of propaganda."

Tran's lawyer, next to her, did not speak up in her defense. Tran thought that was surprising. She wanted to turn to him but dared not — for fear of the woman's attention as much as for fear of what the lawyer's expression might be.

The woman pointed at Tran. "What is the name of this friend of yours?"

The judge suddenly coughed into a handerkerchief, looking away toward the window behind him. Tran saw in his eyes a flicker of something — vulnerability, perhaps. Or was it ignorance? He was trying not to pay attention, it occurred to her. She became aware then of the ineffectiveness of his authority. The two policemen standing at either end of the room also seemed mute and obligatory presences, their eyes trained on some space between them; they appeared to be staring straight at each other without staring at each other at all.

Tran gave a name she had made up. "He is nobody important. He was a locksmith."

"I don't believe you," said the woman, and folded her arms. "What is the real name of your friend?"

Tran replied, "I told you already."

"I will pass an ordinance," interjected the judge, abruptly, as if he had been napping and someone had prodded him. "All the independent newspapers will be required to comply with stricter guidelines. A team of censors will be sent to each office. All pages with any potentially offensive material will be confiscated by the government and burned. Would you like to be the impetus for this action against your colleagues?"

The nausea of hunger churned inside of her, perilous and urgent. Couldn't they see how ill-suited she was for the trickery they were accusing her of having mastered?

The woman asked again, "What is the name of your friend?"

Her lawyer put his hand on her arm. "I must tell you, cousin," he addressed her in a conspiratorial way. "Actually, they are trying to help you."

A moment later she broke down. "I don't *know* his real name," she sobbed, "I just wanted to write a love story."

Later, in another room, the woman gave Tran a lemonade. "Your unborn child. Do you wish to keep it?" She spoke briskly, solicitously. "I can understand if you don't want to; it won't be easy for you, having two illegitimate children. It won't be easy for them, either. If you didn't wish to keep it, I know who might take it. Your baby's father — I know his reputation — has certainly a good mind. We can use children with good minds. Do you know what I mean? Educate them properly. You are concerned with education, aren't you?"

Tran felt around her the stickiness of a web. She had thought she could trust at least the newspaper's lawyer but now didn't know what to think. Every word she said could mean someone's condemnation. Even what you believed to be undoubtably your own could be challenged.

"I want to keep it," said Tran.

"I have a friend," said the woman, with a smile. "He is looking for a wife."

An ordinance was passed and the newspapers began to hold clandestine meetings to discuss their options. Many people were quitting simply out of fear. They did not want to be too clearly aligned with anything potentially dangerous; they thought it safer to appear neutral, even ignorant.

It was 1973. The American soldiers were gone. And though they had left the South Vietnamese Army massively, ridiculously, well equipped, and had dropped another round of bombs on the North in order to reiterate their conviction in the fight against encroaching Communism before flying homeward themselves, the atmosphere in the city was largely one of doubt. A few of Tran's colleagues, it was rumored, had even defected to the Communist Party, or were just now showing what might have all along been their true allegiance, according to speculation.

Giang vanished immediately following the trial. Strangely, Tran's first thoughts were not of finding him or learning where he had gone, but of his wife; what would she do now, did she blame Tran? Once, Tran sent the maid to his house with a gift of rice cakes and wrapped pork and an invitation to his wife — Tran thought they might be able to speak frankly now that Giang was absent — but not surprisingly, she received no reply.

Tran lived for the last month of her pregnancy with a mid-ranking military official who came to be the man her family accepted as her new daughter's father (whether they knew the truth or not, they were ready to accept nearly anyone). Tran had felt she had no choice but to accept the arrangement, despite her wariness of what kind of man her proposed husband might be; Tran knew she was being watched by the government. One month after the birth of the baby girl, Tran's new husband was killed in a military excursion in the southern countryside. Soon after, Tran remembered something from long ago, some prophecy concerning herself and men. Though in this circumstance, the relationship should not have ended in the man's leaving or death (as the fortuneteller had predicted all Tran's marriages before the age of thirty would), as this had not been an actual marriage. Or so Tran thought. He had been a kind man; he had surprised her. There had been moments of tenderness, even. The presence of the baby had affected them and caused them both to surrender — though Tran was aware that their passion was grounded in a heightened sense of reality and that her own emotional state was unsteady — to the roles they had each for whatever reason agreed to play. (Tran suspected he, too, had been coerced into the marriage by higher-ranking officials, possibly as a coverup of some other scandal.) In their private moments, he had revealed to Tran a slight discontent with his career, though he had never expressed it directly; Tran suspected his death had not been an accident.

Giang's wife came to the hospital a few days after the delivery. Some women from the newspaper had warned Tran that Giang's wife would be coming to see her husband's baby. She stood at the side of the hospital bed and fixed her eyes on Tran with what seemed to Tran an undue air of superiority. It struck her that this was a woman who enjoyed confronting other women when they were vulnerable.

But Tran felt at least partly responsible for this woman's loss of her husband. "I'm so sorry he's gone," she said.

Giang's wife made no reply, the tight line of her red lips telling Tran she would not be forgiven. She was holding in her hands the obligatory bouquet of flowers for the baby. Swaddled in a blanket, the baby was asleep in a clear plastic bin the nurses had wheeled in on a cart and positioned at the foot of Tran's bed; the two women looked at the baby's fleshy, closed face. "I came to see our daughter. She is my daughter, too, you know. I harbor no ill will toward her. Children are all born innocent in the presence of God." She set her bouquet of flowers among some others on a table by the window. "It's not her fault you are a weak woman."

Tran named the baby Thuy, a girl's name popular for its gentle sound and its allusion to the kingfisher bird, this her gesture toward freeing the child from the web of ill-fated events that had preceded her entry into the world. But it was only a halfhearted gesture, for Tran felt deep down that there was no conceivable escape from the sorrows of life. When Thuy was two months old, Tran returned to work. Her younger sister came to stay at her apartment, where she helped the maid with the household duties and care of Thien.

At the newspaper, Tran allowed herself to be moved into a research position. She put in fewer hours and did not go out into the field. Occasionally, she wrote a poem for the paper, but it usually explored safe themes: new motherhood, the simplicity of a baby, glimpses of nature.

Soon whether or not they would fold was a question provoking ongoing discussion at the newspaper office. Tran could not avoid it. She listened, though she kept her opinions to herself. What will be, will be, she believed. She felt doom in the air, but she would not quit the paper. She simply could not face the idea of quitting. That would be too much of an admission of shame — which she was not willing to let herself feel about the past year's events.

She attended meetings at various colleagues' houses and stood on the periphery. The meetings usually began with a lot of shouting, which continued until a senior editor or some other commanding personality climbed onto a chair or table or found something to bang on. Then this person would attempt to mediate. Ideas about how to retaliate against or circumvent censorship policies went back and forth; there were those who favored the more subversive tactic of compromise, or appearing to compromise, while extremists in the group favored louder, more outright protestations. At one meeting, an old poet (who had lately been a contributing editor) stood and gave a speech that moved Tran.

"Come out of your bones! What is even flesh or blood worth at a time like this? How come we cling to flesh and blood when what we really covet is ephemeral? What we covet is a concept, freedom? You are always free to think as you will: this is the true aim of freedom. My children, I beg of you — recognize this! Or you are missing the point, you are wasting the beauty of your struggle. I am an old man, and I tell you: only God lives on."

But Tran knew nobody was listening to the old man, mournful-eyed and perched on a plastic stool, speaking in such a soft, defeated tone. The backyard where this particular meeting was held belonged to an aggressive young reporter popular for his willingness to draw hasty and slanderous conclusions about public officials in his articles. Theirs was not a kind of journalism that had ever claimed to be impartial, reporters like him would say. The now passé poet's esoteric philosophy on the uselessness of writing made no sense here.

And now the extremists in the group were suggesting a great protest, a grand collaboration of art. A statement of the very reason, the need for such a thing as writing. Self-destruction, they concluded, was the best way to show the seriousness of their cause. In the end, it was those who spoke the loudest that decided what would be the manner of their protest.

Tran was likely the only person who saw the old poet shake his head, probably dismayed at the wasted passion of the young.

V

The burning began. The reporters, the op-ed writers, the editors, print-layers, photojournalists threw up their arms and whooped. "We will burn our blood before we let them confiscate it!" Soon their voices rose into a chant: *Burn Burn Burn!* and *Blood Blood Blood!*

One elderly man climbed atop a mountain of papers and waved a gun, declaring he would shoot himself in the head if the government so much as touched a single sheet — even though no government police had yet arrived. In the street, editors in chief of competing publications were shaking hands, agreeing that yes, indeed, this was solidarity! This was news! Then the militia arrived, dressed in dull green, and shouted orders through megaphones and pointed rifles in the air. Tran stood watching from the sidewalk, occasionally jogging from one side of the action to another, helping carry a few papers or passing someone a match or lighter.

It did not last long, as fires go. There the demonstrators stood, gasping or leaning on one another or crying up and down the street as they watched their papers burning. Tran was aware of a gathering sense of denouement, an emotional momentum, an unnatural rift. She was caught by it, too, though she had thought she would be able to remain detached. They were both a ludicrous and sad sight, her colleagues, the earnest, expended vitality of the men setting alight their papers; the women, too. These were intellectuals, and this was as close to brutal as they could get; the militia, on the other hand, could easily be violent. Tran stepped out of the way of the soldiers and policemen, stayed on the sidewalk. She watched the fire as it colored the dirty street orange and cooked the facades of city buildings; she watched the air around the flames tremble from the heat.

The policemen and soldiers rushed forward to beat the flames with blankets; other policemen came running with buckets of water. The scene was preposterous. For though it was what they would have done themselves — burn the papers — now the policemen were trying to put the fires out. Some young reporters threw themselves onto policemen's backs and were hauled off, thrown down and kicked, beaten with rifle butts. Ghostwriters charged forward with new torches and tossed them into piles of papers, setting them alight again. Cheers rose. *"Oh, for the liberty of words!"* cried the elderly man as he shot his gun off at the sky and leaped from the stack upon which he had been standing. A group of ten photojournalists stripped off their shirts and danced wildly around the largest pyre. With wiry arms they grappled with the policemen who advanced. The flames licked at the sky and black curls of ash and singed paragraphs rose in a swift and beautiful burning (this is what Tran would recall years later) — the rise into the air of a thousand blackened bits of *papier* like scarred and disembodied butterfly wings, weightless at their fate. Catching on hair and clothes, being rubbed into eyes, skin. That morning the news was everywhere.

Until at last the policemen put the flames out.

VI

The newspaper was discontinued in October 1974, and Tran, now out of work, could no longer afford to keep a maid or to live alone. She decided to move back to her mother's house, where her sisters and cousins could help tend to Thien and Thuy — little more than a year old now. When Tran and her children saw Muoi Bon off at the train station, it was a wrenching good-bye: for hours afterward, Thuy was in a frenzy. When finally she had tired enough to sleep, it was only to wake crying again, wanting the maid who had spent long hours holding her. The little girl would accept no consolation for weeks after the parting. Gradually, though, she forgot as she grew older.

In the first months after the shutdown of the newspaper, Tran wandered the city with her son and daughter, slightly at sea. She bought fruit and toys at markets; she sat in cafés and wrote quietly — thoughts and half-hearted ideas she would later burn in private for fear that these papers might be found and misinterpreted — while her children played with the café owners' kids. Occasionally she ran into a former newspaper colleague doing much the same as she, whiling away days in old familiar haunts, and she was always saddened by their mildly stunned demeanor, their guardedness. It was not safe anymore to speak to anyone, and no one dared ask questions.

Coming home one evening with her children, Tran passed the woman from the adjacent house on her stoop washing her baby in a round plastic tub. The baby sat placidly, its large dark eyes staring up at Tran as she approached, its skin wet and gleaming in the fading light of their small lane. Silently, Tran's children stared back at the wet baby. The two mothers smiled at each other. Tran felt an odd sense of imperfection and peace at that moment, the first such peace she had felt in many months, years even. This other woman appeared close to her own age and, as far as Tran could tell, did not have a husband, either. Probably, though, hers had died in the war, clearly affiliated with one army or the other, thought Tran, stepping into her mother's house.

That night, when Thuy awoke crying, Tran took her out to the stoop to feed her. She had chosen to use the bottle rather than breastfeed because she understood this to be an avenue toward freedom, albeit a small one; it was what most American women chose as well, or she had gathered as much from her few American acquaintances. The lane was dark blue and weighted and still. The woman from next door appeared, leaning her head out the window of her house.

"Sister, I can't sleep tonight," the woman whispered.

"Your baby?"

"No, it's more than that, I'm afraid." She spoke quickly, as if she'd planned this meeting. "I know who you are, I know you are a smart woman and you know about the world. I am afraid. I am not optimistic. Do you know what I mean?"

Tran did.

"I need advice," said the neighbor. "I have money. I've been saving to remodel my house. But I'm afraid. If I spend it, I may not have long to enjoy my new home, but if I don't spend it, I know the Communists will surely take it from me when they come. Am I not right?"

Feeling for something inside herself, the appropriate response, the so-designated wisdom, Tran found instead a puncturing, exhaustive pain. She told the woman: "Spend your money. Regret nothing."

Later she would not forget: the sounds of construction from the house next door — the pounding of hammers, the rhythms of saws and shovels. She would think she should have recognized it as a sign, an omen of reconstruction soon to come. A new home waiting, a new man — an architect. She should have known that just as the rooms of the neighbor's house were being gutted and renovated, so would she be. Many old pieces cast aside, painful new fittings and additions. She would remember: her mother on that fatal last day, sitting up from lying on the couch as alarms rang out over the city, her long hair unraveling from its bun (hair that in Tran's memory would tumble, in a repeated wave, down her back), and the unspoken final wish so obvious right then: that she might be invited to go with her favorite unsaved daughter so that this daughter might still have a chance to be saved. "We'll come back for you, Mother," Tran and each of her sisters had said in turn, as they ran off to meet their various exit sponsors at the prearranged rendezvous points.

Tran and her two children made their exit by plane on April 29, 1975. It was not the narrow escape it might have been a day later, but it still gave Tran a sense of having forgotten something in haste. Tran had packed, telling herself she would soon return, and she left valuables behind to convince herself. Framed photographs of her parents and grandparents, favorite shirts, her old diaries, Thien's baby memorabilia. But the truth was that there was a limit to what passengers were permitted to bring aboard the plane; she had had to be selective. One change of clothing, a handful of old photographs, several books she knew she had to save, some mementos from the newspaper. In those few final days the streets of Saigon were full, chaotic, streaming. People flung themselves on cars, made leaps at trucks and buses that looked like they were headed somewhere, somewhere else. People squeezed against one another at the gates of the U.S. and French embassies, the airports, the radio stations — any facility known to have a connection with the outer world.

For it was plain by this time that Vietnam was a sinking ship, a shriveling dragon. All the world's turmoil seemed concentrated here, with cameras and people running together: here was Vietnam offering herself up, desperate, scandalized. Tran watched the shape and details of the land below becoming simpler — more intrinsic to the landscape as a whole — out the plane window as they ascended. Here was the land, here was the water, here was the gradation of browns in the soil as it proceeded toward the water. Here was the city and here was the countryside, in definitive different textures. Here was the ocean. She could not make out the tall spires of the Notre Dame Cathedral, where a few hours ago she had seen a woman shot by a soldier; she could not see the rivers of people thronging the avenues as she'd suspected she might. Though she could see the wide, winding, mud-brown waters of the Mekong making its way to the sea like a flat serpent. As if eager to dissolve itself in the sea, the river was prematurely dispersing into tributaries that were like multitudinous, fine tentacles.

And the plane, Tran wondered, what was it made of? For though she had seen plenty of them, this was the first she had ever entered. She looked around her at the stiff, narrow seats, the other people silent and crowded there and on the floors, some crying, others clinging to some object or other, or clutching each other. Broad-shouldered Americans stood by the exits with guns. Some uniformed, some not, with sweat rings staining the armpits of their short-sleeved white shirts. The interior of the plane was like the cavernous insides of some great metal monster. They had put their fates into the hands of, well, fate perhaps, is what she felt. Neither of her children was crying anymore, only staring around. She put her arms around them both and held tightly. In the end, she thought, your children are the only crucial possessions you can take with you or leave behind.

VII

In the new country, she will remarry a Westerner. (She will have turned thirty; her debt to prophecy, she hopes, will have been paid.) He will be an immigrant himself, though from Denmark, and though already in the new country for twenty-odd years, sympathetic to her circumstances, but also forward-looking and a believer in reinvention. She will be enamored of him for his authority and confidence — his compassion! — and he will teach them many new things. For instance, he will insist the children speak correct English. *Labrador. Siamese. Department store. One dollar, two dollars. One fish, two fish,* he will tell them. *With,* not *wiff.* And it will be his idea to buy a piece of land in those once fabled hills of gold, where they will build a house with a good view of the valley and raise the children with dogs and ponies and chickens. Here, Tran will see more trees and taller trees and stranger formations of land and grass than she'd ever imagined, and here — for the first time in the five years since their arrival in America — she will feel calm and resign herself to *being there.* She will learn how to drive a car. She will drive the children to track practice, the bus stop, the park, the library, the grocery store, the pizza parlor. Once, stupidly, she will try to return a can of Folger's coffee to the wrong supermarket, not understanding the incriminating details of receipts. The car, she will discover, is a wonderful place for dreaming. Her head will fill with stories, words, speculation, slights. But the need to write will have begun to ebb; she will not commit any of these ideas to paper. She will receive news of her mother's death, months after it has occurred, one afternoon while she is eating a sandwich (and she will try to picture the story in her mind: her mother went to market in the morning, came home, had some soup, complained of being tired, lay down, never woke). On weekends she will do the laundry while her husband changes the oil in the Volkswagen or the truck, mends a fence, brushes the dogs. The old organizations, her old friends and colleagues, will begin to seem inadequate to her. Slowly she will lose touch, the immediacy of old causes now faded, juvenile, surreal — her husband, who works as an architectural adviser for the government, has taught her this: there is little that ordinary people can do in the complex web of a large modern society.

On occasion, though, she will try to explain herself to him. She will talk about Buddhism, the closest thing she has to a religion. Her husband will tell her he is an atheist. (With passion: "I answer to no one, you hear, no one.") She will try to tell him Buddhism is more a way of life than a religion. She will try to explain the concept of the low road, of seeking not to worship but to kill your God, and of "acceptance," of how the highest happiness in life must often come through suffering.

"The highest happiness is saffron," she will say.

He will frown at her. "Saffron is a spice. It comes from a flower. Very painstaking to extract." She will shake her head and say it again. But still he will not understand the last word so they must struggle over it: zephyr? sever? ("Are you dwelling on the past again?") sub-fur? Finally they will go for the dictionary. She will search and search for the correct spelling. And he will laugh.

"Suffering! To suffer! S-*u*-f, you mean!" For she has spelled the word *saffering*. "There is a big difference between an 'a' and a 'u,' Tran. Those are two entirely different vowels." He will demonstrate these sounds for her, shaping his mouth with exaggeration. "A, e, i, o, u," he will recite for her.

2

LUCKY

Our dogs were two large mixed-breed Newfoundlands. One black female that our father had rescued — pregnant already — from the pound, and her son, a dirty white pup with faint brown spots, the only pup we kept from the litter. The largest — thick-furred with shorter ears and tail than his mother. Quiet but strong. We called him "Kee," the most easily pronounceable name my sister, Beth, and I could agree on at the time. She was five, I was eight. No one knew who Kee's father was. All we knew, our own father liked to say, was he must've been some kind of dog to jump over the six-foot fence at the pound to get to Jamie, the mother dog. (Beth and I didn't understand what the "to get to" part really entailed, though our father's approving chuckle as he said it comforted us.) Perhaps Kee's father had been a wolf, our father would hypothesize when Kee howled at the moon or disappeared for days into the woods below our property. We were duly impressed. We took these signs to be evidence of Kee's exceptionality, his uncontainability, his superiority — the commendable result of an enigmatic and wayward background.

Kee had been born just before our family moved to the Sierra foothills; thus he was the same age as the house that our father was in the slow process of building. Because of his job and lack of money and having only our older brother, Thien, and a neighbor to help, only the skeleton of a first floor was standing after an entire year. Now it was October and the rain had come. Shallow puddles formed where the concrete foundation was not even. The rain seeped under tarps and warped some of the lumber. Our father worried hugely over small and large complications alike. The loss of a few pieces of lumber, spider web–size cracks in the foundation, the possibility of landslides or floods over the site. Waiting for spring, he busied himself with other projects on the property, such as stringing barbed wire for the future horse pastures and burning brush and repairing leaks in the storage shed roof. He kept Thien busy as well. Our father was like a thundercloud, swelled with many hopes and plans for our new life here, glowering and desperate to set them loose, to drum them into our heads before — as he seemed to think — it became too late.

It was 1981.

Kee was a beautiful and smart and gentle dog. Our father would point out the integrity in his eyes, his deep-set lupine brown eyes like all the heavy-climate breeds seemed to have — the clear, soulful gaze of a creature who has not only the capacity to live wild but also enough humility and dignity to prevent him from ever harming a thing. (Our father believed this. I think it had to do with his own experience of war, of what he knew he might've been capable of had certain situations arisen — which they had not — in Korea in the 1950s.) Dogs like these, he would tell us, were unknowingly burdened by their own strength, for nothing in their domesticated lives would ever truly put it to the test. Yet that combined strength and reserve was a fine, fine characteristic, he would say, with a kind of trapped passion, and even when I was only eight it struck me he was not speaking just of dogs. He was speaking rather of something vital and exacting that had compelled him to hold himself aloof, always — from a more messily, shamelessly, and duplicitously emoting larger population, as his descriptions made the rest of the world out to be.

I understood the elusive characteristic he spoke of was what had driven him forward — and outward — through his own life. He had fled his family and another country years ago, in the early 1950s, by joining first the Danish marines and then the U.S. Army. "You have no idea, no idea what I've been through," he would tell us. And he wished now to nurture this characteristic in us children

— now that we were his — this kernel of something like goodness or kindness or acumen, it is hard to name in just one word. But I would try to recognize it for myself in some sights or moments I believed my father might commend my noticing — an unusually shaped pine tree on a hillside (it must be something unique perhaps), or the warmth I felt as I began to fall asleep, before I had fallen too far no longer to be aware of the pull of sleep (it must be something inscrutable and intensely personal, then).

But to continue about our animals: we kept dogs and cats because we adored them, we kept chickens for eggs and slaughter. Our father considered chickens to be mainly brainless creatures, and no matter what the extent of their unique talents or strengths or markings, they could never become refined. This was the important difference between chickens and dogs and applied even to our favorite hen, whom we called "Lucky" because occasionally she laid an egg with two yolks. Still, we had to keep in mind she was brainless, ill destined. Our father was the kind of man who held to a hierarchy of nature, who placed his faith only in the indifference of evolution.

One morning, he woke early and walked down the hill to the chicken coop. He had to search for the hens' eggs, which often they tried to hide in corners of the coop or in holes scratched in the dirt underneath. Lucky had found a spot in the crook of the roots of an oak tree some way away, and from under her he pulled out (later, this is how we would always recall this) the largest egg any of our chickens ever laid and Lucky's last complete one.

Our mother was sitting on the trailer steps, smoking her cigarette, looking at the morning view of the mountains. She was small-boned and youthful-looking but possessed a manliness — her flat chest and short hair, her petite, muscular legs, her forward, bright manner that could come as a surprise from someone of her stature. She had (in those years) a lack of self-consciousness that we as children were not aware was unusual for an adult. She was also a willing companion to our father's adventures: the house-building, the purchase of our trailer, our new lifestyle in the foreign countryside. She was unafraid to pick up a shovel, she proudly sported the cowboy boots he'd suggested she buy for the terrain up here.

"On mornings like this, I think we very lucky," she said happily. Her English was still heavily accented.

"Yes," agreed our father as he came up the driveway, toting eggs in the stretched-out hem of his T-shirt. "Look at this." Proudly, he showed our mother that morning's largest egg, brown-speckled and big as one of her fists.

He carried the eggs into the trailer, where he placed the large one on the counter for us children to find when we woke. The rest he placed in the fridge. My sister and I were sleeping tangled like kittens in the sheets of the fold-out bed in the trailer's small dining area, our brother in the loft above us, one skinny arm dangling loose and naked over the side into the crisp morning air. Trailer life for us was like an extended camping trip, after our first few years in the States in apartment complexes and working- to middle-class suburban neighborhoods; we knew it was impermanent, this new, less structured life, and so had set ourselves loose into it, without complaint, with casual abandon, with an eye to discovery. Each routine activity seemed new and alive to us. For instance, we took our baths outside now with the use of a cup and a plastic yellow baby tub, or on a stump. We went to the bathroom outside as well, at the base of the nearest large old oak tree with a roll of toilet paper that we carried back and forth from the trailer (some mornings we made a game of passing the toilet paper off to one another as we rushed out to pee). Mastering the mundane in these new ways dominated much of our attention, and we congratulated ourselves on it every day, our survival of the daily — the mishaps and ingenuities and tiny ridiculous triumphs we'd managed. Or our parents did, at least, while our brother sulked in dismay at having to live like this at all, and my sister and I thought nothing of it, really, for we were too young to know any better. When our father and brother came home from surplus sales and unloaded bathroom appliances in the dirt in front of the skeleton of our house, we climbed into the dry tubs and pretended they were boats. We lounged on the toilet seats and ate lunch. We played outside all day and slept solidly through the night.

It was warm inside the trailer at night and only slightly chilly in the mornings, when we would wake to find the covers kicked off or *stolen. Dimly, through the haze of half sleep, I could hear my father that morning filling the dogs' food bowls — the opening and closing of the cupboard door, the crinkling of the dog-food bag. He set the bowls on the counter. He opened the built-in refrigerator that faced the sink. Then came the sound of eggshells cracking, two over each bowl of dog food. Raw eggs helped keep the dogs' coats shiny and healthy. For a moment our father paused, his gaze on us stirring in our sheets. As he did many mornings, he reached down and rear-ranged the sheets to cover our bare chests. He placed my brother's arm back in the bunk beside his body.*

Then he exited the trailer and set the dogs' bowls down on the hard dirt outside, and the dogs came to him, butts and tails wag-ging, snouts nuzzling against his hands and legs.

Our mother took us into town to do laundry and shop for groceries that afternoon. Our father stayed home to string wire around the chicken coop and make a pen so the chickens would not wander. The dogs lay panting in the shade under the twisted oak trees while our father squatted by the coop and planned his pen, and when he got up the dogs stood, too. They sniffed the ground, shoved their noses around under the fallen leaves.

Our father went up the hill to the storage shed to get some wire. Suddenly he heard a loud squawking and the sound of wings beat-ing and scuffling in the dirt. He ran down the hill in time to see Kee attacking one of the chickens. He shouted and swung his arms at the pup, who cowered backward with his tail low and let go of the chicken. Our father stepped closer to inspect the damage. Lucky lay listing to one side in the strewn leaves, making strangled clucking noises and flicking her feathers. Our father did not see any blood yet, so he leaned closer and placed his hand under the chicken's soft belly feathers and gently he lifted her. The hen's stomach lay be-neath her in the leaves with an egg not completely laid. The egg was broken, its yolk like a filmy yellow eye within the stomach. Our fa-ther realized Kee must've been trying to reach the egg.

Of course. Kee would've never deliberately injured the chicken.

Our father said out loud, "Well, I'm sorry, Lucky." He decided he *would have to finish it for her. He pressed down on her back with one hand and twisted with the other.*

As he was carrying Lucky down the hill to bury her, he spotted Kee hiding under the trailer. The poor pup was already punishing himself. That dogs were capable of shame seemed evidence to our father of an awareness not typically expected of dogs — an awareness of responsibility, or the ability to discern (and thus not act on, if the dog were well trained enough) an impulse. "A test of love and duty" was the lesson he would draw for us out of what had happened that day. And he did not mean love in the mushy sense we wanted to give it, of course; he meant love only as a condition irrevocably tied to how one did or did not act dutifully in a given circumstance. When he told us, he told us carefully, even clinically, what had happened to Lucky. "Love," he said scornfully (when we speculated that Kee had felt bad because "he loved Lucky and knew we did, too"), "bah. Don't let it trick you."

"Not so lucky!" laughed our mother to our brother in the background as they unpacked groceries in the trailer's tiny kitchen space — for she was callous about chickens, understood the butchering of them to be purely practical.

"The egg wasn't ready to be taken yet," explained our father. He gently told us about the logistics of chickens' stomachs.

"Why did Kee do it?" I asked.

"Because he likes the eggs I've been feeding him and he wanted more," said our father. "He wanted more but it was too soon."

His head hunched, Kee was looking at us through the trailer screen door.

"But he's a smart dog," said our father, "to have figured out where the eggs come from."

CHICKENS

The relatives were waking. Hus Madsen could hear them moving around inside the van and the storage shed where they had slept in their sleeping bags. Hus took his cigarettes and headed down the hill to smoke and admire the view. The mid-August sun was rising over the mountains and the silver line of the American River wound soundlessly through the bottom of the Coloma Valley, wheat-yellow this time of year, and pocked with faraway houses and squares of plowed land and the cloudlike green puffs of live-oak treetops and the darker, bramblier heads of the black and blue oaks. Hus walked down the steep driveway, kicking up fresh red dirt with his boots, and stepped onto the concrete foundation he'd had poured the previous week. He stood there and looked out over the Coloma Valley with his arms folded across his chest.

Down there was where gold had first been discovered in California, in 1848, by some other unsuspecting new landowner.

One can only hope, Hus liked to joke.

Behind him, from the top of the driveway, he heard the dogs' collars jingling and their paws scraping excitedly on the ground as the trailer door banged open against the sharp morning air. He began to hear the voices of the relatives. They had arrived just two days ago to visit the Madsens' new land in the foothills of the Sierra Nevada, and it was only the second time Hus had met them in the five years he and Tran had been married and living in Sacramento. The relatives spoke in slow, broken English, or rapidly and loudly in their native tongue, which he didn't understand a word of. Hus had insisted, when he married Tran, that they speak only English in their home. He believed it was more important for the children to speak the language of the country they were growing up in than for them to cling to a culture they had left. It was what he had done himself upon coming to America, twenty-eight long years ago, and if they were to succeed in this society, fluent, natural-sounding English was what they would have to learn as well. As far as he could tell, Tran agreed.

They had both agreed the past would be something best gotten over without much grief, or elaboration to one another or the children.

Of the three children, only the youngest was Hus's by blood. The other two had come with their mother from Vietnam, just four months before Hus had met them. They had escaped on one of the last vessels out of Saigon (and there had been all kinds: famed helicopters, DC-3s, DC-10s, whole squadrons of fighter planes, naval, marine and army air carriers, little rat-trap fishing boats, overloaded rowboats), before the capital fell to the Communist forces. Tran and her two children had been moving between refugee camps, from Guam to San Diego to Sacramento, and while in the last camp, called Hope Village, Tran had written an article about her and her children's experiences that was published in *The Sacramento Bee*. Hus had just relocated from San Francisco to Sacramento through a transfer of air bases (he was now in the civil sector, putting his architectural degree to work) when he read Tran's story. He had heard many of these stories lately, and his sympathies were with the Vietnamese people, the dislocated; he believed these people could prosper if only given the right chance and circumstances. And then it had occurred to him. He had no one else. He was forty-four years old, still living with only a cat. He was not an unattractive man. Women had often said things to him, and men in bars even, long ago, when he'd been first feeling his way around the States. They had told him he might try Los Angeles, that he looked like he should be on TV. The few involvements he'd had with women, however, had been messy and disruptive, or just plainly confounding to him. He had given up. Those women, he thought, were not serious about anything and were too demanding of men; they did not know how to respect — or let alone — the deeper, more important facts about a person. They had refused even to try to understand the hardships he'd been through, or the distance he'd had to put between himself and his former life and home. They listened with consternation when he spoke about his childhood during World War II, and their questions, when they asked them, seemed always unimaginative ("Do you miss your mother? Was she a good cook? Was she pretty?") and designed to elicit only light-hearted answers. As he read Tran's story in the paper, though, something stirred in him, a sense of recognition that was more than personal, that was strangely nostalgic already; he thought, now here is a woman who has done some necessary fighting of her own. Here is a woman for whom life has not been easy, yet she has endured, she possesses character. Sitting up late that August night in 1975 in his small two-room apartment, Hus found himself writing a letter to send to her via the newspaper, typing as if another's hands were guiding his own hands over the keys. He wanted to do something for this woman who was a fighter. What could he do, he asked in his letter. His intentions at this stage were purely pragmatic, he'd thought. But when they met his heart went out to her and to himself also.

They were married two weeks later.

They drove in a rented car out to Virginia City, Nevada, and after the brief proceedings made their way into a shop called the Silver Time Saloon, where they tried on authentic pioneer costumes from the 1800s and had their picture taken. The photo was tinted to appear old, as if they had already shared history together — and a prototypical American one, at that. They spent their honeymoon in a hotel in Virginia City. Then they drove their rented car back to Sacramento the following day. Hus brought back gifts for the children, who'd been staying with some volunteers from Hope Village. Now the new family moved into Hus's apartment near downtown Sacramento. And when U.S. citizenship was officially granted to them all three years later, he encouraged the children to come up with American versions — or at least American spellings — of their former names. The little girl agreed to *April,* the month of her birth (she was too young to choose for herself and didn't fully understand anyway); the boy, however, was less agreeable and insisted on remaining Thien — although *Tim* was a close and nice enough alternative, Hus had tried explaining — but the boy could not be persuaded.

The girls were coming down the hill, holding hands with Huong, the girl cousin, who was maybe seventeen. He couldn't remember all of the seven cousins' names, and couldn't pronounce them all, either. Hus knew Huong because he thought her the most pleasant and considerate. When they ate dinner, the boys left their plates on the table, and Huong did all the cleaning. As she came down the hill now with his daughters, he called out, "Well, good morning! Come and look at the view. I'll bet you've never seen a view like this before." Views like this were, in large part, what he'd been after in moving the family up into the hills, away from the congested, suburban way of life in Sacramento. He held his cigarette away from his lips and made a sweeping gesture at the landscape beyond, as if it were his own painting he was showing.

His daughters, he noticed, were dressed in the flimsy, strapless dresses the relatives had brought as gifts. The girls had been wearing these foolish outfits ever since the relatives had arrived two days before. Even on women with full figures, the dresses would've looked nothing more than cheap, Hus thought. April, the seven-year-old, wore a glittery purple dress, and Beth, four, was in a satiny blue one. Neither had anything up top to hold up the dresses, and the fabric bagged out over their torsos, often slipping to expose a babyish nub of nipple. Tugging at the dresses, they came tottering toward him down the steep drive in high-heeled shoes that were far too big as well. Hus hadn't known what to say about these gifts without seeming rude, so he had decided, from the beginning, not even to acknowledge the dresses.

"Hi, Daddy, hi, Daddy."

"Aunt Mary and I made the girls look very pretty," said Huong, smiling brightly. She was wearing a tiger-striped bathing suit and a floppy straw hat.

"Why don't you show your cousins how to take a bath?" Hus said to the girls.

"We'll show you the way we take a bath in the country!"

"Good idea," said Hus.

He watched as the girls hobbled over to the wooden rack holding gallon jugs of water and showed their cousin how to feel for the warmest. The rack had black sandpaper nailed to it to absorb the sun's heat. They each picked up a gallon jug and started back up the hill. It was good, he thought, to see his four-year-old lugging the heavy gallon of water as well as her older sister and cousin did. He heard April explaining, "See, the sun heats up the water."

He called after them, "Make sure you lather first!"

He spotted his wife coming out of the trailer. Tran was wearing cut-off jeans with cowboy boots. She was laughing and speaking Vietnamese with her sister, the one they called Aunt Mary. Often Hus could not tell, with this language, whether the speakers were angry or happy. The tones of it were so garrulous and aggressive and shrill. Aunt Mary's husband, whom they all referred to as Uncle John, was smoking a cigarette outside the trailer, his shirt unbuttoned to well below his chest. His eyes were narrow, his brown skin mottled, and he had a straight, black moustache. He wore a gold necklace and was a skinny man, at least a head shorter than Hus. Hus had never understood men who wore necklaces. He believed men who adorned themselves to be vain, in an untrustworthy way. Uncle John saw Hus and waved his hand. "Come, eat!" the man said in his thick accent. He nodded his chin and again waved his cigarette in the air.

Hus put a hand on his stomach and shook his head. "No, thank you," he said loudly. "I have to go check on the pups." He pointed to the doghouse on the hill. Then he stepped off the foundation and dropped his cigarette, grinding it into the dirt with the heel of his boot.

Since the doghouse sat on a slope, at night the puppies sometimes rolled down the hill in their sleep and fell into the deep trench that had been dug for the septic system. Hus counted the puppies in and around the doghouse, then walked along the edge of the trench, searching. Usually he would get Thien out of bed in the mornings to do this. That morning, two puppies whined and clawed at the fresh dirt at the bottom of the trench. Hus felt some irritation that the boy had not been out here first thing to help the puppies. But Thien was a teenager, fourteen now, and what more could one expect, these days especially? Hus hopped down into the trench and picked each puppy up by the scruff of its neck. They kicked their legs and yelped. They were so young that they had not yet opened their eyes. As he held them up and looked into their soft faces, he realized how, in or out of the trench, the world was still dark for them. Hus wondered, could they sense him helping them even when they couldn't see him? And later, when their eyes opened and they could see, would they recognize him as the man who had helped them?

Hus carried the two puppies back up to the doghouse where the mother dog was nursing, and carefully set them down.

Heading back up the hill, he heard voices and splashing. At the side of the trailer around the stump the girls usually stood on when Tran bathed them, the cousins were loosely gathered, bathing, each with a gallon of water, and the girls were instructing them, teetering on their high heels and still tugging at those dresses. The cousins wore their bathing suits, the boys small and scrawny in their swim trunks. They giggled and stomped and shook themselves as they poured water over their heads. They looked a little like chickens. Hus was struck by the realization that these people were his relations.

He walked toward them, lighting another cigarette, and he called out to them that it worked best if they poured the water slowly. "Just enough to get you wet first," he said. "Then put the gallon down, and lather up and shampoo. Then, rinse. Out here in the country, we have to conserve water." As they paused to look at him, he made lathering motions around his body to illustrate what he meant. They smiled and laughed. They put down their jugs while they rubbed shampoo in their hair. Then, one of the boys picked up a jug and splashed water at his brothers. They began to shriek and laugh and chase each other around. Hus waved his arms. "Hey, hey," he called, "we have to conserve water here. No horsing around now."

This was Hus's design for their sewage system: a large septic tank buried deep in the ground and twenty feet of pipe running the length of the trench across the hillside, attached at one end to the porthole of the septic tank and the other — when it was ready — to the sewage pipes beneath the house. In the meantime, however, Hus planned to leave one end of the pipe loose, so it could be dragged up the hill and attached to the waste tank underneath the trailer at least once every week. Thien, wearing thick rubber gloves, would be in charge of this chore. Hus had already shown him the lever that opened the trailer's sewer tank valve, how it released the smaller tank's contents into the long pipe, through the trench, and into the larger septic tank.

Thien had stared glumly, silently, at the coils of pipe as Hus explained all this to him. Hus had tried to make a joke of it, nudging the boy's shoulder and commenting, "Hey, you may hate it now but one day you'll realize, this might well be one of the most interesting experiences of your life! How many kids get a chance to man a septic tank every week, anyhow?"

Of Tran's two children before Hus, only Thien had been old enough to be aware of the changes they had gone through in coming from Vietnam and his mother's remarriage. While Tran's daughter had accepted Hus easily enough, Thien was gloomy and reticent. Hus worried that the boy might be unresilient, one of those simply fated not to adapt well to changed environments. Hus had tried to teach him about fishing, cars, model airplanes — things Hus thought should have interested a boy. But Thien always seemed to listen rather unenthusiastically, though in private, Hus soon discovered, Thien worked intently on the model airplanes Hus brought him, or pored over the photos of cars in books and drew countless pictures of them. Hus took it personally, this stubborn, reclusive enjoyment of his gifts. It startled Hus, how effective an insult from a child could be.

The septic tank — a huge, black, submarine-shaped hunk of iron and aluminum — now sat at the top of the driveway. Today Hus and Thien were to drag the tank down the hill and maneuver it into the hole they had dug for it next to the trench. With two thick coils of braided rope, they fastened a harness around the body of the tank. The cousins were playing soccer with a deflated ball on the concrete foundation, the girls running barefoot after them with the hems of their ridiculous dresses flapping, and Tran had set up lawn chairs in front of the trailer for Aunt Mary and Uncle John, who were lounging in the summer morning sun with glasses of iced tea to watch the touted septic tank event (Hus had been proudly expounding on the details of this task to the relatives since the day they'd arrived). As Hus and Thien finished attaching the harness, a black Chevrolet truck appeared at the top of the driveway, its engine was cut off, and a man climbed out.

"Howdy, there." The man greeted them in the comfortable drawl Hus had grown used to hearing in these hills. People talked much the same way they walked around here, he had noticed, in ambling, calmly investigative tones, so unabashedly, enviably John Wayne American.

"Hi, there," said Hus, with a little peremptory nod. Hus couldn't recall having seen this man before, though he recognized the truck from having passed it occasionally on the roads. The man was tall and wiry, not much younger than Hus, dressed in dirty blue jeans and a white pocketed T-shirt with a red design of horses raging across the front. His muscles showed like knots through the thin fabric of the T-shirt, and his forearms were dark with tattooes. The skin on his nose was peeling slightly, his hair was curled tightly against his head, the same unlively brown as tree bark, and he had a beard. His appearance made Hus think of the black house he sometimes passed on one of the nearby roads, with the Harley-Davidson motorcycles always parked out front, the lawn furniture decrepit. Hus had been entertaining a suspicion that a cult lived there.

The man walked down the driveway with his long hands dangling loosely.

Hus stopped halfway up. "Hello," he said expectantly.

The man slowed and stood a guarded distance from Hus. He looked at Hus, then behind him at the relatives and the children and Tran. He hooked one thumb in his belt loop and rubbed his beard with his other hand. When he spoke, his voice was surprising, deep and mellow and natural. "Hello, neighbor," he said. "It's a beautiful morning, isn't it?" And there was something cheerful and knowing to the way he clipped his words, making *isn't it* sound more like *itn'dit*.

"Certainly is," said Hus.

The man stroked his beard, glancing around amiably enough. "Now I hope I'm not interrupting your party or anything here, sir, but I am conducting a little personal investigation of my own. If you like, maybe you could help me. You see, sir, my dog was shot last night." His eyes shifted, and that was when Hus noticed his motionless eyebrows, betraying the smile on his lips. "She was a damn fine dog, too, never would hurt a fly. A little mean-looking and big, sure, but still no one had the right to go and shoot her in the night like that. Now this morning, I'm just going around to ask people if they seen or heard anything unusual about eleven-thirty or so last night. That's when I heard all the commotion."

"I'm afraid I heard nothing out of the ordinary last night," replied Hus.

The man stood quietly for a moment, one hand still on his chin and the other hooked on his waist, and studied Hus. "Well, sir, she was a nice dog is the fact," said the man, "and she wasn't so easily replaceable, you see, as she was partway wolf. I raised her from a pup, after some roaming free agent hopped the fence on one of my German shepherd dogs, made her a mama." Then slowly, lowering his hands, in gentle, amused disbelief he said, "You mean to tell me you didn't hear nothing when I heard a great big commotion of barking and strange voices and real live gunfire? You may be on the other side of the hill, sir, but if you've noticed, sound carries across this lake. And if there was people out driving, they'd have surely driven past this piece of the road, too. I would think so."

"I assure you I heard nothing," said Hus.

"Well, then," said the man, "could I ask you, then, what you and these folk were up to at about that time last night?"

"We were asleep," Hus replied briefly. "I'm sorry I can't help you anymore. Good luck, however." He turned his back to walk away, but the man raised his voice to call out after him.

"Well, sir, I have to tell you I've been hearing maybe otherwise. Some other fella gave me your address, says you're the new people here. And he's seen your truck drive by my place a number of times."

Hus's eyes swept over the relatives, who had come up the driveway and were standing now midway up the dirt road, staring at him. He turned to face the man again, but the image of the relatives had stuck in his mind and he saw himself as the man must have seen him, with all his brown-skinned, slant-eyed company in a scattered line behind him, dressed in their cheap secondhand clothing, the scrawny boys in their swim trunks and Huong in her floppy hat and tiger-striped bathing suit, his wife squatting on the ground with her knees in her armpits, in that way he tried to discourage, as she smoked her cigarette. Hus could read the man's disgust at the sight, and felt a shameful anger flare up inside himself. He understood all too well that feeling of repulsion. Suddenly there was a pain in his stomach. He was terrifically sensitive to stress and different foods and had recently developed an ulcer. Sometimes when the pain occurred, it made him furious at everything, regardless of his true intentions. Hunger and lack of discipline could do this to dogs as well, he often thought. Especially those not-entirely-domestic breeds.

"Now I don't mean to jump to conclusions," said the man, "but I don't know many other people around here who would go out in the night and shoot a man's dog for no good reason."

"As I already said, we were asleep."

"How do I know that for sure?" The man took a step forward and held his palm up toward Hus. Hus felt a flash of apprehension shoot through his body like heat. He saw the man's other arm hanging at his side, swaying, as if it had been caught by surprise. His skin looked smudged beneath the tattooes, which were a faded, inky, dark green tint — and for some reason this led Hus to think the man must be an alcoholic. "What proof have you got?" the man was demanding, the drawling tones of his voice now in anger sounding fatuous.

"You can ask anyone here," said Hus.

"And anyone here could be goddamn lying to me," said the man. "How am I to know what people like you might like to do for sport?"

"You are an insensible man," said Hus as calmly as he could, "and you are wasting my time." Behind him then he heard a soft, petulant "Hey!" He twisted around — conscious that the man was looking, too — and was met by the sight of his wife standing a few feet behind him with her hands on her hips and her feet spread. In her broken English she was exclaiming, "I his wife! He was asleep with me last night, I know!" Her eyes were beady beneath her thick glasses.

The man made a hooting noise. "Oh, mama," he chuckled.

Hus was mortified, on whose behalf more he was not sure. Tran's face, too, was red and her gaze flinched beneath the man's mocking attention. Her mouth was fast becoming a thin, disappearing, injured little line.

Hus broke. "What did I just tell you!" he turned and shouted at the man. As Hus strode forward, he was vaguely aware of the fact he had not just told the man anything to justify his shouting this question. The man jumped immediately backward into a fighting stance, fists raised and bobbing in front of his face, and said, "Yeah, c'mon, you sucker." For Hus there could be little satisfaction in striking an opponent who behaved like this. In Hus's experience it seemed this was the way most American men fought — with a scrabbling, brutal, at-all-costs type of strength that was effective but lacked any finer sense of — how else could he put it — *athletics*. He had encountered it first in the U.S. Army.

Hus stopped two feet in front of the man and chose the option of pointing at him firmly and menacingly. "You get off my property this instant," demanded Hus. "Or I swear you'll regret it. You do not know what you're dealing with if you don't get your filthy person off my property this instant." The blood had drained from his face, and he felt cold. He didn't want the girls to see him like this.

The man was still bobbing up and down in front of Hus. "You chicken, man? You afraid I might knock you on your chicken shit ass?"

They stared at one another until the man pulled himself upright, with a glowering, unfinished look. Hus didn't budge. The man spat over his shoulder, glared at Hus once more, then turned with an abrupt, jerking motion and strode back to his truck. He climbed into the cab and turned over the ignition, and the truck roared. Its grill hissed. The man rested his tattooed forearm on the window frame and leaned his head out. "Listen, I won't forget this, you hear me?" he shouted. Then he put the truck in gear and backed out of the driveway, tires spitting pebbles.

Hus turned and walked stiffly back to the septic tank. His wife and the relatives and the children were all looking at him. Thien was kicking at the septic tank with the toe of his sneaker. Tran, her face flushed, still had her hands on her hips.

"That not a very friendly man," said Aunt Mary, who stood in front of her lawn chair. She looked with concern toward Tran.

Hus said, "She's all right now. She just has to learn that not everybody in the world is friendly." He caught his wife's glance and noticed a darkness in her expression. He didn't know if this was because of what he had just said or if she was upset about the whole incident. He told himself irritably that she did not understand, that she shouldn't have stepped in and given the man more to make fun of.

"I just try to help," she said, seeming to read his thoughts, "that all, but you no appreciate anything I do." She headed back toward the trailer and Aunt Mary, her back to Hus as she spoke. Sometimes when she got upset she was like a child herself, Hus thought.

"You *do not* appreciate." He automatically corrected her grammar. "Of course I appreciate your efforts, but I don't think you understand what people like that are truly like."

His wife did not respond. She spoke in Vietnamese with her sister, and again Hus couldn't tell if they were quarreling or not. Tran was speaking in a curt voice, and Uncle John joined in, also with a raised voice. Hus watched them for a few moments. He tried to chuckle. Loudly, he interjected, "Tell them, Tran, that's not how everyone out here in the country is." He realized this would be the story the relatives would tell when they went back to San Diego. They would tell other Vietnamese people they knew, this is what people in the country are like, and this is what Tran Trinh's new husband is like.

"Tell them now, Mom," Hus said cheerfully.

∎ ∎ ∎

The man returned about half an hour later, carrying a bottle of wine. Hus and Thien had dragged the septic tank to the edge of the driveway and were beginning to ease it down the slope. The relatives were gathered around watching, and Hus felt he was educating them by allowing them the chance to watch this work being done. Though he didn't know exactly what to make of their loud and animated, even joyous, exclamations at some moments, as when the tank began to teeter sideways on the slope, or when the ropes caught on an overhead tree branch — what were they cheering in hopes of, he wondered, a rescue or a fiasco? The girls sat above them in a tree with their prized second-hand Barbie dolls that'd been given to them by some previous neighbors in Sacramento (otherwise Hus would not have allowed them to have Barbies). The girls had strung ropes in the branches of the oak tree and were straddling each their own branch, pretending the branches were ponies.

The mother dog was barking as the man came down the driveway.

He raised his arms over his head as he approached. "I came back to apologize, is all," he announced, and held the bottle of wine out to Hus. "I was jumping the gun earlier and I just wanted to come say how sorry I am for making a mess of your morning like I did."

Hus looked at the bottle. He was reminded of his ulcer, the reason he no longer drank alcohol.

"That's fine," said Hus. "Tran," he called to his wife, "why don't you come take this?"

Tran came over from the trailer and took the bottle, smiling politely. Hus thought he should tell her later never to smile so sweetly at a man like this.

The man wiped his hands on his jeans. "My name's Will, by the way. William Bentley. I live over toward Crooked Mile Court. I do apologize for this morning, truly." His voice was measured and controlled once more, but now Hus heard a falseness in it. He shook the man's hand reluctantly, finding it thin and sticky.

"Hus Madsen," he said. "My wife, Tran."

"Hello, missus." The man tipped his head slightly. "I do hope you'll excuse my rotten behavior this morning."

"Well, we all okay now," said Tran brightly. Hus looked at her.

"So, you folks all Chinese or Japanese?" said the man conversationally. "I knew a Chinese family back in Tracy where I used to live for a while. They were nice people. The missus was a real good seamstress, actually. She could patch any rip in a matter of minutes. She sewed some pretty dresses for my wife." The man glanced around briefly. "Now all of you don't live in there, do you?" He nodded toward the trailer.

"No, it's just my wife and I and our three, the boy here and the two little girls," said Hus. "My wife's side of the family is visiting from down south." Hus made a gesture to Tran, to send her back to the trailer. She went, seeming oblivious.

"And they're Chinese, too, huh?" said the man.

"Vietnamese," corrected Hus.

"Is that so?" The man declared this with genuine surprise and a spark of something else. He met Hus's eye only briefly as his glance skated over the relatives. "Well, Hoss," said the man (and Hus didn't bother to correct his pronunciation), "I was on my way over to ask if you wanted to accompany me on a little visit to somebody. You see, I went over to a man named Curt Hopkins's place just now, and the way he was acting, it occurred to me he might well be the culprit I'm looking for. And I just thought I might enlist a little help talking to him." The man paused a moment, then focused again on Hus. He did not disguise the growing nastiness in his tone. "But I see you're probably much too busy for that right now."

The dog had approached them and was nuzzling Thien's legs as Thien, at the other end of the septic tank, dropped the piece of rope he'd been holding and knelt beside the dog to absently stroke her head. The dog panted and wagged her tail happily.

"Yes," said Hus, "we have far too much work to do here right now. I'm sorry about your dog, however."

"Well, I thank you," said the man, bowing with a mock salute, two fingers to his forehead. "Enjoy that wine, now." Then he turned his back and left them.

Hus and Thien got the septic tank down the hill and maneuvered it into position above the hole. They had to brace themselves against the weight of the tank, Hus in front pulling the rope over his shoulder and leaning so far forward his knees almost dug into the ground, and Thien at the back of the tank, pushing. Hus wondered if Thien was pushing hard at all. Soon they would have to pull backward on their ropes to keep the tank from sliding too fast into the hole in the wrong position. The girls had climbed down from their tree and were running about, chasing the chickens out of the way of the oncoming tank, waving their dirty, half-dressed Barbie dolls in front of them. Hus was afraid the girls might fall into the hole or the trench, and it was making him nervous and distracted. "Get out of the way now! Now!" he shouted, when he heard the truck again.

William Bentley walked to the edge of the driveway and stood with his feet spread and his fists on his hips. "Hey!" he called down. "I gotta talk with you, Hoss!"

Hus wiped his brow with his forearm and released the rope. He moved calmly back up the length of the tank to its end, and stopped beside Thien. They both shielded their eyes and looked up the hill at the man. Hus folded his arms across his chest. For a scant moment it felt as if they were in this together, father and son, both of them sweating and dusty.

"What's the problem?" Hus called.

"I got a problem with my here dog that was shot last night," yelled the man.

"I thought we discussed this already," said Hus.

"I gotta say now, Hoss, I believe you've been lying to me."

Hus took a deep breath. He stared for a moment at his dirty, worn work boots.

"Yeah, I believe you been lying to me," the man repeated, "and Curt Hopkins isn't the one who done it, and I know because he proved it to me by giving me some other pertinent news —"

"You need to get off my property right now," said Hus, raising his voice.

The man paced a few steps back and forth at the edge of the driveway. "What you got here on your property, Hoss" — he gestured at the relatives and their kids standing around — "I know better than to trust a man who's running a refugee camp on his property. I know what's normal or not. And I know if anyone shot my dog, it was someone on this here property."

"No one here shot your dog." With contained vehemence, Hus got this out.

"Yeah?" The man nodded his chin in the direction of the trailer, where Uncle John was standing. "What about him? I know something you oughtta know, Hoss. I know that boy of yours is damn sneaky enough to have sent someone out to shoot my dog last night, behind your sleeping dumb-ass back, Hoss."

Hus stared incredulously at the man. A short distance behind the man was Tran on the doorstep of the trailer. She had poured herself a glass of wine and was holding it with both hands, looking at the man's back. Beside Hus, Thien shuffled his feet. Hus wondered suddenly, how had he gotten himself into this situation, into this life? "If you don't get off my property, I am going to have to call the police."

"Oh, no, I'm not leaving yet," shouted the man. "I'm not leaving until you tell me yes, my people shot your poor dog, and then you give me some money to repair my damages. I want at least five hundred dollars, you hear me? Five hundred. Because my dog was a *rare* animal, goddamn it." The man paced. He then strode back to his truck, reached into the bed, and dragged something out, something that Hus could not see clearly until the man had heaved it over his shoulder, carried it onto the driveway, and thrown it down on the rocks. The large white dog's body was limp and the bullet wound was visible in the middle of its rib cage, where the fur was stained red.

Hus glared at the man, furious.

"I'm leaving her for you now, see? She's all yours now."

Suddenly, Hus was on the driveway, shoving the man aside

and reaching for the dog. He lifted its cold furry body and felt the weight and softness of it against his forearms and chest as he began to walk with it up the driveway.

The man shouted, "Hey!"

They all watched Hus. He continued to walk, not knowing himself what he would do, down the road. It occurred to him what he was at that moment: a forty-nine-year-old man carrying a dead dog down a dirt road. How had this ever become an impasse at which he had arrived, and what did it say about his future? Everything he had done — for years — had long been motivated by the wish to separate himself from any risk of conflicts such as these, and from people whose prejudices were based, like this man's, on fear or rage or spite. This was the consequence of righteousness, it seemed to Hus, his own as well as this man's. But how could Hus not view this man as a lazy worthless person, after he had thrown his own dead dog on the ground? Surely this was a person not capable of understanding a desire for peace, a man who had allowed his dog to be shot in the first place. As Hus continued to walk, it dawned on him that the man had probably shot his dog himself. Drunk and mad at the dog for harassing the neighbors, or mad at having been accused by the neighbors of some harassment or other by the dog, this man, William Bentley, had probably on an impulse gone out and shot the dog, then regretted it. And by morning, he had convinced himself that someone else must've come and shot the dog. This was what Hus believed, the farther he walked holding the dog, as if its contact with him were imparting to him this version of the story.

The man yelled after him, "You lousy son of a bitch! You go and keep her!"

Hus stopped in the middle of the dusty road. He looked around at the trees and the brilliant blue sky and the sunshine. He gently set the dog's body down in the tall, dry grass and starthistle on the side of the road. Then he turned around slowly, his eyes sweeping over the tangled oaks and pines descending in thickening clusters down the hill on one side; he saw his family and relatives scattered up the road watching him, slowly trailing after him, the man pushing through them and swinging his arms. On the other side of the road was a driveway that led to the Nerwinskis' house. A retired old couple, the Nerwinskis were nice enough to allow the Madsens to fill their plastic gallon jugs with water from their outdoor spigot once a week or so, and they also had a telephone the Madsens could borrow. In the pastures alongside their long, gently winding driveway, the Nerwinskis' sheep were grazing.

The man caught up to Hus and stepped over the dog's body in the grass without glancing at it.

"You bastard fucker." The man slammed his fist into his palm, but Hus did not feel threatened. "What do you think you're doing?"

"I think it's time you removed yourself and your dog from here. I think you've overstayed your welcome by now, don't you?"

Hus's family and the relatives trickled down the road toward them. Thien and two of the cousins came and stood a few feet behind the man, glancing from Hus and the man to the dead dog. Hus saw the girls and Huong holding hands at the back of the crowd. They looked pitifully disheveled in their silly strapless dresses, and they were barefoot now, like urchins.

"I've got something to say to you, Hoss," the man said quickly. "I've seen your boy going by my place on his motorbike before. And I just found out that last week there was a boy out on a motorbike chasing my dog around with a BB gun. I was told that just today when I was out asking questions of my good neighbors."

Hus didn't believe him. "To be honest with you, it's probably best your dog was shot. It was most likely mistreated and vicious because of your mistreatment." He caught sight of Thien staring open-mouthed at the man. Hus felt the pain in his stomach flare to his ribs. He straightened his back and tried to stand taller. He faced Thien with a piercing look.

Thien's gaze immediately dropped to his feet.

The man laughed.

"The dog was chasing me," Thien mumbled, "but it was a long

time ago. I was on my motorbike one day and I fell off because he was chasing me and he almost bit me."

"And then you fired at this animal with your BB gun, did you?"

Thien shrugged, not looking up, and shifted his feet in the grass. "I didn't hurt his dog. He made me fall off my bike. And it happened a long time ago."

The man stood between Hus and Thien, looking from one to the other triumphantly. He folded his arms and narrowed his eyes with what looked like concentration. Maybe, Hus thought, it was best in life to just suspect everyone of holding out on you.

"And what were you doing driving around with your BB gun on your motorbike? Don't you know how stupid that is? That is a stupid, stupid thing to do!" Though he knew he should not berate the boy in front of a stranger, Hus could not contain himself — it was with kids as it was with dogs sometimes, he thought, that you had to punish them on the spot or they might not remember what you had caught them at. Hus leaned toward Thien. "*Stupid!* I would expect you to know better, Thien. Is that what you do? Answer me. Why were you driving around with your BB gun on your motorbike? Is this something you do regularly?"

Thien shook his head. His shoulders moved up and down.

Hus again demanded an answer.

"Yeah, you tell him now," added the man. Hus ignored him, but he was irked by the feeling of the man joining him.

"Do you, Thien," Hus repeated meticulously, "drive your motorcycle around with your BB gun?"

Thien muttered, "I wasn't, I didn't have it with me. I came back and got it, all right?" He glared briefly at Hus, then looked away.

Tran was beside them now, trying to step in. "Let me talk to him, Daddy," she said, addressing Hus as she usually did in front of the children.

"No, he needs to learn," said Hus. "So you came back and got your gun. You meant to come back and specifically shoot at this dog. That is what they call premeditated, do you understand? That kind of thinking, and the choice that you made is equal to a crime, do you realize? How do I know you didn't decide to do this again last night? I can't be sure of anything now, can I?"

"No, you can't," the man agreed.

"I fell off my dumb bike, okay? I almost got bit. That dumb dog was trying to bite me. But I never *shot* him!" Thien's face twisted up and he crossed his arms tightly over his chest and hunched his shoulders. He began to cry.

For a moment the only sound was Thien's sniffling. Hus didn't know what to say next. He stood staring at the boy with his eyes so fiercely focused, they ached. He stepped back in the grass.

"You do a thing that stupid again and you'll be sorry," said Hus. But he meant it not as a threat — he just wanted Thien to learn something, something about life, this. He said sternly, "You don't make dumb moves like that. Let me tell you."

Thien was crying and wiping his eyes.

"Go on home now," said Hus, and Thien turned quickly away and shouldered past his mother, who was reaching for him. She glared at Hus, and Hus believed they were all, the relatives and kids, glaring at him in the same hateful manner. Even the man was leering. Hus felt sick to his stomach.

"Aw, shit," said the man suddenly. "What the hell are you yelling at him for? He's just a kid. He didn't shoot my dog. Sure, I believe someone here did, but it wasn't that poor kid. You should be yelling at that other guy." He gestured toward Uncle John.

Tran spoke up. "Yes, you being too hard on Thien. I think you being unreasonable. We go home now, we forget everything."

Hus could hardly believe what he was hearing. He watched as Tran headed back up the dirt road, and Aunt Mary and the cousins started to follow. Hus noticed his younger daughter, Beth, was crying, and Huong knelt beside her. The older girl, April, was glancing between Hus and Tran, and Hus saw her dark hair swinging against her neck. It looked cheerful and nonchalant and so innocent, that motion. Uncle John and a few of the older boys were hesitating, still interested in the conflict.

"You got some problems," said the man, "beyond the five hundred dollars you still owe me."

Hus looked at him with pity. "You take your animal and leave now. You disgust me. You are a low and common form of human being." He gestured toward the driveway across the road. "I am going to go call the police. You can decide what you're going to do next."

Hus stepped over the dead dog and crossed the road. The man didn't stop him. The fight was over for both of them. Hus walked up the Nerwinskis' driveway. The sheep grazing in the pastures raised their heads briefly as he went by. He stepped onto the Nerwinskis' porch and rang the doorbell. The wind chimes dangling from the eaves tinkled like water rippling — and for one second an image of a snow-covered mountain meadow crystallized in his mind with excruciating clarity. Mr. Nerwinski let him in, nodding pleasantly. The TV murmured in the living room and Hus could hear the sound of some crockery being set down in the kitchen, could see a section of the sheep pasture through the open front-room window, as perfect as a painting on the wall itself. Mrs. Nerwinski came out of the kitchen to join her husband.

Sweaty and dusty, Hus's clothes emitted a bad odor. "There's a man harassing my family" was all he could say. "May I use your telephone?"

The old couple directed him to the phone and he tramped across their clean floor, tracking clumps of dirt from his boots.

As he laid his hand on the phone, he caught sight of the dirt. His stomach turned painfully and he abruptly moved his hand to it, frowning. The couple looked alarmed, and Hus could not answer immediately when they asked what was the matter. Mr. Nerwinski brought Hus a chair. It was a simple, sturdy wooden chair, Hus noted as he sat down, leaning back and breathing heavily. He was unable to thank them or apologize right away, either. Mr. Nerwinski went back to stand with his wife, and Hus saw them, the old couple, in the middle of their living room, watching him with wondering eyes. He saw them among their weathered furniture and full bookshelves and framed pictures on their walls, pictures of children young and grown, and a strange melancholy washed over him. He remembered then an incident from his youth. It was winter, and he was at the train station awaiting his father's return from a business trip, when an older boy approached and began taunting him about his family. Hus had become so angered he had beaten the other boy until all he could see was the blood red against the white snow, and his own hands bleeding and red from the cold. Slowly, the roll of pain in his stomach subsided.

"It's nothing," said Hus. "I'm very sorry. I'll be just a minute." He tried to chuckle to ease his awkwardness.

Mrs. Nerwinski smiled tenderly and shook her head. "Poor young man," she said.

Hus raised his chin. "No, no, I'm fine," he said and nodded briskly. He sat with his back straight and reached for the phone again, but knew he would not make the call. He laid his other hand on his thigh, and tried to keep his face from clouding.

The man and the dog and all of Hus's family were gone when Hus came down the Nerwinskis' driveway. He walked back up the road home by himself. He felt drained and mentally exhausted, but there was peace in the tangles of wild oats that grew beside the road and in the sound of sparrows in the trees.

When Hus reached the top of his driveway, Tran and the others were standing about the trailer. They stopped talking when they saw him. April and Beth ran to him, exclaiming, "Daddy's back!" and he patted their heads and said, "Yep, we're all home now." He picked up Beth and carried her on his hip. When he reached the trailer he set Beth down, nodded briefly at Tran, and went inside. He poured water from the gallon jug by the sink over his hands and rubbed them together, then wiped them dry on his jeans. He spotted the bottle of wine on the counter and thought they should probably throw it out.

Outside again, his family and the relatives were gathered around the front of the trailer. They all looked at him, their eyes dark and blank, except for the girls, who were bumping hips in the dirt and twirling their dresses around their legs. Thien was standing with his arms crossed, staring off down the hill even as Hus spoke.

"Everything's all right now," he said, and gave a reassuring chuckle. He wondered if they still cared what he thought or not, and half hoped they did not. "He won't be coming back, that man," he said, feigning confidence. Then he added, addressing the girls, "It's time to feed the animals now. There's no reason to forget that." The girls ran to get the dog dishes and he added, "Make sure you give them fresh water, too."

Hus looked at his wife. She was pulling on the galoshes she used to walk in the chicken coop. She didn't like to walk on the chicken droppings in her good boots. Hus waved at her. The relatives had begun to talk again among themselves; Hus wondered whether they were discussing him. He needed to keep busy, to get away.

"No, no, Mom," he said, making a face. "I'll do it. I'll feed the chickens today." Outside the coop, he scooped up a cup of poultry feed and entered the chicken pen. As he scattered the yellow kernels around his feet in handfuls, the chickens surrounded him, scratching and clambering frantically over each other and the tops of his boots. He closed his fist, stemming the flow, then stepped over their backs to another part of the pen to scatter the rest of the feed.

to notice that there was now one pine tree less — it was another dig-
ger, admittedly — on the hillside of the empty horse pasture to the
east. But trees are heedless. I realize that now. It is only humans
who worry over the necessity of being heard.

TREES, HANDS, LEAVES

I

In August it rained for two weeks straight and the gray sky made it seem as if it were already fall. The long yellow grass dying on the hills all summer was wet and bent. Usually dry in the summertime, the creek that ran through the ravine at the bottom of our property filled with water. One afternoon I explored the ravine. I went across the creek and through the berry vines and manzanita trees and up the hill on the other side. Should I say this now about the trees? The hillsides where we lived were so steep the trees on them grew at precarious angles, slanting and leaning almost sideways out of the slopes, trying very hard to grow upward, perfectly, toward the sky, but not quite making it because of the pull of gravity from the valley below. The pine trees especially looked strange because their trunks were tall and straight and rigid. They looked frozen in the middle of falling.

I climbed to where the hill leveled into a meadow of thin yellow grass and scattered boulders. From here I could see the mountains and the American River winding quietly along the bottom of the Coloma Valley. This was the view my father had built our house to look out on. The only sound I could hear was the creek running. I opened my mouth to scream into the silence then, and I tried to make myself sound like a red-tailed hawk. It was a game Cody Walker and I had been playing lately. We used the sound to call to each other — our families lived just over the hill from each other. Sometimes you could not tell the difference between us and real hawks, and that made me proud. That day, I let out a couple of sharp cries, pretty high-pitched, and after a few seconds I heard a cry come back to me. I knew it was Cody. He came walking up out of the trees at the same place I had, wearing jeans and his father's boots that were too big for him and a ratty knit sweater that hung to his knees. His blond hair was thick and messy and fell over his forehead like a pony's forelock. Cody Walker and I were both almost eleven, but we were only friends, really, in the summertime and after school; I had skipped a grade, and so we were in different classes. The other truth is that home and school were two different worlds and in school Cody was popular, so popular he did not have time for me when we were there, though sometimes he stuck up for me. Cody Walker was the only kid in school who knew what I was like at home (sometimes I wished this could be more widely known) — how I was more adventurous and talented than others might think, how I was not just a little brain.

Cody was swinging a stick at the grass and grinning. "I knew that was you," he said.

"Well, I knew it was you," I answered, happy to see him.

He sat down on one of the rocks and poked his stick into the ground. He started gouging up clumps of the yellow grass. When he bent his head down, I could see the back of his neck was red. He rubbed it with one hand.

"Why is your neck red?"

"I got sunburned. I guess you don't ever burn. You're lucky."

I walked a few steps away into the grass. I broke off a branch of a manzanita tree that was hanging over my head. The bark was smooth and deep crimson red. You could peel it off like the skin of a fruit, and the wood underneath was white and soft and delicate and pretty. Suddenly I felt like fighting. I stuck the branch in my mouth.

Cody was watching. "You're acting weird, April," he said, "you're chewing on a stick."

I shrugged. We didn't talk for a few moments. Cody kept digging at the ground with his stick and I stood with my ankles crossed and watched him. The dirt turned up in wet, dark redbrown clumps with pale yellow slivers of grassroots poking through.

"My mom turns red as a turkey every time she goes out in the sun," said Cody. He laughed slightly. "This one time my dad and her were lying by the lake and my dad fell asleep with his hand on her back and when she got up later and went inside, she had, like, a white handprint mark in the middle of her back and the rest of her back was all red. My dad called it the hand of God!" He laughed more, but I didn't feel like laughing with him. "It was so funny, though," he said.

"Did it go away?"

"'Course it went away."

I sat down on the other side of the rock next to Cody, imagining a big white hand mark on a person's bare back. "Who do you like better," I asked, "me or my sister?" My sister, Beth, was seven, three years younger than we were.

Cody shrugged. "Neither, I guess."

"But you have to like someone better," I said. That year I had begun to be scared about possibilities and had to seek security sometimes. By myself, it seemed any disaster, any atrocity was possible. Often in the afternoons I would be overwhelmed by dread. I don't know why or where it came from. I'd be inside, thinking a crazy person might have broken into the house while we were away and that he was hiding there watching me, so I would go outside. But there might be a storm blowing and then I'd envision the whole side of the cliff next to the house collapsing suddenly and burying me. You just couldn't know. So often it felt as if there was nowhere safe to go.

"I like you both the same," said Cody. He glanced up abruptly. "Whoa, lookit. Wish I could do *that*."

Two red-tailed hawks circled in the sky far overhead. Their cries came across the valley toward us, faint and lonely sounding.

Cody made a squawking noise in his throat.

We came back up along the blue gravel road and sat down at the top of my driveway. The dogs waddled up the driveway and walked around us, wagging their tails and trying to lick our faces. We kept pushing them off and finally they lay down, panting. Their big thick coats smelled like the mucky parts of the lake, but they felt good to lean against or lay your head on.

We were there on the driveway with our heads on the dogs, looking up at the gray sky, when Cody's Uncle Michael walked by on the road. Uncle Michael was about fifty years old and brain-damaged from all the drinking he'd done. At least that's what I remember being told. He lived in a trailer next to the trailer the Walkers lived in, because Cody's mom was Uncle Michael's niece and had to take care of him. The Walkers were also building a house on their property, nicer than ours, though, a log cabin. The logs the Walkers were using for their home were honey brown, like the color of pancakes.

Uncle Michael was known for taking frequent walks down the road. He dragged his feet when he went by and he slouched. He never talked to anyone, and if you said "hi" to him he would just lift his hand at you and not blink. He wasn't supposed to drink or smoke anymore, but when he took his long walks down the road you could spy him sneaking cigarettes. (That is how the older girls in the neighborhood picked up the technique, actually, of holding their lit cigarettes carefully, backward, in the cups of their hands as they walked; they told Cody so.) And Uncle Michael wasn't really brain-damaged, we knew, he just didn't want to talk. He sat in his chair in front of his trailer and played cards by himself all the time, too, and didn't that take thinking? I'd decided something must've happened to Uncle Michael, something terrible when he was young. My parents on the other hand explained to me that Uncle Michael was a vegetable, a human vegetable. Maybe before he had been an avid card player, an expert, reasoned my father, and that was why this skill was now automatic to him. His having been a card player would explain his drinking, too, said my father.

I didn't always believe them, though, my parents.

Cody and I waved at Uncle Michael and he waved back and went on walking. A few seconds later, Rebel Johnson and her little brother, Davy, who was four, came walking up from the opposite direction. They lived down the road, and their father, Travis Johnson, was a contractor who'd been helping my father build our house for a couple of years; he still occasionally helped. Rebel was one year older than me and Cody but in the same grade as I was. She was the first friend I'd made when we moved up here.

"Your uncle just flipped me off," she told Cody.

"No, he didn't." Cody rolled his eyes.

"I swear to God he did." Rebel had straight, shoulder-length blond hair and freckles. She wasn't popular in school, because (the other kids liked to say) she had a big butt. She was also a troublemaker and a kleptomaniac. Otherwise, maybe people would've thought she was pretty. I'd been told by some girls in school that more guys might like me if I didn't hang out with Rebel so much. Those same girls wouldn't have believed I actually hung out more with Cody Walker when we weren't in school.

Rebel walked up and stood over us, Davy behind her with his fingers in his mouth and his face all dirty. He was barefoot. Davy was always barefoot. Once in the middle of winter even, he walked down to the creek by himself and went in naked. He was only two years old then. He got poison oak all over his body and had to be put in a cold bath.

"April, I have something to tell you," said Rebel, her hands on her hips.

I squinted up at her. "So, tell me."

"You have to c'mere. It's a secret."

"So," I said, fixing my gaze on her.

Rebel's eyes got a little wide. "It's *important*, April. Like, majorly."

I got up, and she took my arm and pulled me aside. The dogs also got up, so Cody stood, too. I noticed his blond hair was messy in the back from lying down and for a single moment I felt protective of him. Rebel put her arm around my shoulders and her bangs touched mine. "Amy Abraham died," she whispered. Amy Abraham was a girl in our neighborhood and a classmate of Rebel's and mine.

I knew enough to be cautious about believing anything Rebel said. I narrowed my eyes at her — a thing I'd recently picked up from watching one of the older girls, Leann DeOlivera, do it while she was talking back to her parents.

"A tree fell on her. I swear to God, April. My mom just got a phone call from Dana Morrison's mom, and Dana Morrison's mom said Dana'd just been on a Girl Scouts camping trip, and the park ranger said they camped under a dead tree. Dana Morrison was there like right next to Amy, and she saw Amy's legs sticking out from under the tree. She said her legs were totally blue."

I didn't speak. I was thinking about Rebel's reputation for making up stories and stealing things from people at school. Many times the teacher kept the whole class after to search through all the desks. Once, I was remembering, Rebel stole a holographic dinosaur ruler from Amy Abraham, and later I gave it back to Amy in secret. But I told Amy I'd just found it on the ground somewhere. Usually people suspected the truth about Rebel anyway.

"Cross my heart, swear to *Jesus,* April," said Rebel. "It's true, true, true." She got in my face and nodded three times. "Amy's gone. Aren't you sad? You should be sad, April. We're never going to see her again and we didn't even get to say good-bye. Isn't that awful?"

I thought then that I should feel like crying, but for some reason nothing moved inside me. The sound of my father's pickup truck growling up the road broke the air then. He came home from work each day at five o'clock. The truck looked very white on that gray day. Cody and Davy moved off the driveway, and the dogs ran up against the driver's side window, wagging their tails and barking and panting.

My father leaned out the window. "What are you skunks up to?" He was in a good mood. He pointed to Davy, who still had his fingers in his mouth. "Hey, he has no shoes on. Rebel, your brother could get ringworm running around barefoot like that, you know." The truck rolled slowly forward.

"Dad," I had to say it before Rebel could, "Amy Abraham died."

"A tree fell on her when they were out camping with the Girl Scouts last night," said Rebel in one breath. "It was a dead tree, a Ponderosa pine. And it wasn't even windy. The tree just fell because it was dead."

My father sat with the truck idling. He shook his head. "Oh, Jesus," he said, his mouth turning down as if he were about to get angry.

Cody walked over to where Rebel and I were standing and looked at us with a blank face. He was still holding his stick, and he drew some lines in the road with it in front of his feet. I felt my eyes start to water a little but, I have to say, that was the only time. Not just with Amy's death. With the next one, too.

At the bus stop a lot of kids used to tease Amy Abraham because she was sort of a goody-goody. Some mornings I sat next to her on the bus and tried to make her feel better by attempting to be her friend. But most days, to be honest, I walked straight to the back of the bus, where I sat and tried to be more like all the others. The back of the bus was where it was at. Laughing and sticking my foot out in the aisle to trip boys like Todd Parham and Bryan Nichol as they boarded. Nothing that happened on those bus rides counted for very much once you arrived at school, though.

And at school Amy Abraham had nothing to worry about; she hung out with other girls more like her, who wore prettier dresses and colored hairbands, who'd come in on the Highway 49 bus that went almost into town, other girls who were not too popular but not unpopular, and who were affiliated with things like the Girl Scouts because their parents knew about these things. Girls who had events like first communions in their lives, and annual bake sales.

Amy Abraham lived down Winding Mile Way (which went on much longer than a mile), clear on the other side of the lake we all lived near, Lake Miwok. Her mother participated in the carpools to and from the bus stop with the other mothers, and her father was a professional baseball player but also a contractor. Amy had two little brothers and a white pony named Snowcone, and one year Snowcone got sick and had to be put to sleep, and the following day in school Amy was crying a lot in the middle of class. I remember standing around with the other girls who gathered to comfort her, but I didn't have the nerve to put my hand on her shoulder. We were all sometimes friends and sometimes not, in those days.

After dinner on the evening Rebel had told me the news, my sister, Beth, and I sat at the edge of the dirt bank behind our house, eating cantaloupe halves. From there we could watch the faraway strip of sky (across the valley where it was not as overcast as here) fading to orange, then purple, then blue, over the hills. My hands and legs were sticky with cantaloupe juice.

My brother, Thien, came and stood to our side, throwing rocks down into the ravine. "You know what this guy Victor called me at the pool today? This guy from school who I hate? He called me a Indian."

Our mom, who was sitting behind Beth and me on a turned-over bucket, said in a surprised tone, "You're not a Indian."

"No, duh," said Thien, and threw another rock. The dogs kept pricking up their ears at the sounds the rocks made landing in the brush and grass. They thought it was deer or porcupine or some other creature down there.

Mom laughed. "Well, whatever they say, you just tell them 'thank you!' and 'good-bye!' and pretend you don't care, because they don't know what they talking about."

"I'm not going to *thank* people for that," said Thien, with disgust. "God, Mom."

"They don't know what they're talking about," I agreed, thinking about a mistake my teacher had made. She'd written "America" on the board and told us to come up with words we could spell out of those letters. She hadn't believed me when I raised my hand and said "camera." She just skipped over me with a look that said she thought I didn't understand the exercise.

My brother said, "Well, I told him at least I'm not a stupid ugly albino." Beth and I laughed, even though neither of us knew what an albino was.

Thien glared at us. "It's not funny."

"I know you are but what am I," I said as quickly as I could. I didn't know why I said it.

Thien's face wrinkled at me. "Shut up, loser," he said, then walked off up the driveway.

Later, I walked down the road a way to find him. I was feeling full of love and worry because, honestly, I hated seeing my brother get mad. When he got mad he always looked more like he was getting sad. I didn't like his silence at those times; it terrified me. When he got in fights with our father, it was this way, too. He would just get very, very quiet while our father yelled. Sometimes he wouldn't answer a question, and our father would repeat it again and again, and I would stand nearby praying Thien would say just one word at least. The trees were blue now in the late evening light. I saw the shape of a person coming, but it was too tall to be Thien. I ducked down on the side of the road and the grass poked at my legs. It was just Uncle Michael walking by, smoking his cigarette. He lifted his hand in his stiff wave and hardly looked at me, as if he'd known all along I was there.

I finally found my brother in his trailer. The rest of us had moved into the house only a month or so ago, but he'd stayed in the trailer. Inside was my brother's own world. He had hooked up his speakers so that the whole inside of the trailer filled with sound whenever you turned on any music. We listened to The Beatles a lot, since they were Thien's favorite band. I liked to lie on my stomach on his floor and draw while he did his homework or whatever. Sometimes if I needed to draw something difficult, like a hand or a foot (the hardest things to draw realistically, said our mother, who had read this in a book about art), I would ask Thien to draw it for me. He was good at everything. He was always copying pictures out of comic books and science fiction novels whose plots he would tell me. There were many stories about men who could travel through time or to different planets but were lonely in their regular lives.

"Thien, I'm sorry." I stood on the dirt outside and called through the door.

"Stupid," said Thien, opening the door. "I'm not mad at you anymore." He was smiling.

Inside, the music was warm and loud. I stood on one of the seats and pressed my body to the wall and felt the wall trembling, as if the music was inside trying to get out. I felt so cozy for a moment, it felt like Christmas.

"You know that girl, the one who died?" asked Thien. "You should never sleep under any trees, okay? And if you're walking and you ever hear branches creaking over your head, from now on run. Fast, okay?"

"Okay," I said, feeling serious and a little proud about the possible danger.

"It was careless of the Girl Scout camp leaders not to have realized those girls were sleeping under a dead tree." Our dad had already said this.

I closed my eyes for a second to feel the music more strongly.

"You wanna know a secret? You can't tell Mom or Dad, though."

I opened my eyes. "Swear to God, hope to die." I swore it, but then I crossed my fingers behind my back, just in case.

"I hate living in the trailer. I hate building the house. I hate Dad."

"I hate it, too," I said. But I wasn't sure which part I meant.

Amy's funeral was on a Saturday. Mom said we should go, since everyone in the neighborhood was going, and Dad said he'd rather not, because he didn't like big occasions, which he said people were always putting on to make themselves feel better about things that had nothing to do with them in the first place. Plus, he had work to do.

That morning he was laying tile in the kitchen, and Thien was helping. The floors of the house were still concrete. There was no gypsum board on any of the upstairs walls, so you could walk between the beams and if you weren't careful, you could fall. The tiles our father was laying were like big, square, textured stickers — the cheapest kind. When our father built things, he either made them makeshift or like the humongous cat carrier we couldn't even carry, as the pine wood he'd built it with was so heavy. Beth and I used the box as a house for our dolls instead.

I stood on the bottom stair and ate my toast, watching Dad

and Thien peel the paper backing off each square and stick the tiles straight onto the concrete. Tile by tile the kitchen was starting to look like a kitchen was supposed to look, but it still seemed unfinished to me. It was like watching chickens grow up. I was so used to seeing them as baby chicks, I couldn't tell at which point they became adult chickens.

Dad pointed at one of the tiles Thien was about to lay down. "Not straight," he said tersely, then took it from Thien and placed it himself. Thien sat back on his heels and watched. "Now, like that," he directed Thien. "Concentrate."

I didn't want to watch anymore, so I went out the sliding glass door and made sure to close it gently behind me. I did not even leave my fingerprints on the glass.

Beth was riding her bicycle around and around the house, raising dust. The bike was ancient, and it rattled. It had no seat so she pedaled standing up the whole time. She was singing and wasn't watching where she was going.

"You're gonna fall if you don't concentrate," I told her.

My mother drove Beth and me and Rebel to the church, and we sat near the back. Other kids we knew were there, too, kids we hadn't seen since school let out in June, kids from our bus stop who used to tease Amy. It made me think I would not want for someone to be mad at me and then die.

Maybe Rebel was thinking the same thing, because as we were watching people come in, she whispered, "I said sorry to Amy before she died."

The ceiling of the church arched above us, the walls a cool pale blue that cast a diffuse glow over all the faces. Everyone watched Amy Abraham's parents enter and walk quietly to the front of the church. Crying, Mrs. Abraham walked beside another woman, whose arm was around her shoulders. Both wore black dresses. Their black clothes and their nearness to our pew as they passed made their bodies seem very large; I could not foresee myself ever becoming so large. Amy's father followed, carrying Amy's two-year-old brother and holding the hand of her five-year-old brother. Their black outfits, it occurred to me, were appropriate. My sister and I were not wearing black. We were wearing green and brown T-shirts and blue jeans, and we had our swimsuits on underneath, because afterward we had to go to our swimming lessons. Our mother had told us it would be good enough if we just wore dark colors. She was in a gray pantsuit with a black pointy-collared shirt underneath. Beth leaned slightly forward with her hands pressed against the edge of the bench and swung her legs, a calm look on her face. Though she was probably old enough to understand what was going on, I don't think she did.

Rebel's mom had dressed Rebel in a black dress, and Rebel's blond hair looked shock-white against it.

At the front of the church stood the priest in a black robe that was so long, I couldn't tell where his feet were. Surrounded by white roses and abundant long-petaled yellow flowers, the white coffin rested off to the side. The priest began to talk.

"We are here today for a very grave reason. Please" — gesturing with his arm so his sleeve seemed to flow — "let us pray."

As the priest spoke I swung my feet and gazed up at the high ceilings, at their smooth curves meeting at the center. I looked at the backs of all those people's heads in front of us. It was so quiet I heard shoes scraping the floor and stifled coughs. I felt as if I couldn't even breathe; I would make too much noise. I held my breath then and imagined a loud noise coming suddenly from the ceiling. I imagined a man, or a boy, or many boys — an *army* of them — suddenly breaking through the ceiling to take me away. They would whisper their plans to me, and we would slink together under the pews, around calves and ankles and shoes, to the back of the church, where they would tell me to hold tightly onto this rope — it would be a certain boy who would close his hands over mine, guiding my grip, one boy who would know the answers to such things as where the planets came from and why I sometimes felt scared looking at the night sky — and then I would be hoisted above everybody, through the ceiling, outside, not even gravity holding me down.

I tried to picture what this boy would look like, but the only boy's face I could come up with was Cody Walker's. Slowly and intently, I let out my breath and glanced toward my mother (who often scolded me for sighing, because she said I was doing it unnecessarily), but this time she didn't notice.

After the service we drove in a motorcade down Main Street to the Weatherwood Memorial Park, where we watched the pallbearers ease the white coffin into the ground. At the graveside I stood and looked around at the kids and their parents. The sun shone, interrupted occasionally by giant roving shadows from clouds. The mothers hugged each other. Many were crying.

On the way back to the car, Rebel and Beth and I walked past the rows of headstones, making sure not to step on any of the graves.

"Because they can feel you," Rebel warned us.

We waited at the car for my mother to say good-bye to the other mothers. She was not one of those crying. She was smiling sympathetically and laughing when it was appropriate (their laughter rising suddenly like exclamation marks into the air), but the truth is our mother did not look anything like the other mothers, even when she did what they did. They looked like plastic while she looked like wood. And this was when I much preferred the unspoiled new look of plastic things to the antiquated look of wooden things: wooden toys, how wistful and undynamic.

Rebel pinched me. "It's Jennifer Harsh."

In normal circumstances, Jennifer Harsh would not be coming toward me or Rebel Johnson to say hello, but here she was now. She had a long chestnut-brown ponytail I'd always envied and bright eyes and a big mouth, much fuller and prettier than my thin lips. She was one of the two most popular girls in our class. The other was Nicole Henley, who was the kind of popular person who could stop and talk to anybody. But Jennifer wasn't. Jennifer was looks-popular while Nicole was personality-popular.

"Isn't it terrible," Jennifer said to us, "and she lived so close to you two. How *are* you guys?"

"I'm okay," I said. I hooked one foot on the bumper of my

mom's car and raised my arms and laced my fingers together behind my head.

Rebel was staring at Jennifer, then she looked at me sideways.

"I just can't stop crying," said Jennifer, and she wrung her
fingers around a tissue and wiped at her eyes. "It's so sad, I'm so
sad for *everybody*. It's like, like everything suddenly has *changed*.
I didn't know Amy that well, but when I heard? It was like all of a
sudden I felt like she was my own sister, it hit me that hard." Her
eyes were gentle and wet-looking as she peered at us. "I used to
think we were different, but we're all the same, you know? So I
don't want to ever be mean to you guys ever again or anybody."

Rebel said, "I cried so much when I first heard," as if she was
admitting something secret, or making an excuse for herself.

"How could you *not* cry?" exclaimed Jennifer.

I stayed quiet with my fingers laced behind my head and my
arms up like a brace. I felt frozen. Beth was glancing back and
forth among the three of us, listening. I knew she had not cried,
either.

"I can't stop thinking about it," said Jennifer. "I hope she
wasn't in too much pain, you know?"

"I think it killed her too fast for her to feel it," said Rebel.

"Oh, God, please don't say that." Jennifer put her hand to her
chest and shut her eyes briefly. She looked pretty even in shock, I
thought.

I looked past Jennifer then and saw my mother standing with
Kathlyn Walker. Cody was picking up his little brother, Danny,
and turning him upside down. Danny was hollering, "Stop it,
Cody, you jerk!"

I lowered my arms and folded them across my chest. I could
feel my hair against the back of my neck and my body breathing.
In my mind I was a loose horse. I saw things in ways Jennifer and
Rebel could not, I thought.

Jennifer was saying, "I have to go now. You guys have to give
me a hug."

She kissed the top of my sister's head and hugged Rebel and
then me. She was sniffling a little as she patted my back with her

hands in a very adult way, and for a second I pictured the mark of her hand staying there on my back, though I didn't want it to.

"You guys take care now," she said, waving as she walked off.

Rebel waited a couple of seconds, then said, "She's such a fake."

That afternoon it rained on the swimming pool in town while we were having our lessons. The raindrops splashed on top of the clear pool water and made circles ripple and collide on the surface. Above us the sky was roiling and gray. It began to rain harder. Some kids shrieked and laughed and jumped up and down. The rain coming down made everybody turn their faces up together. The mothers in the deck chairs on the patio put their books or their kids' towels over their heads, or they just laughed. Something was happening and I didn't understand it, but I thought it was wonderful. Like the feeling of looking at a tree or the lake through the hair falling over my eyes and realizing no one else could have that view exactly ever; and how the poignant but amazing thing about that was this: *I can't show it to you.* Or like the mysterious sense I got sometimes in the late summer sitting on our driveway, looking at a blade of grass and feeling: *I am very close to the ground,* the dirt dusty on my knees and legs and darkening the skin where it'd rubbed into my knuckles. I wished we could be frozen in time — the rain, the voices, the pool. The water came down on top of my head and face and already surrounded my whole body, and I thought: *Maybe this is what it feels like to be buried.*

> I can't show it to you.
> I am very close to the ground.
> Maybe this is what it feels like to be buried.

A few days after Amy Abraham's funeral, we went with my mother and Kathlyn Walker to visit Amy's mother. It was Kathlyn Walker's idea, and she had invited my mother to come. All the mothers in the neighborhood were doing it in pairs and threes, calling on Mrs. Abraham every few days or so. It was still gray outside. Our mothers sat in the living room while Danny and Beth went outside to play. Cody and I went down the hall with Amy's little brothers.

Amy's bedroom was the same as it'd always been. I sat on the floor with her little brother, John, who was five, and he asked me did I know where his sister had gone, and I said no, and he said she had gone to heaven. I felt he was wrong (my own parents had told me heaven was just a story), but I understood this was how his parents had explained it to him, so I didn't correct him. Besides, I had no better idea about where Amy had gone.

"Can you read, John?" Cody was looking at some books on the floor.

John pulled one of the books out of Cody's lap. "I can read this one."

"Well, why don't you read it to us?" said Cody. John shook his head, and Cody pointed to himself. "You want me to read it?" He winked at me. "But April's a better reader than me. April's real smart. Will you read it to us, April?"

I took the book. Inside was a drawing of some people in a boat, and in the water all around them there were other people with their arms up, waving or floating on their backs. I knew it was just the Swiss Family Robinson but something about the picture was unsettling to me. "You read it, Cody," I said, holding it out to him.

Cody put his hand in his pocket and nudged John. "Give you what's in my pocket if you read to us, John. It's a surprise."

John took the bait. I set the book in his lap, and we looked on as he started. "*The family was at sea for many days,*" was all he could get through. "What's that word?" He pointed. "*After the...*"

Cody sounded it out. "Ex-pol-shun."

"Ex-*plo*-sion," I said.

"That's what I said."

"No, it's not."

Cody rolled his eyes. "I'm so sure. How would you know? I was only joking when I said you were smart."

I got up to leave. "I'm going outside." I walked down the hall into the kitchen. Our mothers were sitting with Mrs. Abraham in the living room, and they looked toward me.

"What're you kids up to?" asked Kathlyn Walker as I went and sat down on the couch next to my mother.

There were framed photos of Amy on the coffee tables and on the walls. I felt uneasy looking at them, as if I had to be very careful. "I miss Amy," I said, and leaned against my mother. "Amy was pretty," I added. And then I thought maybe I had said the wrong thing because I had said "was." Amy's mother was sitting forward with her elbows on her knees. Her face changed color, the skin on her forehead wrinkled. Then she put her hand over her face.

"April —" said my mother crossly, abruptly. She made a strange, half-apologetic noise with her tongue. "Go outside now."

On the long gravel driveway my sister, Beth, and Cody's little brother, Danny, were racing from the top of the drive to the gate, back and forth. The Abrahams' dogs were running alongside them, barking. Beth was older and bigger than Danny and beating him every time.

It was late afternoon and dead brown leaves spiraled down from treetops and landed brittle and curled on the yellowed ground. The grass had been bitten to nubs by the Abrahams' horses and goats. I sat down and picked at the leaves, concentrating on stripping them as close to the veins as I could without breaking the stem or the veins, but the stems were too thin and dry, and they broke.

Beth dropped down in the grass next to me. She started picking at a leaf, too. "I like this weather best," she said, "don't you?"

"Yeah, it makes me want to drink hot chocolate and sit and look out the window."

"Yeah."

"I have a serious question to ask you," I said. Beth looked at me and nodded. I motioned for her to come nearer and then I whispered in her ear: did she believe in God?

"No," she replied. I don't think she even understood the question. "Why?"

I shrugged. "I was walking home from the bus stop this one time because Mom wasn't there to pick me up, and I was really worried something bad had happened to her. So I said in my head, 'God, please let my mom come for me and let her be alive and well.' Right after I thought that, I swear to God, Mom came driving around the corner."

I looked up the hill toward the Abrahams' horse pasture. A big white wooden cross stood there, and I knew what it was for, because Amy had told me. It was where her pony Snowcone had been buried. The Abrahams still had two other ponies and they were standing close to the fence at the edge of the pasture with their heads low, blowing out their lips and swishing their manes.

I heard a hawk cry. Cody came walking across the gravel, grinning. "I'll race you, April. Bet you can't beat me."

"Beat you where?"

"Down to the end of the driveway."

"I don't feel like it." I could usually outrun Cody, but just barely. We were about the same size, but lately he was getting taller.

Cody stood in front of me. "Come on, are you scared?"

"What would I be scared of? I'm not scared of you." I stretched my legs out straight on the grass and leaned back on my arms.

"Bet me," he said.

"Screw you."

"Bet me," he said again.

"I don't want to. Stop it, dipwad."

Cody was kicking the bottom of my shoe. Behind Cody, Danny said, "Yeah, c'mon 'fraidy maple–April."

I made a face. "That is the lamest thing."

"That is the lamest thing," Danny mimicked me, and Cody was still kicking my shoe.

"Stop it now." I pulled up my knees.

"Stop it now," said Danny in a girl's voice. He stepped around Cody and stuck his face out at me.

I jumped up and pushed Danny in the face with my hand. He gasped and started crying. Cody looked surprised. "What are you doing, April?" he exclaimed, and for just that moment I liked him even more because of how he was sticking up for his little brother.

"I'm not doing anything," I said, suddenly embarrassed.

"Yes, you are." Cody's blue eyes narrowed at me.

"I'm leaving," I said. I turned toward the Abrahams' house and started walking, but Danny ran after me and shoved me in the back. He grabbed onto my waist and wouldn't let go. I twisted around and dug my fingernails into his forehead. I was so mad, my eyes started to water.

"Leave him alone, you bitch!" Cody shouted, and began throwing rocks at me. He broke into a run and lunged. Both Danny and I fell down. My knees were skinned, but I told myself it didn't hurt.

Beth was screaming at us all to stop it. Then she jumped up and headed for the house at a stiff walk, as if she was trying to move fast but not to run.

Danny was really crying now. "Cody, you hurt me!"

"Shut up, Danny," said Cody.

Danny struggled to stand up, rubbing his eyes and whining, "I'm gonna tell Mom!" I looked Cody in the eye and said, "Cody deserves it," and Cody yelled at me, "Well, your family is refugees," then took off after Danny, who was now running toward the house on his short legs that were never going to beat Cody across the lawn.

My eyes were still watering and I didn't want anyone to see, so I walked down the driveway. I was mad and it was burning in the inside of my head. My knees stung, but that wasn't what was making me mad, that was just what was making the being mad come out. I sighed like the horses do. I brushed leaves off my shirt.

II

On a night five years later, I was pulled out of a Sacramento dance club called Maximillian's by police officers, who informed me my mother had been taken to the El Dorado County General

Hospital. The police officers had had to track me down through a web of excuses my friends and I had set up in order to go out dancing; in smugly reprimanding tones, they told me this. The drive to the hospital took forty-five minutes. I arrived still wearing my cat's-eye makeup — exaggerated rings of black eyeliner — and black lipstick, and my black clothes felt garish under the glare of the fluorescent lights. I thought: onlookers will say the teenage daughter knew all along, was waiting every day for the mother's end to come, was *celebrating* death, even. Just look at her!

Outside it had been cool and dark as I got into the patrol car, and the lights from nearby neighborhoods and shopping centers had seemed mute and pretty. Inside the hospital it was like geometry, the lines and planes and corners absolute, stifling. The waiting room was full of old home furnishings, to make it cozier, I supposed. My sister and father were seated on the most uncomfortable chairs anyway, the ones most resembling classroom chairs. On the walls were posters of Snoopy or ordinary-looking people smiling, urging you to ask your doctor about rubella vaccinations, cholesterol, birth control, incontinence — all these issues were hinted at tactfully, however. A grinning overweight man held a spatula over the caption: "Are you watching what you eat?" The hazards and statistics of each condition were listed in small print; you had to walk closer to read these. On an end table in the corner was a cardboard display of religious brochures, with a photo of a child's praying profile and a caption reading: "Prayer does help." The "does" was underlined.

And suddenly I was recalling a story about a boy — was it someone I knew or had I read about him? — who had a terminal illness and was told that if he went to sleep with his forearm propped up by pillows, his hand raised, then the angels would know he was ready to be taken and would come get him. Eventually the boy knew he was too sick to go on living, and so his grandfather or mother or friend helped him arrange his pillows, and that night the boy died peacefully. I must have believed this story at least slightly: I could remember being afraid to fall asleep unless my hands were firmly at my sides and beneath the blankets. Had my parents told me the story of the raised hand as part of a ploy to keep me from sucking my thumb at night? I had also been intrigued by the potential power of making death a willed decision. What a relief to a young child's mind.

But I was not so young anymore, and as I floated into this waiting room I was still slightly high on other things — the music, the perfumed smoke, the colored lights, the alcohol, that night's social games. My body was still warm from dancing.

My mother had had what we thought was a protracted flu for weeks — she suffered often enough from colds or allergies. None of us had thought to pay much attention.

Beth was sitting on her chair, not talking or even looking at me. She wore sweatpants and a T-shirt, her hair a little messy from sleep. She clutched a plastic fish necklace, the most recent thing our mother had bought for her. Beth made her decisions according to a mystical logic sometimes. I never would've thought to bring something like that along.

Our father was sitting impassively, too, his hand on his stomach. His eyes flickered toward me. "Your little old mom," he said with stern cheerfulness, "was sicker than we thought. It was imperative we get her to the hospital when we did. She'll pull through, though, she will." I noticed he didn't stand to greet the two police officers who had escorted me there. And the police officers were men, exactly the type my father usually stood to talk to, in the way men do.

"We learned her whereabouts after talking to four different sets of parents who also did not know where their kids really were tonight," said one officer. "Only one parent out of the whole group of them knew, if you can believe it. A divorced single mother. They're always the liberal ones, of course."

My father nodded. They exchanged more words and my father thanked them for responding to his call. Once they'd left, he turned on me. "You are a disgustingly selfish creature."

I didn't try to respond and he asked no questions.

"Can I see her?" It was the most straightforward — the most pressing — question I thought I would ever ask.

It looked as if violence was being done to her chest. Thick clear tubes protruded like viscous ropes from her torso. Her breasts were bared, soft whitish bags of flesh sloping toward her ribs, the nipples like dark eyes. Her eyeglasses had been removed. Her face was half covered by the hands of the doctors and nurses surrounding her bed, and more tubes stuck out of her mouth. I recalled more fears I'd had in plush-carpeted waiting rooms with magazine-coated tables, alone, listening to soft music tinkling from speakers I could never spot, while my mother went down a quiet hallway to her dentist appointment. Already I knew she was no longer my mother; she had abandoned this role. She hacked horribly from somewhere deep inside herself, some garbled esoteric message, as the nurses closed the door. Her hands — were they at her sides or raised? I had not seen them at all, I realized.

A nurse put her hand on my arm, her fingers firm. "You need to go back to the waiting area now, get some rest."

"What are they doing? Is she going to be okay?"

She smiled a nurse's smile at me. "She is in good hands," she said. It sounded ludicrous to me, all those references to hands so close to the fact of death. Like an ad for insurance, I thought.

I went back out to the waiting room, where another family now sat on a couch across from my father and sister — a big lady with curly hair, wearing a jacket over her nightgown, a heavy-set man with a moustache, a little boy in Spiderman pajamas holding his stomach, and an older boy looking sullen at the far end of the couch. A door opened and a nurse called, "Travis Frailey?" The little boy and the mother got up to follow the nurse, leaving the other two in the waiting room. These two turned on the TV. I could tell this annoyed my father; he frowned and placed his hand higher on his stomach.

Beth and I turned our heads to watch the TV, and our father glared at us. One of those late-night talk show hosts was telling jokes, the fake cityscape behind his desk glittering and tinny. I thought I would never feel the same about these shows again; they would always seem to me cruelly comforting.

At one point our father went to telephone our brother. The nurses allowed him to make a long-distance call from the phone behind the front desk. Thien now lived with our cousins in southern California and had since my father kicked him out of the house four years ago because he'd discovered my brother was cutting school to work at a garage in Sacramento. My father had said that if Thien thought he was smart enough to make this kind of decision about school, then he should be smart enough to live on his own, too. My brother was eighteen with one more year of high school to go; I was eleven.

We waited I don't know how long.

Later, I went to the bathroom. In the stall, the water in the toilet had risen and was swirling and someone's slightly bloody tampon floated on top, a smear of red on a string, like some version of a tadpole in the bowl. This struck me as something I would remember; it jolted me. From now on, I told myself, I would be the kind of person who always checked to make sure the toilet had flushed completely behind me. I used a different stall. Then I ran the water to wash my hands and looked at my eyeliner-smudged face in the mirror. I look okay, I thought. My thoughts were like this, jumpy and cold, one at a time.

In the hallway, Beth was talking to the sullen-looking older boy. He was her age, a spiky-haired blond with a faceful of pale brown freckles. The two stood by the drinking fountain.

"They said she may have an advanced case of secondary tuberculosis," Beth was telling him, very seriously and quietly. (Beth was often willing to talk about our family issues to anyone, anyone who would listen.)

The boy furrowed his brow. "Does your family have AIDS?"

"What? You asshole," said Beth quickly.

"No, man, no. I just thought people only got tuberculosis if they had AIDS."

"Whatever," said Beth, and then she caught my eye.

We had to face the drive home with one person less. It was the reverse of going there to have a baby, likely the only other time my father had to drive her to the hospital in the middle of the night.

The world outside the hospital, after our long wait inside, seemed suddenly bright with morning and insane and extremely dangerous — it was no wonder she hadn't survived, I thought. I sat in the front seat by my father, Beth in the back. As we pulled out of the parking lot, Beth said softly, "Bye, Mom," as she looked out the window, as if that place was where we had left her; we had only to go back and pick her up later. Beth was also the one to make the suggestion about the library lawn. "Mom always liked it there. Let's drive past." The Honda, which we were so used to riding in with our mother in the driver's seat, idled like an obedient kitten as my father steered it slowly by these familiar, soon-to-be-so-different places. We were meandering. We were on our own time now, in our own sphere of the newly unknown. Still, we stopped for the traffic lights.

"Well, then," said our father after the library lawn, "how about a hamburger?" And he pulled into a Jack in the Box, but it was closed.

We hadn't realized it was only seven thirty in the morning.

We ate at a twenty-four-hour diner. My father told us about some antibiotics we would have to take, a preventive measure; he worried aloud about our brother, living around our cousins and other recent immigrants who might be carriers of tuberculosis. My father talked about how people who'd died from diseases such as these had to be buried under slabs of concrete because their bodies might still have been infectious; he said this was costly and cremation was a better idea all around (though the smoke probably had to be monitored somehow, he added). "One must be extremely cautious," he said. "One should have a dignified exit from the world." I wasn't sure if what he was saying about the slabs of concrete was true, but it filled me with a familiar dread. He had said similar things when my mother's father died. My grandfather had been sponsored to come to the States from Vietnam some years ago by my mother and her sisters in Los Angeles (he hadn't wanted to emigrate but his children had insisted), and he had died of cancer or tuberculosis or pneumonia, or a combination of all these ailments — they eventually decided — not two months after his emigration. My sister and brother and I visited Los Angeles with my mother around that time, and while all the adults were at the hospital, we played

"Bloody Mary" in front of the bathroom mirror, all of us crowded together in front of the bathroom sink with a lighted candle. We'd say her name three times out loud, then one of the older cousins would claim he'd seen a face appear in the mirror, and we would run screaming out of the bathroom, delighted by our fear. The one time our mother took us to see her father, he was an ancient silent man in the hospital bed, breathing laboriously, with a deeply lined brown face like *National Geographic* photos I'd seen of people from other — lesser, I'd thought then — parts of the world. His collarbones stuck skeletally up beneath his old skin. In the flower-dotted white hospital gown, he looked like a withered and hapless, overly sentient child. My mother ordered my sister and me to give him a kiss on his cheek. He touched our faces with his long, bony hands.

Later, over the phone, our father had questioned us intently and told us to wash our hands and faces thoroughly if we had been near our grandfather. My father's fear of disease was not so uncommon then; this was the mid-1980s. A time in which all types of contact were purported to have resounding consequences. When it was our mother's turn to speak to him, she had cried and talked angrily into the phone.

Our father was being irritable with the waitress. "What're you doing back there, hey, taking a shower?" he said when she was slow bringing him an ashtray.

She half laughed, trying to show a good face. Our father raised his eyebrow, took out his cigarettes and lighter. The waitress cleared our plates, asked if we needed anything else. Our father gave her a brutal no. He stared out the window as he blew smoke over our heads. Beth coughed, just a little. He turned on her suddenly with wide-open eyes, grabbed her by the arm.

"Do not, do you hear? Do *not* play with me like that."

Beth cringed, hunching up her shoulders. I watched as her face sank into itself. She was the only one of the three of us, finally, then, to cry.

Once home, the first thing my father did was call our neighbors the Walkers. Our brother was to fly in that afternoon, and the

Walkers offered to pick him up at the airport. My father called our other neighbors, the Johnsons, whom we actually hadn't spoken to in years, not since Rebel Johnson stole our horse, Chip, and rode him lame on the asphalt roads and Animal Control had to take him away. My father told Mrs. Johnson he thought they should know. There were no other local friends of my mother's to call. He opened her address book but the names inside, of all her Vietnamese friends, were indecipherable to him; he passed the book to me, but I was not much help, as I'd never bothered to keep track of the names or faces of my mother's friends, and I couldn't read or speak Vietnamese, either. Except for one or two visits years ago, when they first married and when we first moved up here, my father hadn't had to interact very much with any relatives on my mother's side of the family. (For that matter he'd hardly interacted with his relatives, either, the ones still back in Denmark.)

I didn't know what to do with my mother's address book. It was not long before the phone rang anyway. It was one of my aunts. She had been with my brother when my father had to tell him the news over the phone the night before.

She spoke half in Vietnamese to me, half in broken English. She must've forgotten my sister and I couldn't understand Vietnamese; Vietnamese people we knew generally took it for granted. "You must to come live with me now, you and your sister, two of you. I take good care of you. I your mother's oldest sister. Tell your father I say so. I your mother's sister."

"Dad," I said, unsure how to handle the situation, "Aunt Mary says she wants me and Beth to come live with her now."

My father was leaning on the kitchen sink, smoking another cigarette. He looked exhausted. "Absolutely not. Tell her I said no."

"He says no," I said into the phone.

"Can't we talk about this later?" I heard Beth ask no one directly. She was sitting at the end of the couch, still holding her fish necklace.

"You let me talk to your father," said my aunt. "I tell him, I make him to understand, I do this for your mom. She my little sister."

I relayed this to my father. "You tell her to call back later. I can't talk to her right now." He made a face and shook his head. Then he turned and walked out of the room.

The minute I was off the phone, my sister grabbed it to call the Newmans. Lisa Newman was her best friend and Beth spent a lot of time after school over at the Newmans' house. Lisa's mom, Katie Newman, was a pretty, red-headed, but slightly ditzy woman who our parents had said was like a child herself, simpleminded. She dressed her daughters in girlish clothes and often instructed them to pretend their house was a castle, their property a fenced-in kingdom. Katie Newman liked to claim that she was Beth's "second mom" and sometimes announced when Beth arrived at their gate, "Oh, my long-lost daughter escaped from her evil stepparents at last!" My father had warned Beth not to take Katie's games too seriously; he thought them harmless but foolish.

"Dad, I'm going over to the Newmans," my sister called out once she was off the phone. She was crying again.

We heard the bathroom door open, our father come back down the hall into the kitchen. "You are not going anywhere," he said. "No, no, and no." He pointed his finger. "You call back and tell them your father says you are not going anywhere. No, I'll call and tell them that." He walked over to the phone, looked for the Newmans' number on our phone board, dialed it. "Listen, Katie," he said, "the girls need to stay here right now, do you understand me? If I find that Beth is sneaking over to your house without my permission, let me tell you she is going to be in a whole lot of trouble."

Beth and I sat down on the couch. There were people I would have liked to call, too, but my nerve was gone. For some reason I was thinking about other things, normal things, the people I knew at school, the fun I'd been having dancing, the satisfying, curious way I was looked at by other kids last night in the club as the police officers took me away.

It kept feeling as if we were just waiting for our mother to return. There was still, of course, evidence of her daily activities everywhere: a folded-open magazine on the end table by the couch; her toothbrush and floss-holder in a cup in the bathroom; her cluttered desk in the corner of the living room; her closet full of newspapers and stacked milk cartons of more papers and her books, shelves of them, all paperback with extra thin pages, the Vietnamese words printed small and too close together, three- and four-letter words most of them, and consisting often of consonants in a row: *nghi* was a word, for example. They seemed confounding and unbeautiful to me, these crude things she had left behind. And then there were her shoes — this was what got me — by the back door. Cheap, beige, high-heeled, open-toed slip-ons she used for walking out onto the deck, resting now at slight angles to each other where she must have casually kicked them off.

The Walkers arrived, all except Mr. Walker, who was on his way to the airport to pick up Thien. Mrs. Walker was effusive, red-eyed, and sobbing enough for all of us. She was an expressive and outgoing woman whom my mother, out of her own shyness, truthfully, had tended to avoid.

"Anything you need, anything *they* need," Mrs. Walker told my father over and over. She sat between Beth and me, clutching our hands in our laps, and we sat rigid in a row on the couch as if it were a seat on a roller-coaster and we had to hold on to each other tightly.

Cody and Danny sat down at the dining table and looked at their feet. Cody had grown to be tall, athletic-bodied, and begrudgingly blond and beautiful, the type of good-looking fifteen-year-old boy who gave you a quick, disdainful glance if he caught you looking at him admiringly — something I'd seen happen frequently between him and girls at school. Danny was a younger, lesser version of his brother. I knew better than to want from Cody Walker what other girls wanted. Our social personas were antithetical: he was everything I hated about the status quo; I was everything he could not understand about the aberrant.

"God has taken her. It is so sad but we must believe He has His reasons," Mrs. Walker said urgently to us. "You girls are so strong. So strong."

"It's nice of you to try to make us feel better," I said, "but that honestly doesn't help me a lot."

"April," said my father curtly, though I knew he felt much the same as I did on the matter of religion; he just wasn't saying so to the Walkers' faces.

"God will forgive you," said Mrs. Walker. "You are, of course, angry with Him."

Beth said, "I believe in Him, sometimes."

Mrs. Walker released my hand to use both of hers to squeeze Beth's shoulders. She said, "Good girl, good girl," almost as if she were praising a dog.

I caught Cody glowering in his mother's direction from across the room, and I gave him a cold stare. I was not sure whom I wanted to criticize more.

Beth went on, "I mean, of course I want to believe she's somewhere happier now. Like maybe she's sitting in a beautiful meadow with a blue sky and birds singing and she's eating anything she wants to."

"And what do you think that would be?" asked Mrs. Walker.

"Probably some cream cheese toast," replied Beth, with a gratuitous, sad little laugh. One of our mother's staple snacks, cream cheese toast was toasted sourdough bread topped with cream cheese and soy sauce. "Maybe if we made some it could be like something to help her rest in peace. Like fruit before bed."

I felt appalled by this whole exchange, as if Beth had betrayed me somehow. I tried to catch her eye, but she didn't notice.

"Well, any time you want, you can come over to my house and we'll make a peace offering to your mother, all right? We can even do it now if your dad says it's all right and it'll make you feel better," said Mrs. Walker judiciously.

"Sure, sure," said our father. He was standing by the kitchen counter with his hands in his pockets, looking agitated and vulnerable.

"But maybe we'd better wait," Mrs. Walker continued. "I think your father needs you girls here with him right now." Her tone was gentle and watchful and diplomatic.

Our father made a sound like a balloon letting out a spurt of air. It was unconvincingly dismissive. "We need to all be here when your brother arrives," he said finally.

We sat on the couch a while longer with Mrs. Walker, trying to make conversation in the strained silence. Cody and Danny stubbed their sneakers against the floor, swung their legs, rubbed their noses in awkward boredom. Mrs. Walker decided coffee would be nice, and food shouldn't be forgotten, either; it was about lunchtime after all, if our father wouldn't mind her nosing around the kitchen some.

He said, "No, Kathlyn. No, please," with a firm frown.

Mrs. Walker insisted. "You go sit down, Hus, you've had a long night. Or go outside and get some fresh air. I'll take care of the girls." She stood up and walked over to him and put her hand on his shoulder.

My sister's and my eyes went to his shoulder, her hand. Was this the proper way to offer comfort?

We watched our father acquiesce. His shoulders looked soft and big for the first time. His hair had drifted out of place onto his forehead. The lines in his face were long and beginning, elegantly, to droop. "I don't know what you'll find in here," he said. "God knows where Tran kept anything."

"I have a way with kitchens," said Mrs. Walker gaily. "I can find anything in anybody's kitchen. I can."

My father took his cigarettes and lighter and went outside on the deck to smoke.

"So are you guys still gonna go to school on Monday?" asked Cody, from the table. Beth and I hadn't moved from the couch; there was a gap between us where Mrs. Walker had been just a moment ago. "You don't have to, you know," added Cody. "People don't usually, when someone in the family dies." He didn't look Beth or me in the eye as he said this; his gaze drifted around the space between us. He scratched the wood of the table with his thumbnail.

Danny pushed back his chair, got up, and leaned over the kitchen counter. "Hey, Mom, I'm thirsty," he said in a low voice. We heard the refrigerator open a few seconds later.

"It helps to believe in God," said Cody, in the same drifting, almost sullen manner as he'd made his last comment, as if he was trying to be sincere but would quickly turn angry if anyone we knew were to catch him talking like this. "April, I could lend you my Bible or something. If you want." He shrugged one shoulder.

"I don't think so." There was a small feeling of triumph in saying this, the triumph of being able to refuse someone who would normally never offer you anything.

"Well, I'm just saying," said Cody, shrugging again.

I narrowed my eyes at him. I was sitting with my legs crossed, my arms folded. Then it occurred to me what I wanted to say. "You're only being nice, Cody, because this is exactly what people do when something bad happens. They think they're supposed to act all sad because it's the nice thing to do, when really it's the totally fake thing to do. The honest thing would be to just act normal. I'm not sad, okay? I'm not really that sad right now. I feel fine, in fact. I feel the same way I did yesterday."

Mrs. Walker said from the kitchen, "Let's give April some time, Cody."

"Whatever," said Cody, back to his old self. "I think she's a bitch, though."

"Cody Michael," warned Mrs. Walker.

Beth got up suddenly and headed for the stairs, walked up them loudly.

I sat very still, looking straight ahead. On the bookshelf opposite me was my mother's picture in a frame, staring back at me. It was unnerving, and a feeling like nothing I had ever felt before imploded in me. But I still wouldn't say I was sad. It was not that.

I had not always been an unbeliever. Around the time I'd started to fear almost everything, when I was about eleven, I turned to God for a while, secretly. I made up a prayer that I wrote in my diary; it was seven pages long, and I would read it every night before bed, though never aloud. I praised and prayed for all the usual things — thanks for the safe passing of the day; protection from all the dire possibilities of tomorrow — but I prayed for it in the utmost detail, each night adding to my list of concerns. I racked my brain to imagine every ill I could (the mentioning of it was key in warding it off), and I prayed that I and those I knew be spared from earthquakes, falling trees, landslides, lightning, floods, rabid or wild animals, rape, murder, kidnapping, sudden disappearance, assault, car accidents, brain damage, contagious diseases — my list went on and on. And I would ask God for these graces in exchange for certain sacrifices.

I promised to forgo stealing candy from the Lotus General Store for one day; I would walk, not gallop, my horse over a stretch of field where I usually loved to gallop; I would make a one-week pact not to cry even if I felt like it during an argument with my parents — I would vow absolutely not to cry whenever being spanked by my father with his belt (I would tell myself it hurt just the same as falling off a horse, and I'd done that plenty of times and even laughed). It was not so much that I saw these actions — crying or enjoying candy or galloping across a field — as sinful. It was simply that I associated piety with restraint. My understanding of God was that you bargained against whatever was your most basic nature or impulse in a given moment in order to remain on the "good" side of life; the safe, blessed, loftier side. And whether or not this proved the existence of God, the fact was no grave ills befell our family in that period of time.

Then something happened, between twelve and thirteen. I woke up. Boys had begun trying to put their hands on me underwater at the city pool; I was finally permitted to wear makeup. I outgrew my fears, lost interest in praying. I even went back to my diary and erased all the pages of "I HATE ME" I had written (self-loathing was another deal I'd thought to make with God — this was how I had interpreted penance) because now I needed the extra room to write down new lists — records of boys' names and memorable glances and gestures and other tiny but significant instances I didn't want to forget.

I guessed if it were still in me now, that brief allegiance I'd had to Him then, I might've felt it was my fault somehow, my mother's end. But I had no doubts about my disbelief — not that, at least — though I did still believe in some rhythm of sacrifice. Which is why at the back of my mind there was the thought, almost guilty, that my mother might have been the biggest sacrifice of all. I may have been meant, then, to have other things: stranger, more remarkable, unlikelier things. Fame. A gorgeous boyfriend. ESP or great beauty or an adventure.

Kathlyn Walker was making us sandwiches. She was brewing coffee. My father was out on the deck smoking a cigarette.

In the end, we did not take up Kathlyn Walker's invitation to come over and make toast. Ted Walker returned with Thien and the Walkers left us, and in the days to come it was just the four of us, dealing, retreating, speculating, bickering. We watched our father hang up the phone with his other hand on his stomach a number of times. We watched helplessly, not offering much and knowing he wouldn't allow us to help anyhow. After some deliberation, he decided against having a funeral service. Maybe a small, private ritual, but my father would not stand for any priests or ceremony (technically, my mother had been a Catholic) because he scoffed at all organized religion. In fact, he was opposed to it. Church-centered gatherings such as funerals and weddings had always made him uncomfortable and compromised his sense of emotional integrity; he felt that mourning or celebrating as a group tainted the experience — which was private, or should be. This was just how Danish people were, my father explained. In Denmark you left a family alone after they'd had a tragedy; you did not come knocking on their door with a basket of fruit. You could offer assistance, certainly, but only if it was appropriate and necessary. Americans, on the other hand, seemed to want to make everything public, and our Vietnamese relatives were proving to be not much different. They had been calling, trying to intervene. They wanted to hold a Vietnamese Catholic service in Los Angeles because there were too many of them to make the trip north, they said. My father insisted she would be cremated.

That first night, my brother and sister and I curled up on one bed upstairs and talked about our mother. My sister and I expressed our dread at living alone with our father; our brother expressed his worry about us; we expounded on these fears. We agreed our father had always been the more difficult parent, our mother the soother. Without her to allay his moods, we imagined he would become a tyrant, a demanding and unyielding person. We couldn't conjure many specifics of this future, though; our fears were, it seemed, based more on a general sense of void. My brother repeated what our Aunt Mary had said over the phone, that we should go to live down south. He said he loved it down there. The weather was nicer, and our cousins' house had consistently running hot water, a big-screen TV and stereo system, was in walking distance of malls and beaches. Aunt Mary even had him going to church (though this part, I argued, would never happen to me). I was almost excited, being able to blind myself to the fact of her absence, turning everything, our lives, into the idea of a vacation of sorts. Beth was more sensible, remorseful, attached. "But Dad'll get lonely, too, you know," she said. We could hear him downstairs coughing and moving around and talking to the dogs. We heard the squeak of the sliding glass door as he opened it to let them in and out, the clack of their claws on the tile floor, the rush of their happy panting. It was March, still cold in the house at night and freezing in the mornings.

A couple of times in the following days, Kathlyn Walker sent Cody and Danny over with a pan of baked lasagna, a large glass bowl of spaghetti, boxes or bags of various sundries she and a few other neighborhood mothers thought we might need. She was discreet, tactful — right, actually — and in the bottom of one bag was a supply of feminine items for Beth and me. These items were placed at the foot of the stairs (we knew they came from Mrs. Walker because we had seen the bags earlier), uncommented upon by our father, but we took them to mean he understood what we would have to deal with as girls, alone now; or he was trying to, at least.

And it would be weeks before we started to put away anything our mother had left out, the folded-open magazine, her deck shoes, the washcloth in the bathroom we each suspected the other was using until at last it occurred to us it had been dry for weeks. Objects would just go on waiting, we realized.

▪ ▪ ▪

There was no official service for my mother. We would dress nicely and drive to the funeral home to pick up the ashes; we would accept some visitors; we would mourn in private. Once, the Walkers invited us over for coffee and tea and passed on to us condolences from other neighbors and friends' parents and teachers at school. Beth and I sat on our chairs, sipping hot chocolate and looking across at Cody and Danny, dressed in slacks with their shirts tucked in, slouching on the couch. Thien sat in an armchair and drank coffee and answered Mrs. Walker's occasional questions about San Diego. Ted Walker and my father stood the whole time, and at one point Ted took my father into the kitchen to show him their new cabinets. Uncle Michael called for Kathlyn from the other room, and she took him some cookies.

Aunt Mary and Uncle John had expressed their wish to fly our mother's ashes back to Vietnam. This was a traditional idea: where one's ashes lay, one's soul may rest. Our father thought this appropriate and agreed to pay half the airfare. He was "absolutely *not* sentimental" about such things as adjacent burial plots, and when asked was appalled anyway at the thought of being buried himself. ("Is not marriage a morbid enough union as it is?" he said at one point, his usually wry jokes like lumps of lead at this time.) He couldn't comprehend the benefit for anyone involved of all these proceedings — not even death could bring him to admit a God or the good of spiritual measures. He would talk only about the disease, and in general about her. He arranged for the ashes to be transported to L.A. on the same flight as my brother's and allowed Beth and me to go, too, for the memorial service our relatives were arranging down there, though he declined to go himself.

"Your mother, her largest concern was always for Vietnam," said our father on our drive home from retrieving the ashes, "and the Communists. She wanted nothing more than to see Communism defeated, you know." This was something I did know about my mother, but I'd never considered it her largest concern; to me it had seemed she, like all adults, had many concerns, many ongoing projects of vague nature that she easily picked up or set aside whenever we came in or out of the house. "She was obsessed by it, in fact," my father went on. "It was a vital, crucial part of her being and without it, without that sense of struggle, she was not a whole person. She was always feeling embittered about her homeland and what the injustice of Communism had done to it. She used to lash out at me sometimes in incomprehensible bouts of anger." He fell silent, as if he had just caught wind of some other news beneath his own words.

The ashes were confounding to me. The funeral home director handed them to my father in two separate vessels — a large, Egyptian-looking vase, and a second box that was heavy though small enough to be held under one arm, small but dense as a chunk of metal. The ashes themselves were as fine as the finest, driest mud. So easily could the pieces of my mother slip away now — a puff of them escaped as we lowered the lid back down: what did that mean? What part of her was that and where had it gone? That a person could be so dissolved was no comfort to me. I tried to imagine the essence of my mother floating around, pleasantly uniting with others who had passed on beyond the physical, but all I could imagine her soul to be — if it existed — was simply the outline of her body and features as they had appeared in life. This seemed no better — just a continuation, not a passage.

But at least this box and vase were tidy, were *right*. It was done.

I remembered something in the car. "Mom had a story she was telling me that she wanted to write someday," I said. "It was about a character who drives past a beautiful field of sunflowers on the side of the freeway. All the sunflowers are open and facing the road, and she is so in awe of the sight that she wants to stop her car and pull over and take a picture of the field. But she tells herself she'll stop next time. Each day she tells herself this. Until one day the flowers have turned away from the road, they're following the sun, and she can see only the curved backs of their stems now, which is not as picturesque, and she realizes, in a poignant and self-reflective way" — I used the exact words my mother had used to convey this moment in her story; it was imperative to me to be acutely honest — "that she has missed an important opportunity in her life."

My father made a "hmph" sound. "Told so cryptically, April," he remarked, almost thoughtfully.

My brother sat in the passenger seat next to my father. "The flowers died?" he said, sympathetically.

"They weren't dead, they just turned in the direction of the sun," I explained, leaning forward in the backseat.

Beth leaned forward with me. "I have a story about something Mom told me, too," she said. "A couple of days before she had to go into the hospital, we were sitting upstairs in my bedroom talking, and she asked if I would miss her if she had to go away. I said, no, I wouldn't, because I don't believe in missing people. If where they went would make them happier than where they were before, I mean. And you know what she said then?" We were quieted by Beth's words, humbled and envious and skeptical altogether. Without a note of incredulity, Beth finished, "She looked at me really softly and said, 'I knew you would understand, Beth.' And I looked at her and I didn't understand totally then, but I do now. She knew she was going to die, see."

The service took place in a large banquet room above a Vietnamese lawyers' office and an Asian grocery in a shopping plaza in Santa Ana, otherwise known as Little Saigon. The room was rectangular with one bank of windows overlooking the parking lot. We sat on metal-framed, red-cushioned conference chairs set in rows facing the front of the room, where there was a carpeted stage and large black speakers aimed outward. The service would've been held at a local Vietnamese Catholic church, but our relatives were afraid the church wouldn't be large enough; there were nearly a hundred people attending. The Vietnamese Catholic priest wore a long white robe; he wore thick eyeglasses and his skin was pockmarked. Beside him on an easel was displayed an 8 by 10 photograph of our mother's face, smiling and made up (as she never was in daily life), taken by a photographer friend of hers. In it, rouge had been applied in circles over her cheeks; her lips were glossy; her hair up in hairpins. Her face looked masklike and tranquil, and older than it had usually appeared. The frame was ringed with flowers, and on metal TV trays beside it were candles, red-tipped incense sticks, red envelopes, rice, fruit, flower petals, and a hand-bound book of uneven, coarsely textured paper, inside of which were pasted clippings and photographs. All our mother's brothers and sisters and some of our older cousins wore white head sashes. Their clothing was formal, rustling, perfumed, white, or floral. The aunts were so thickly made up you could read the boundary, clearly marked along their jawlines, between the orangey brown of their facial foundation and the natural brown of their necks. All this adornment, all these mourning accoutrements — to me, it was as if our relatives had put on what they thought were the adequate masks of grief. They dabbed at their eyes; their husbands next to them looked heavy-lidded and piggish and irate and stared straight ahead.

I had wanted to wear black but it was not acceptable. When I asked why, one of my uncles said, "It is just Vietnamese custom." He did not look me in the eye, and his expression was disapproving and disgusted. Sitting through the service, I felt not like myself, uncomfortably ordinary, in the khaki pants and white button-down shirt I had finally agreed to.

My sister was wearing a white dress; our cousins had taken her shopping. Thien wore a white head sash, willingly, with the rest of them.

All in Vietnamese, the service was a mix of the traditional and the sentimental. A woman thinner and prettier than most in the room stood after the priest and a number of my mother's sisters and brothers and friends had spoken, and she began to sing. She sang with exaggeration, dipping and swaying and tilting her head back at the appropriate moments, the accompanying synthesized strings and guitar solos piped into the speakers from a soundboard to the side of the stage; a spiky-haired boy in a white shirt and skinny tie sat over the controls. Onstage in her nearglittering white ao dai, the woman had hair that was a sheer black mane down her back; her hands were small and clasped gently round the bulbous black microphone. It was a vulgar and incongruous sight; tacky but excruciatingly well intentioned. A memory occurred to me: the melody was familiar. One of our cousins leaned over to tell us, "It is old folk song from Vietnam. Your mother like this one very much, when she younger. Very famous song." He paused, listening, then translated for us:

> Because I love you so, I give you my shirt —
> When I come home my mom ask,
> I say the wind blew it away,
> as I crossed over the bridge

"Oh, something like that," he cut himself off with a sheepish laugh. He was gay (everyone knew this except his parents). We had always referred to him as "the card maker" because our mother once noted he had a talent for it, handmade greeting cards, though actually he worked as an engineer. "It is very serious love song, like oh-I-die-for-you love song, you know." He spoke earnestly, in a whisper, but with an undertone that denoted an easy awareness of and even a comfortableness with absurdity. "Maybe the girl very poor, own only one shirt, who know."

The singer's voice was tremulous and sincere, the words guttural yet delicate-sounding, as if her tongue was attempting to strangle them before they got out clearly. The song seemed literally to drip, as all these songs did. I thought this but was transported nonetheless.

Their hands were upon us like a flurry of moths, and only occasionally did I comprehend a word or two as they surrounded us, held us, positioned us. They were a people unafraid of handling one another. There was a casual disregard for personal space. Cruelly I thought, this is how come they can crowd together inside small cars, laughing about it and unembarrassed. We were told we must pose for photographs in various ensembles: all her sisters, all her brothers, brothers and sisters together, children separately, the whole family together standing close, tall ones in the back, little ones in the front, the three generations of women, the three generations of men, et cetera. The adults straightened their white head sashes and kept their mouths solemn. Afterward it was the hands again, on my shoulders, on my back, this aunt saying go with that cousin; that aunt saying come with me; this old girlfriend of my mother's insisting on another snapshot, clasping my hand in hers, squeezing. Her skin was thin and dry. The little nieces wanted to hang on to my arms; they thought Beth and I were pretty, they told their mothers, who were our older cousins or cousins-in-law, and I overheard. I knew some of their names but not all. Once my mother had tallied them and counted forty-eight. First and second cousins, that is. You might think this was something I'd have felt the weight of, but I felt as light as paper, a scrap of ash among them. My mother was the sixth of eleven in her family, which put her exactly in the middle. Five older and five younger than she. (I'd heard that middle children are always the ones cursed.) She had been the third of her siblings to die: there were two older brothers who had died a long time ago, when they all still lived in Vietnam.

In the parking lot, the male cousins and uncles and in-laws shouted back and forth in a mix of Vietnamese and English; they seemed joyous and argumentative, raising their voices over the roofs of their cars, trying to give directions or make plans or finish a joke, something. I didn't know. I stood quietly and waited wherever I was pushed. So did my sister. They will sweep you into their fold invitingly and entirely oblivious to the dangers of anonymity, I thought. It was not for me. Something in me struggled like a snake, choking me from the inside. My brother was off with the other boy cousins, ducking his head into the car to ask, "Okay, you guys are okay, right?"

"I lost my virginity to a married woman," said my brother later that night. The two of us were in one of the upstairs bedrooms of a cousin's house, watching MTV, a treat for me, since in our father's house there was no TV, let alone cable. Downstairs the adults were eating around the kitchen table, laughing and crying and bantering loudly. Beth was off in another room with our cousins, and music was playing down the hall in another cousin's bedroom. It had been like this all day and evening, the comfort and chaos of a crowded house. I sort of liked it but sort of didn't. Every now and then some new adult came in to touch our heads or offer us food, insist, really, and I found it irritating that all they could think to offer us was food, not conversation.

"Six months ago," said Thien. "Don't talk to Beth about this, okay? Her name was Janice. She was my boss's friend's wife. Twenty-seven years old." He said this proudly; he was only twenty-two. "She wasn't happy in her marriage. She still isn't but she's still married to him, of course. When she told me she couldn't see me anymore, you know what?" He was lying on his back on the bed, hands tucked behind his head, staring at the ceiling. "I cried."

"Really?" The thought of my brother crying was almost too much for me to manage. It was like seeing my mother without her eyeglasses when she woke in the mornings or right before bed — how beady and vulnerable her eyes looked then. I wanted my brother to share more with me. "Did you cry in front of her?"

"She cried, too. It was sad."

I could not fathom this form of pain, try as I might. I had liked boys, some of them a lot, but never to this point. I thought it must have to do with him, my brother, some inherent flaw.

"We only slept together once," said Thien, "but we were kind of hanging out a lot before that. It seemed like we were getting to be good friends. It's hard for guys and girls to stay friends, though, I think."

"Is she Vietnamese?" I asked, trying to picture the kind of woman — no kind I could easily imagine — who would go so far as to cry for my brother.

"No. She's white," he said. "That's the funny thing. I can't help it, but I tend to be attracted to Caucasian girls. Even though all our cousins date Vietnamese girls, I just haven't met any I actually like. They're all kind of the same. They care about what car you drive and money and clothes, they're kind of shallow like that. It sucks, though, because how often do you see a Caucasian woman dating an Asian guy, you know?"

I agreed, though I thought maybe I should act more encouraging toward him.

"I think I have low self-esteem," said my brother, making "low self-esteem" sound like one big word, a phenomenon. As if one should be proud to stake a claim here. "Because of Dad," he went on. "I didn't really realize it till I came to live down here, how badly he speaks about other people all the time, especially Vietnamese. He used to call Mom's sisters 'peasants' and 'barbarians,' when the truth is he doesn't know the first thing about them, really. Our aunts said Mom was a bad mother, you know? For letting Dad kick me out of the house and not keeping us all together and then not helping pay for my college or anything. I loved Mom, though. I think she just didn't have the strength to leave Dad. You know that's what it takes to leave someone, strength. You wouldn't think so, but that's the truth. Janice didn't have it, either. Her husband is a jerk, too. Dad used to say so many mean things about Mom. I remember once he said she smelled. That was the reason he had to stop sleeping in the same room as her. Because he couldn't stand it anymore, her smell. That's what he said."

There was something in this admission, this glimpse into my parents, that repulsed yet didn't surprise me. I didn't turn away from the TV, but I narrowed my eyes, to concentrate on what my brother was saying.

"Dad didn't like her cooking," I said noncommittally, just to keep my brother talking.

"Dad doesn't like a lot of things," said Thien. "You know what I think? I think Dad is a racist." This was another of those words. He pronounced it with an almost proud horror.

I twisted around to look at him.

"You could be one, too," he said. "It's like a disease, you know. Kids learn it from their parents and they grow up and pass it on. You can have it even toward your own kind, even toward yourself, and not even realize it. It's like low self-esteem. It's a disease, really."

"Thien, what are you talking about?" I said sharply. It came back to me at that moment, the small feeling of power I'd felt when I said "I don't think so" to Cody when he tried to offer me his Bible on the day my mother had died.

"I'm talking about Dad. What do you think?" Thien retorted, flustered. "I've been talking about Dad for like fifteen minutes now. Because I'm worried about you and Beth. I think you need to look at yourselves. I did. And I realized a lot about Mom and Dad, how they messed us up in a lot of ways. Everyone has to look at themselves someday, I just think."

"I've already thought about all that," I said, and just then I believed it. "A long time ago," I added. Then I turned back to the music videos.

What I couldn't tell any of them, though, was what I kept inside myself — it might be a flood or a flowering, this feeling that might just as easily break as enlighten me, I thought, as I tried to understand myself emotionally in relation to the rest of my family. I didn't trust any of them, I found, couldn't remember when I last had. I had always wanted to turn to strangers. (Dimly I could remember crying in a department store as a young child — somehow I had become separated from my parents — and a kind woman gave me a package of M&Ms, like a reward for getting lost, that burned brighter in my memory than any other part of the experience.) Now I wanted someone to hold me, someone who would never show me his weaknesses, who in fact *had* no weaknesses. Yes, I thought this must be possible. A being with no needs, no complaints, no overwhelming desires, and together we could go forward independently. He would be kind and wisely discriminating. He would be beautiful in a subtle way. He would be clever yet profoundly, ironically compassionate, with the capacity to take in everything and not bat an eyelid. He would be sympathetic when a woman lost a piece of jewelry but restrained when saying good-byes or hellos. He would be playful and wisecracking on the surface but deep in hidden pain beneath. We would recognize each other in trivial asides, without speaking directly about anything. And he would also pity and slightly admire — but no longer feel attached to — his own parents, as would I. For they had been our guides into this world and had taught us the pain of humanity, but now they had led us as far as they could and we would have to go on without and despite them.

The plane had to circle above the Sacramento Valley fog for months, it seemed, before we were able to land. My sister and I walked up the long enclosed passageway to the terminal gate on precarious, sleeping legs; we blinked into the fluorescent lights. Our father was waiting in the terminal, his hands clutched around dog leashes. The dogs were in the car, fogging up the windows because he could not leave them at home alone, he said.

Years later, I found some words my mother had written in a yellow spiral notebook. I don't know when exactly she'd begun writing this, or to whom, if anybody, these words were directed, don't know whether it was a journal entry or the start of a story. It was only one line, not even complete, and it was on the first page. The rest of the notebook was empty. The words were in Vietnamese: *O my dear T, how many tired nights we* and that was it. Who was the mysterious T? I could believe it was myself she was addressing, using my Vietnamese birth name *Thuy,* but with such angst, why? Or maybe it was my brother, the other T? Or was it some oblique address to herself or to an old friend, unnameable, an old lover maybe, a code for some other topic or affair she'd had reasons not to share with us? I ransacked her other papers for answers. I read many of her books. I asked her sisters to translate letters she'd written. Nothing has revealed as much as those few words, this barely begun line — the hazards, the contingencies of it. Often I have thought: How shall I respond? And I do.

4

*My brother has told me about clinging to the legs and riding on the
boots of American GIs in the refugee camp in Guam where we
waited a month for passage to the States in May 1975. They were
impressively large, these men, and utterly fascinating to my brother,
who was nine. The soldiers assisted the Red Cross workers, hauling
supplies, setting up tents, handing out blankets, food rations, medi-
cines. With rifles on their shoulders, they patroled the fenced pe-
rimeters of the camp, and my brother and the other boys he played
with would watch them. Sometimes they would dare each other to
run up behind and touch the soldiers — on the leg, the hand — or
say one of the few English phrases they'd recently learned: "Hello,
how you do?" or "You number one!" or "Goddamnit." The soldiers
would say words in return and make friendly gestures, but my
brother could not understand English well. The first few times this
happened he froze in shyness, then took off running again the second the soldier's conversation paused. Steadily he grew bolder,
though, and lingered longer, as the other boys did.*

*The GIs gave them small items — packs of gum, a cigarette or
two, a candy bar, magazines or comic books, a pencil, a dogtag,
wallet pictures of themselves in uniform, and, occasionally, swigs of
soda or beer. Some soldiers played with the boys, swinging them
around, turning them upside down, hoisting them high onto their
shoulders. One time, a boy, as he was being let down, wrapped
himself around his soldier's leg, and the soldier proceeded to walk
with him sitting on his boot. The other boys thought this was hilar-*

124

ious. Soon it became a ritual game between the boys and the soldiers. Each time the boys saw a soldier walking by, they would run after him, and whoever reached him first would throw himself at the soldier's khaki-covered leg and clamp on. The soldiers mostly humored them, plodding on without pause, or feigning confusion and effort at walking. The boys would hold on for as long as they could, usually just ten or twenty yards, from one end of a row of barracks to the other, then would fall away, rolling across the ground and dramatically acting out a death. There were one or two boys who were clingers to a more severe degree, however, and inadvertently Thien became one of these. Something in a particular soldier's presence caught him one afternoon. He could not let go. For more than half an hour, he clung to this soldier's leg, and the soldier took him on all his errands, to the laundry room, to the post office, to the area behind the mess hall where GIs and kitchen staff stood to smoke, to a building full of other soldiers to get some papers signed. The soldier never glanced down to acknowledge Thien, but his silence was powerful — it exuded a manner of benevolence that was extremely mellow, personal, and unusual. Thien hung on despite the discomfort of sitting so long in this position (his hands were leaving sweat marks on the soldier's pants) and the soldier let him. When others passed and made comments or pointed, the soldier responded only in brief, semiserious tones; that he did not laugh or joke with his peers told Thien something. There was an agreement between them, he and this soldier.

The ride ended when an older American, not in uniform, passed them crossing the commons and barked some commands at Thien's soldier who, now, at last, turned his face toward Thien. His eyes were small in his wide, smooth face, giving the impression that they looked out from somewhere hidden. His look was apologetic but conspiratorial. Thien grinned in understanding, let go, went on his way. For days afterward, though, this soldier's expressions and mannerisms stayed with Thien. He tried to copy them, to smile with a small upturn of his lips and exude the same mysterious, accepting silence. Remembering the soldier was slightly pigeon-toed, Thien began to turn his toes in when he walked. He looked for the soldier to pass their area of the camp every day. Finally, he spotted *the soldier one evening outside the mess hall, standing beside another boy, one of those whom Thien played with regularly. The soldier had his hand on the other boy's shoulder. When Thien saw this, a bottled fury rose inside him. He rushed at the other boy, knocking them both to the ground. The two wrestled and rolled in the dirt, pulling hair and clawing at faces.*

The soldier broke them apart. His expression was startled but amused. He held them apart with a hand on each boy's chest, his arms stretched out wide.

MECHANICS

One day a deer got caught in a fence down the road. Only three hours earlier, while he was chainsawing oak and pine trunks into big chunks of firewood, Thien had had an encounter with some other deer. It was the end of summer and a breeze was rustling through, making the tall treetops swish their branches like bellows at the sky; it surged across the long grass on the hillside like an invisible giant's foot, pressing down upon the slope and crushing the grass for just a second, then lifting, leaving the grass to sway, dazed, upright again.

Invisible giants, lowing trees — he was growing used to being the sole witness of such entities and anomalies up in these hills where the trees and grasses were taller than any he'd seen before, and where the mountain views could set one immediately to wishing: this place with no sidewalks, no culs-de-sac, no reasonable places to ride a bicycle, no Kmart or 7-Eleven, no friends. Thien hated their new home and thought house-building a bewildering idea (why, when there were so many far nicer ones already built and available?). He missed the television programs they used to watch in their first two apartments in Sacramento, the easy glamour and humor that was, it had seemed, offering promise of what life in America should be about. He imagined it must be fun and inviting and warm behind those yellow-lit windows in the nicer Sacramento neighborhoods they used to walk through on some evenings, where the driveways were wide and garage doors open and kids rode bicycles round and round in circles in the street. In all of Thien's earlier knowledge of America there had been nothing about chainsaws and dead trees, or the cold of these hills at night, or the discomfort of sleeping in a trailer in a tiny bunk with his nose four inches from the ceiling, or no running water or electricity, just a wheelbarrow of old plastic milk jugs to push, full and empty, up and down a gravel road. At least he was developing muscles, sometimes he thought, but this country was not much different — in terms of being easier, or at least more comfortable — than Vietnam; this was the strange, inescapable truth. At times Thien hated his mother as much as he did his new father, for what she would not take them back to — unclear as the concept of return was to him.

His ears were full of the grinding, churning buzz of the chainsaw, muffled slightly by the helmet he was wearing, when he saw out of the corner of his eye a flash of gray-brown movement, then the dogs bounding up from their resting place in the grass. His upper body jerked, too, almost dangerously, and the saw slid, the groove he was making in the log in front of him swerved, and the log rolled almost onto his feet, as he cut the chainsaw motor quickly. He pushed back his helmet, and his ears, his whole head, filled immediately with the immense rushing sound of silence, a few crackling twigs, then the sudden great rustle and crash of a heavy, swift body plunging through the pallid yellow grass and brown leaves, down the steep hillside. A family of deer (he saw them now) had passed not more than an arm's length from where he stood, a large sleek doe followed by her two fawns, leaping effortlessly over fallen logs and brush, eyes panicked and bright yet still like stones glued into the sides of their mulish faces. The three seemed to be surrounded by a nervous, quivering rim of light, and their bodies were papery, thin-boned, thin-coated, tapering neatly at their noses, hooves, tails. They were graceful and deliberate even in their fear. The dogs pursued them with zeal; the pup's white ears flopped comically, joyfully, while his tongue lashed about between his jaws and his barks came out in eager, unusual yelps. Jamie, the mother dog (named by Thien after the Bionic Woman), was more dutiful in her chase, barking with conviction, with a guard dog's earnest recognition of an intrusion. Then they were gone, disappeared into the tangles of trees and grasses and viny growth that shrouded the ravine down where the hill ended. For a few seconds more Thien saw the pup's white stump of a tail bobbing like a flag through the undergrowth, then the dogs gave up and came, noses first, out of the trees, tails wagging, tongues long, dripping, and the corners of their mouths creased into what looked like dog smiles.

Thien didn't tell anyone else about how close the deer had passed or the slipping of the saw almost to his foot. He had felt it would be a breach of his relationship, however momentary, with the deer; and he was sure his stepfather would've had to make something of it, either about the boldness of the deer or his own clumsiness with the saw. Thien had learned not to talk about everything he saw, and to hide the things that might be construed as mistakes.

Now he came down the road with the wire cutters Hus had sent him back to retrieve. He saw the entangled deer, tugging and hopping frantically on three legs, its fourth leg stretched out behind it, skinny and brown and crooked like a branch, twisted in the wires of the Garrett property's fence. It was a young deer but larger than the three young ones he'd seen earlier. Gray-faced with large black eyes and two nubs of white just beginning to protrude out of its brow. A male deer, Thien observed. Hus and Thien's sisters were standing on the roadside a few yards from the deer.

"Don't touch it," Hus warned the girls, who wanted to move forward for a closer look. "If it gets the scent of humans on it, its mother and the other deer won't go near it ever again. Smell is very important to animals." He directed them to stand back, in the middle of the road.

Hus sent Thien forward with the wire cutters — Thien's arms were small enough to reach through the fence — and meanwhile stood behind Thien on the bank, giving instructions. *Cut there, no there, cut closer — you're cutting his skin now, not the wire!*

But wire and animal leg were well entwined. Thien felt himself caught between the worry of following Hus's instructions and the utter reality of the animal in front of him, closer even than the family that'd passed him earlier on the hill, like an omen, he thought now. The deer was panicking yet not making a sound, just pulling and pulling against the fence. The wires and his leg shook so badly that Thien could not make a clear cut. He could smell the animal, though; it smelled somewhat the same as horses, not a bad smell but also not a clean smell. Its coat was wet with sweat that made patterns like the shapes of continents on a map across its gray-brown back. Thien snipped at a piece of wire far from the leg; he was moving tentatively but wanted at least to appear to be making progress — for in truth he saw only impossibility in the redness and rawness where the wire had submerged itself in the deer's leg, but Hus was not close enough to see that. Blood spattered on Thien's arms and face, and he would have backed off and run were it not for his even greater fear of Hus. He knew Hus would not allow him to leave until the task was completed, and he even began to believe in the dire necessity of the task himself, with Hus's conviction so strong and contagious behind him. It was Hus's conviction as new father at the helm of this family that had brought them to the trailer in these scrubby-treed hills in the first place. (YOU ARE NOW ENTERING GOLD COUNTRY, said a sign along the highway at about the point where the land began to heave itself upward, like flat water stirring into waves, or like a great yellow blanket laid out and beginning, gently, to catch gusts of wind from below.) The deer lurched, stumbled, and fell away from the fence suddenly. It struggled like a creature on stilts upright onto thin legs, then bounded away, leaving half of the fourth leg still in the fence. The leg swung, then fell down into the grass with an unceremonious plop. The crosswires were bloody but still taut.

"There he goes, oh-oh, lookit that! There he goes!" Hus exclaimed. They watched as the deer cleared the far side of the fence on its three legs with no hindrance, powered now by the new strength of fear, and disappeared into the trees. "Well, I suppose a deer can survive on three legs," remarked Hus, "I suppose he can. That is, if the coyotes don't catch the scent of his blood first, of course." He seemed grim but pleased — almost satisfied.

Thien didn't say anything as he pulled his arms back out of the fence and let the wire cutters fall to his side, heavy against his legs. His sisters were standing in the road, he noticed, their hands over their eyes. They never saw anything, it occurred to him.

Years later this was not on his mind as he came out of the movie "Hearts of Darkness," and his eyes had to adjust to the new level, albeit dim, of light in the movie theater lobby. The high flat ceilings were lined with neon tube lighting; shiny faux-sculpture mobiles listed idly in the breeze of the air-conditioning. The reflections of people moved eerily, transparently, across the large glass windows, blocking any view of the darkened parking lot outside. He paused to pry at an eyelid; his contacts itched. The dim outlines of angled walls and movie posters and people grew steadily brighter in his vision. What was on his mind at this moment was the movie, the mood it had put him in — detached, apprehensive — and the feeling of a wheel at the back of his mind, turning, trying to enlighten him about something just beyond the reach of his awareness. It was like a déjà vu of sorts. He could almost pinpoint it, could almost recognize what the mood reminded him of — but then he couldn't. So he had walked with everyone else, not looking at anybody else, out of the artificial dark back into the artificial light.

It was a documentary of the making of a movie about the Vietnam War. Though it wasn't his apparently relevant connection (the subject matter) that he felt strangely toward so much as it was an encompassing revelation about movies in general — the awesome but absurd confluence of the make-believe and the actual that happened on a set. The oldest of his younger sisters, who was eighteen, was currently in film school; she was the one who had recommended this movie. Though he thought he might've gone to see it anyway, regardless of her opinion. (She had developed a particular attitude lately, as if her education had made her privy to some secret knowledge. She laughed at points in movies now where there was nothing to laugh at, he had noticed.) He thought of the actors and their fireworks, their fake ammo, their massive, elaborate fake explosions, their drugs. He thought of Marlon Brando's ugly squished face, remembered how funny it was to see Marlon Brando say candidly, "I swallowed a bug," and how that funniness had opened into something else — weirder and bigger and sadder — the sensation Thien could not pinpoint. He thought people involved in making movies stood somehow at the edge of the world, enlightened and twisted, both, by the range of their power, their famous faces. The movie's subtitle was "A Filmmaker's Apocalypse," and the filmmaker had been exceedingly emphatic about his own torment over the difficulties — financial, logistic, artistic — of shooting an American movie in a Third World country. He had compared the making of this movie to the experience of soldiers in Vietnam. "This is not a film about Vietnam," he had insisted in one interview. "It is Vietnam."

Thien tried to picture his sister amid people like that and felt cheated because he could believe she might get there — to an unlikely, highly coveted lifestyle — but had no similar vision for himself.

He had been enrolled in community college on and off over the years and worked in a garage as a mechanic, a skill that came to him with uncanny ease, had always. He understood them, machines. If he studied any piece of machinery long enough, he could figure out how it worked, how the parts had to come apart or go back together (the only problems he couldn't figure out were the nonmechanical ones, those computer-run parts found in so many newer cars lately). This mechanical comprehension occurred in a strange region of his brain: he had only to turn off his thinking and set his hands in motion. It was the same with firing a gun — he enjoyed it and his aim was unfailingly accurate — another quiet exercise in simultaneously concentrating and letting go.

As he resumed walking after adjusting his contacts, he noticed a textbook inside the ticket-seller's glass booth. She was obviously a student, young, self-preoccupied looking (she reminded him of his sister), also Asian. Her textbook was propped open on the counter before her, the book's front cover reflecting in the window of the booth so that he saw its title backward: it took him a moment to unscramble the letters. *A World of Asia,* the book was called. In his mind the title coincided with the landscape of the movie, dark jungle and greenish mounds of mountains shaped like large reptiles' backs at the edges of murky waters. He saw the words of the book's title imprinted on top of these images, but again he reminded himself, this was always what it was like when he came out of a movie.

He thought of the term "sea legs." He waited for his mind to reorient itself.

His companion, not exactly a date, was waiting for him by the door. Valerie was the only girl he had ever encountered who knew how, and was willing, to change the oil in her own car. But she was not very pretty, and in general he was confused by his feelings for her. The fact was, they spent more time together than he liked to admit, and the terms of their relationship had become ambiguous. But it was not her looks solely that were inadequate — he didn't like to think of himself as that shallow; it was something about her entire demeanor, a certain oblivious candor she possessed. She had a horsey laugh; the tackiness of her clothes made him cringe; she did not mind talking loudly or intimately in public. Sometimes when she came to bed she removed her underpants before her bra, and Thien was revolted by her unabashedness, the utterly frightening gaucheness of her lust. She was also taller and heavier than he was, but then he was a small, slight-bodied man.

"Did that movie remind you of China?" she asked as they exited into the warm early October air.

"Vietnam," he corrected her. She was always getting them mixed up. This was another thing about her he was wary of — her slight, though totally unmalicious, ignorance. She had never been farther outside of San Diego than San Bernadino, one hundred nine miles to the northeast where she'd grown up, and Florida, once, to visit Disney World. How could he blame her when he hardly desired to go much farther himself? He had moved from his aunt's house in one suburb to his own house, a rental, in another suburb just a few months ago, though his aunt wouldn't have minded if he'd stayed till he was forty, it seemed. As for the rift that had sent him out of his stepfather's house in northern California nine years ago and brought him south to San Diego in the first place (he never actually referred to Hus as his stepfather, had done so only for a short period of time three years ago following his mother's death, when he'd been trying in every way he could to claim himself independent of Hus's influence — he was no longer so vindictive, had matured, he believed, past the point of blaming one's parents for everything) — that rift had been largely glazed over, healed by time more than anything. Their animosity toward each other simply wore out. Thien now understood it'd become necessary, then, for both of them, to see him leave. He could remember, after an argument, entering the kitchen to find Hus's bottle of ulcer pills in the middle of the counter, the cap screwed on crookedly, powder from the crushed pills visible on the countertop. Seeing that had always made Thien feel guiltily, tentatively triumphant. He had understood it as evidence of Hus's vulnerability — a rare admission — and possibly the only unadulterated expression of emotion he would ever get from Hus. Now, though, when Thien and Hus talked on the phone occasionally, Hus became lucid, surprising. "I was quite miserable in those years," he told Thien once. He never spoke like this when they spoke in person; self-disclosure could be sanctioned only by phone, it seemed. Thien often didn't know how to respond. He wanted Hus's openness to continue but was also aware of the concentration it required on his own part. The wrong tone of voice or too probing a question could send Hus immediately back into one of his usual modes — sarcasm or bravado or speeches.

"That wasn't really filmed in Vietnam," Thien replied to Valerie's question, as they crossed the parking lot. "It was filmed in the Philippines. The credits said so in the beginning." He felt a little annoyed with her.

Then he realized his car was not where he had left it. They were where he had left it, but the car was not.

This is not happening, he thought immediately. *This is not happening again.* He had had three previous cars stolen in as many years. "Of course this would happen to me. Of course," he said.

"Thien, maybe it was just towed."

Thien almost wanted to laugh. He put his hand to his head, paced the perimeter of the parking space several times as if to confirm its emptiness. There were few cars in the large parking lot. The streetlamps were tall and curved at their tops, like metal swan necks, their heads wide, buzzing bulbs of glaring, yellow light.

Thien cast his gaze around, into the distance, at the headlights of cars going by on the strip, the winking intersection lights. His was a black car, a small one. It wouldn't be easily visible, a Honda CRX with only a few adornments. It should not have been that appealing to thieves — he had resisted his usual desire to fancily adorn the rims, the fenders, as he had done with cars in the past; he had adorned them conservatively this time. As a security measure on one of his previous cars, he had removed all the knobs, inside and out, leaving only one knob that could be easily attached and detached when he himself wanted to get in and out; whenever he left the car, he would put the handle in his pocket and carry it with him like a second key. But even that car had managed to vanish. A Datsun 510. He had belonged to a Datsun 510 car-enthusiast club but had vowed not to buy another 510 after the last one had been stolen. He had then bought a vehicle that was factory issue. He sighed, hooked his fingers in his belt loops, met Valerie's eyes.

"Another one bites the dust," he said.

"You had insurance on this one, didn't you?" She was equally unfazed, had been through it with him before.

He thought of something then. "My Ruger. Should I tell them? It was under the seat. It cost me a lot. I want it covered."

"Say it was in the trunk. Say you were on your way back from the shooting range. Lie." Then, with one of her bold, presuming smiles: "Say you had a stereo in there, too. I could use a new one."

But it was not purely the loss of things that bothered him, was it? he thought later that night, after the police report had been filed, after Valerie had pumped herself to exhaustion atop him and then fallen asleep with arms and legs flung across more than half of the bed. It was her bed anyway, and he was indifferent to its comfort; he hoped he would leave it to her entirely soon enough, for good. Her dyed blond hair fell like a mop over her face, her brown roots showing like some grave aspect (he frankly didn't want to know) beneath her brassy personality. He glanced at the bedside clock and recalled the scenery from the movie and the title of the book. His thoughts had been carried away with the movie, he remembered, and maybe the sight of that book had been meant to pull him back, then, into the situation at hand. Maybe it had been meant to tell him *A World of Asia* existed not so much on the cover or even in the contents of that textbook — or that movie — as it did in what was beyond the reflection in the glass, and notably that was the parking lot, the absence of his own car, which he could not see for all the reflections upon the windows. It was unnerving to him, the sense that one may not always be looking at what one thinks one is looking at. It was also unnerving that one could not leave one's vehicle unguarded for even ninety minutes, without the possibility of returning to its absence and the consequences that entailed. He'd been told he was too emotional about his cars. But he couldn't help it. It flooded him with dread to lose a car. He wanted it back. He wanted the things inside of it back, too, intact. Maybe he was "materialistic" (his college-sister's word), but so what, he thought, so I am.

The truth was he had been driving around for months with the gun under his seat, within easy reach, just in case. Car-jackings, whatever. He kept the safety on, but it was loaded and not in its case, as the law required. Some nights he had even driven with it lying on his lap, or tucked under his leg. He was uneasy enough about this to realize that he shouldn't be doing it, that he was crossing a boundary. But he had succumbed to the security of it, a gun under the seat, as a person might succumb to candy or pornographic movies; juvenile, guilty pleasures that did not actually eradicate lust, or fear.

In the morning they ate breakfast in front of the television on Valerie's kitchen counter. She would drive him to work, she had said.

A commercial jingle for dog food came on, and she got up to dance across the kitchen floor with the dogs, the two little brown mutts. She held them upright by pulling on their front paws, and they followed her lead with stiff, earnest focus. They had short, peppery-brown fur and pert, compact bodies, but around their muzzles the fur was long and straggly, making their faces look like those of bearded old men. She wore a pair of Thien's boxer shorts and a tank top. Her breasts looked large and loose beneath the thin fabric. He had thought before that her body was nicer-looking than her face.

Sometimes a contentedness with her descended upon him — and he felt as abashedly guilty about this as he did about the gun under his seat. It made him angry.

"I'm going to be late," he said.

"Is it my fault you wouldn't get your skinny butt out of bed?" she returned, almost gaily.

"You aren't even dressed yet."

She stuck her tongue out at him, like a child, he thought. She twirled one of the dogs, the dog's hind paws taking a dozen tiny, pained steps to make one tight circle over the floor.

Digging for some morsel of harmless — still, he wished to toe the line of sensitivity — malevolence, finally Thien found it: "What dumb-ass dogs."

He worked quietly that day, taking the usual number of breaks to smoke his cigarettes, half listening to the usual songs on the radio, half thankful when every now and again the few he liked alleviated the monotonous sounds of revving engines and rolling wheels and slamming hoods, the long whining rise and sighing descent of the motorized jack. How many times a day did he reach under the hood of a car with his fingers, find its trigger and then lift, to be met by the sight of another vehicle's gaping innards, asking for interpretation? Some days dragged more than others. He could do much of this work without thinking and so his mind wandered. It followed the good-looking businesswoman with the Miata, pacing in her tight skirt in the waiting room while talking on her cell phone; it followed her as she flipped her buoyant hair while walking to the restroom around the side of the garage and as she delicately stepped back out; it probed her clothing for chance glimpses of the skin beneath; it followed her later as she drove away with her top down, sunglasses on.

At his lunch break he made a phone call to the police department, gave his license plate number, waited. He was told: no news. "Usually they turn up in forty-eight hours or so if they turn up at all," the officer had told him the previous night.

It had been eighteen hours. He imagined the joy-riders still whizzing about; they could've been to Mexico and back by now.

"Bummer about your wheels, man," said a co-worker named Jerry, who was one of the younger boys, maybe twenty, and the only white employee at this company (the rest were Mexican or Asian). Jerry was sociable, would chat up customers, laugh loudly at dumb jokes, snap his oil rag at the others when he should've been working. Harmless. Still, Thien didn't like him.

In fact, the only co-worker Thien did like enough to call a friend was Ramone, whom everyone called simply Mone. Mone claimed his heritage was a mixture of Mexican-Indian, American-Indian (or "Native American," though he preferred the former term because of its more to-the-pointness, he said), German, and Irish; he was also a Catholic. He was twenty-nine, slightly older than Thien, lean and of medium height with skin the same glowing color and texture as burnished pale oak wood; his eyes were dark green, his long hair a unique shade of brown. Women stared at him, Thien had noticed, though sometimes almost with fear, with curious mistrust. Mone spent much of his spare time on his back underneath or bent over the gaping mouth of his own 1970 Datsun 240-Z, one of the most coveted of the Datsun Z car series, rarer and sportier and more expensive to restore than the 510. Mone kept his car locked in his mother's garage and drove it only on rare occasions.

Mone lived with his mother, who spoke only Spanish fluently. He paid her bills, carried in her groceries, ran errands to pick up her prescriptions, took her cats to the vet, et cetera. At times Thien became annoyed by Mone's dutifulness, these activities, their meandering and stalling effects on their friendship; he never waited for Mone to go somewhere with him, he would just leave. And Mone was always unperturbed — by Thien's impatience as well as by the undependable clock of his own life. So the two remained friends. Often what they shared were silences: watching a sports event on the couch, with Mone's mother moving about the kitchen in the background; working on one or the other's car while listening to the radio; going to a movie. Mone did not date (Thien suspected it had to do with his mother) and they rarely talked about girls, or any personal facts of their lives. Maybe a thought dropped here and there — but neither was the kind to question further, or to talk willingly about such matters unless prodded.

Mone carried a hunting knife strapped to his shin, which on occasion he had unsheathed for Thien's sake. "Could skin a baby with this edge," he had said once, but these sounded like words he had heard someone else say and was repeating.

Mone was the one who had let Thien in on the secret — the option — of driving with a gun under the seat. And Mone had been serious, entirely sincere in his paranoia. "You never know, man, when some crazy is gonna pop up in your window. I'll shoot through the glass if I have to, I'll be all cut up by glass if I have to, if it means protecting my own life. Shit, yeah."

Thien had seen the drama in this, at first, and then the inkling, the disturbing seed, of its possibility. He began to keep his gun loaded in the house, then in the car. One of his cousins was robbed at a traffic light as early as seven P.M. in a decent neighborhood, and you could blame it on the fact of his BMW, sure, but still. Sometimes when Thien thought about the world he saw a grid, an immense terrifying grid of objects — like city lights, computer chip boards — viewed from a long distance. The sight made him agoraphobic. There were too many available turns to take; too many people; it was impossible even to imagine the depths of abnormality into which one human being might sink, unnoticed. You just never could be sure.

In the break room Mone nodded to Thien. "Check this out," he said. He was watching the television that was mounted high in one corner of the room, on the wall. "Some guy just went berserk and took a video store clerk hostage in Mira Loma. Look. The TV crew got hooked up to the video store's security cameras somehow. This is live footage, man. They already caught him, though. Trying to run out the back door."

"No one got shot or anything, though," said Jimmy Liu, who was also in the break room, sitting back on the sagging car seat they used for a couch.

"What kind of gun did he use?" asked Thien.

"They didn't say," answered Jimmy Liu.

"A nine-millimeter Ruger P-89," said Mone eagerly, because he knew this was exactly what Thien had lost.

"Yeah, right," said Thien. He patted his pockets for his cigarettes, headed outside to smoke.

On the blacktop after he had finished smoking, he stubbed his cigarette under his shoe, turned, and walked toward the restroom around the side of the garage. It had never been clean here, next to the Dumpster and fence that separated the service station from the apartment complex next door — but he was used to it. The door, when he tried it, was locked. He wandered back to the corner, debating his need to wait, when he heard the door open. A man had opened the door a few inches, to peek out, it seemed. Thien caught his eye, and the man pulled the door shut again. But this glimpse of him stayed in Thien's head: a long-faced man, light brown skin, short, frizzy black hair, apathetic expression, some scruff along his jaw and above his lips, long, thin fingers lying on the doorknob. Thien decided to walk away; he could use the restroom later. But then the man exited, striding swiftly past Thien without a glance, and climbed into a pickup truck (red, Toyota Tacoma, V-6, probably an '88) parked among the other cars in the lot; he pulled out and drove off. Thien had an unclean, a sickly feeling, yes, but told himself it was silly and would be inappropriately discriminating not to use the restroom after this man just because of, what? The look of him, his skin color? Thien told himself: the man was tall, a little skinny; he was dressed in normal, clean clothes. He drove away in a decent vehicle.

When Thien went to pull open the door, he was surprised to find the restroom still occupied. A woman. Her appearance was ruffled, her expression surprised and apologetic. She was gathering what appeared to be Band-Aids from the floor and stuffing them hurriedly into her plastic bag — a bag that seemed to contain other plastic bags. She was not totally despondent-looking, but he assumed she was a homeless person. She wore jeans and dirty, thin-soled sneakers and several layers of big flannel shirts that didn't match. Her blond hair was uncombed. In her thirties, he thought. She was wiping her mouth with a paper towel, and her eyes looked a little raw at the corners. Spotting Thien, she rose from the floor with the courtesy of a drunken person trying to conceal her drunkenness with an overt attempt at manners. "Oh, excuse me," she said and, brightly, "There you go, now," as she ducked out the door. He was holding the door open for her. He wished that if he let it go, it would swing shut fast enough to hit her — a complicated anger had risen inside him — but it was a heavy door, a slow one, on a hydraulic hinge. He noticed the crumpled paper towels on the floor. He felt helpless, foolish, his imagination racing. He used the restroom nevertheless.

Later that afternoon, when he called the police again about his car, it was this man's face he pictured looking furtively out from behind the wheel, although he was aware this was an unfounded suspicion.

Thien had told his sisters about the deer's leg twirling up into the sky like a baton over the fence not to scare them as much as to shield them: he'd understood (if only instinctively rather than consciously) that there was a need for embellishment in such situations, that if you sufficiently dramatized an event to a point of near impossibility, you could be saved. You could be saved from a more private and difficult processing of the event.

He had created a grotesque cartoon image of the deer's leg spinning upward like a fire baton, except that blood instead of flames made colorful arcs in the air. He had told them how the blood had wheeled everywhere; it was like a sprinkler, like rain. He had told them this with a tone of pleasure, the kind of tone he knew his little sisters would respond to with "nuh-unh's." Neither could remember seeing any blood. *You're gross,* they said, and *Eew,* and so the fact of gore had been attributed to him, and the actual incident pretty much forgotten. And Thien was fine with this. He was, in fact, relieved.

Maybe one day he would tell them more, he thought.

Hus had talked in theory about the deer. Deer were *astounding* jumpers, he said. This deer must've been sick, weak already, if unable to make that easy jump. Or he said: the fence was of a poor design. The crosswires stuck out too far from the fence line, and it was easy for animals to get caught; the Garretts should've known better when they built the fence. Then Hus went further. Where was the deer now? he speculated. Probably it had died, shunned by the other deer because of the human scent on it and left to fend off coyotes and mountain lions and wild strays. The accusation burned in Thien's mind.

And Hus made other accusations (Thien had begun to notice them around this time, when he was fifteen years old) about people in general. Fallibility was a fault that couldn't be corrected, his comments had made it seem to Thien, the tendency toward mistake or failure or sloth — it was like ugliness. Unfortunate but undeniable; probably a result of unfit genetics. Just as Hus praised certain breeds of dogs for having good temperament and looks and acumen in their ancestry (the Rottweiler, the German shepherd, the Newfoundland, the Saint Bernard, the Great Pyrenees, and Bernese mountain dogs, as well as any mixture of two or more commendable breeds, because Hus was also wont, on occasion, to praise the surprise strengths of an anomaly), so had he constructed similar theories regarding geographies — races — of people.

You could view the world as you viewed the body, Hus seemed to think, when it came down to it: nether and upper regions, hither and yonder. What went on below was cruder, base, potentially and problematically violent, irrational; what went on above was loftier, better intentioned, better planned, *cerebral*. Of the continental states, for instance, Hus despised Texas most of all, though he'd flown over it, and maybe stopped in it once. Nevertheless he was certain it was a wasteland of bad taste, backward manners, crass Americanism, inbreeding — he had met Texans in the U.S. Army (had shared a bunkhouse with a boy from Lubbock who was the first to expose Hus to the most unbelievably idiotic kind of music he had heard in his life, a wheedling, grating kind of music that was, it had seemed to Hus, especially aimed to promote mediocrity and praise only the virtues of ignorance and self-satisfaction. Hus had also been appalled by his roommate's speech, how it seemed the boy spoke through a mouthful of rocks that contorted his face from the inside with each word). Hus had glimpsed the poor conditions of the South while in boot camp in Alabama (ramshackle wooden houses, haggard-looking women on sunken porches, junk in the front yards, poorly dressed kids, derelict automobiles yawning open alongside potholed roads), though he claimed one could've surmised it all just as well from the topography, the weather reports, the bird's-eye view out the airplane window. Because for Hus it was mountains and seas that held the most distinction — striking, noble vistas and dramatic elevations and expanses sure to create people of respectable composure and unflinching vision. (The hush and grandeur and clear air of northern regions versus the squalor and heat and density and small-animalia of southern regions; civilized, advanced methods of warfare versus cowardly, subversive guerrilla techniques.) For Hus, it seemed a crucial, personal matter to be able to explain the world so categorically. And it put him at ease, made him amiable, actually, if Thien listened and agreed.

Still, Hus's attitude got under Thien's skin. It had not been lost on him that he and his mother (and April) came from that *lower* category, that southward one. And Hus's criticisms were inconsistent. He had cursed idleness yet called their mother "ruthless" when she buried herself in a book or got lost in her notebooks. He poked fun at her for being sedentary and inept at housework, yet spoke negatively of more apparently domestic mothers in the neighborhood, calling them, with disdain, "domineering women." He didn't allow Thien's sisters to play dress-up in certain clothes he deemed provocative, yet had bought Thien the *Sports Illustrated* swimsuit calendar each year for Christmas after his fourteenth birthday.

Thien had not always known how to regard his mother while she was alive. The way she dressed in secondhand clothes from the 1970s; her embarrassing habit of asking people questions to which they'd already given answers, and, especially, the way she looked whenever she attempted something new — she was small, determined, vulnerable but utterly unselfconscious. When she decided to take up power-walking as other women in the area were doing, Thien became aware of smirks on the faces of boys he knew passing by on their motorbikes. There was his mother in a white sweatband, her childish padded body in unseemly white sweatpants. The worst part was that Hus cringed, too, discreetly (but Thien saw it), and in public had begun to call her "Tran" in the casual way other parents called each other by their first names, although she still addressed him as "Daddy." Sometimes Thien could find a comforting humor in the odd details he attributed to his mother (her bell-bottom pants, her taste for what seemed to Thien "old-lady" purses, her candor when she asked him to explain certain slang phrases or figures of speech), but in the next moment these things could fill him with a sudden, terrible humiliation.

When he came home with the blood of the deer on his face and forearms, his mother had looked at him curiously, blankly. Arms submerged in the tiny kitchen sink, she had listened as Hus hooted, solemnly though, and again brought up the threat of the coyotes, their hunger, their wile. When it registered with her that it was the deer's blood and not Thien's, she had laughed, dried her arms, and gone for the camera. The whole trailer felt it when all of them came in or moved about at once; the small thin floor gave, the walls seemed to breathe, to rattle and shrug. She loved her son and saw his blood-spattered state as something to document, another small calamity in the frail course of their lives together — a strange adventure; a story to tell later. Thien didn't always know what to make of his mother's quick recoveries, or her cheerfulness sometimes in the face of such events. It left him feeling shot down, as if he'd just given a wrong answer in class. He wanted his mother to look with concern at him once more, to linger. But he said nothing; and keeping silent made a knot of his heart. He felt guilty and angry and distraught altogether. He would go back to the fence eventually to look for it, whatever might remain of that deer.

He was rinsing the wire cutters with water from a plastic gallon jug when his sisters came up to him later that evening. The sun had dropped below the line of the hills and everything was a fast darkening blue. The girls made their Barbie dolls tiptoe over the rocks as they spoke to each other in some kind of code.

"Hey, Harry, I think I see a waterfall ahead."

"Gee, George, what's a waterfall?"

"Harry, what are you asking me for? I don't know."

"Duh, George, what are you asking me for? I don't know, either."

They were manipulating their dolls' heads and making them pause to turn their torsos and swing their permanently bent arms. Thien was familiar with this routine, though he had no idea what the reasoning behind it was; the girls just seemed to enjoy speaking the names Harry and George out loud. Sometimes they even ran up and down the driveway, calling out to one another as Harry and George. April was usually George and Beth was Harry.

"I used to be as blond as that," Thien said, wanting to feed them another fantasy, to hear their protests. He pointed to their Barbies. "When I was you guyses' age back in Vietnam. Then I ate some burnt dog and got sick. I had to stay in bed for three days straight and when I woke up again, my hair was black. It's been black ever since."

Beth, who was five, looked quizzically at him. "Hotdog?" she said.

"No, *dog*. Regular dog. Woof-woof dog," said Thien. "Where do you think hotdog comes from?"

Immediately the girls threw themselves into a frenzy of gagging sounds. Thien smiled. He stood, leaving the wire cutters to dry at the edge of a nearby pile of lumber, conscious to place them out of at least Beth's reach; April was old enough by then to know better. He never felt spite toward his little sisters (even though the amount of work Hus made him do while they played could seem unfair), just the desire to make them laugh, to see them act silly. It was not that they didn't act silly often enough. Hus told them made-up stories, too, and occasionally did things like swing them through the air holding on to their arms as they screamed in delight. For Thien it came as a relief to hear his sisters laugh. He could open himself up to them, in a gentle, playful way, a side of himself he didn't dare show his peers or parents. And, he had noticed, it seemed to be somewhat the same for Hus. Whenever Thien saw (observing from a distance, bent over his homework or another task) his father playing with his sisters, a feeling of security and hope entered Thien. This Hus was charismatic and theatrical, a compelling storyteller, full of inventive ideas and hilarious facial expressions. Thien had wished the girls would go on intervening in Hus's plans for the house and property, would keep stalling the rhythms of their work, would never grow up.

"Hey, you see that guy earlier today, that black guy? He go into our bathroom with some *puta*," said Jimmy Liu, as they locked up the garage that evening. "I see them walk in the bathroom together, I no see nobody come out right away. Sick!" he added, with pleasurable disgust.

Thien didn't admit he had witnessed this, too; he offered only a smile of agreement, a lift of his eyebrows, in reaction. For if he admitted it, he realized, he would also have to admit how close he had come in behind them, the suspect couple. And he didn't want to let on how that had made him feel — implicated, curious — about their activity in there.

It was Valerie who had pursued Thien when they first met; she wasn't the one he'd been watching initially. It happened at the beach, nearly two summers ago. Thien was playing volleyball with a group of friends from community college. He had come because of a girl, a pretty brunette communications major he was interested in. Her name was Tammy, and to this day he remembered she was wearing a red bikini. He also remembered the pained, surprised expression on her face when he mentioned going for coffee with her and her evasive, noncommittal reply: "Oh, my friend drove me." Her friend, a strident blond girl named Melissa (too sassy and thin for Thien's taste), had, it turned out, just run into another friend whom she soon brought back up the beach to the volleyball game. This was Valerie, and it was Valerie whom Thien fell most naturally into conversation with that afternoon. The other girls didn't like her — this was made plain later, after Valerie had gone her own way again. She was too weird, too loud, and had no style, they said. Thien had felt a pang of chagrin at having been seen talking so readily to the less desirable friend. But in their conversation Valerie had mentioned changing the oil in her car and he had been impressed, had felt compelled to tell her he worked as a mechanic and was always respectful of women who knew how to take care of their own car, because so many didn't, and they often ended up as victims as a result. A few days later she appeared at his garage, having tracked him down not through the obvious channels (she could've asked Melissa or Tammy) but through her own deduction (he'd mentioned certain nearby streets). And as there was no one from school present to witness him saying yes or no to her invitation to go for a drink, he had said yes.

They had a few other things in common. Valerie's mother, too, had died — years ago, when Valerie was a child — and she was estranged from her stepfather, who still lived in San Bernardino and, she claimed, verbally and physically abused her and her sisters. She'd never known her real father. She was also the eldest of her siblings. She'd left home early before finishing high school and taken up with, first, a motorcycle gang and then various drug-dealer or drifter boyfriends or groups of friends. When she was twenty-one she finally mustered the determination to get herself together. She joined AA, got her GED, said so long to her friends. Thien was struck by her resolve, her clarity and self-knowledge. So what if she was not great-looking, she had other qualities, he would tell himself. At first he enjoyed her axioms about life (lessons from AA), but after some months, after he'd heard her drop these phrases often and indiscriminately enough, they began to annoy him, began to strike him as generic; or was it the way she adhered to them, perhaps, that was generic?

Though he believed he wanted to, he still could not stop seeing her.

He had grown too accustomed to beating himself up in her presence, to her blunt, questioning manner that drew him out of himself, forced him to speak. He despised himself for the things he told her as much as he despised her for being willing to listen.

Mostly, she was oblivious, joking, sardonic, mildly grating but easy to be around. Her understanding of him wholly inadequate. He would find himself explaining his personality to her — pedantically, meticulously, idiotically. This taught him to stand up for his own opinions, but it also reminded him of the way Hus had spoken to him when he was an adolescent ("You don't know the first thing about the kind of person I am"). Thien would have rather emulated Mone, his stolid friend, and his self-accepting silence, his holding back; his form of celibacy. "What I like about Mone is that he's a self-sufficient person," Thien would attest to Valerie, painfully aware of the lame hint he was making about what he truly wanted to say to her. "He has no need at all for intimate relationships."

But Valerie was speaking now. "He's like a bird without a nest. A wheel without an axle." She sat over her menu in the booth at Denny's where Mone had joined them for dinner. They were also expecting April, who had phoned Thien from the road an hour earlier, saying she was near San Diego and needed a place to stay for the night. She had driven down to Las Vegas from San Francisco the day before; she was location-scouting for a film project in the desert, she'd said.

Thien gave Valerie an agitated glance. "I don't know what you're talking about, Val."

"I mean you without your car." Her eyes brightened abruptly. "No. An *egg* without a *shell*," she said with delight.

Mone glanced over the rim of his water glass, then set the glass down on the table. Thien watched him watch Valerie and couldn't guess what Mone might be thinking. Mone's eyes were always a bit hazy, hazy but shrewd. Mone smoked pot. Thien usually found an excuse to leave whenever Mone offered him some. Thien had never been comfortable with people who were too obviously having a good time.

"So I'm worried about my car," said Thien, "so what? You would be, too."

"No, I drive a totally crummy piece of shit," she retorted. "I drive a crummy piece of shit because I don't give a shit what people think. I wouldn't give a shit if it disappeared, either. I'm just like that, Thien. I'm different from you. I'm free, my mind is free, my heart is free!" She said this with a vehemence Thien found both infuriating and contradictory to the very concept of carefreeness she was proclaiming; he wished he could point this out to her but didn't know how. So he slapped the side of his head and pretended to grimace.

"Man, Valerie, you are loud." He laughed for a second, self-satisfied.

Valerie brought her hands to her face and announced in a mock-sobbing voice, "Oh, I'm so sad about my car! I can't sleep, I can't eat! Oh, oh!" Even louder than before.

"Stop it." Thien was genuinely irritated. He felt childish.

But Mone was the kind of friend they could bicker in front of. He made no comment and continued to read his menu.

After the waitress took their orders, Thien looked out the window for his sister's car (1973 Saab, fixed up as a whimsical side project and given to her by Hus, who also paid for her college,

Thien knew, as he never had for Thien, as Thien had never expected he would), but he saw no sign of it, its unmissable electric orange. It was a cool, odd little car with a lot of problems — a completely unpragmatic vehicle to give an eighteen-year-old girl who knew or cared nothing about automobiles. She drove it around on long trips as if it were a Chevy Sprint, and more than once it had sprung a leak or popped its ignition coil, leaving her stranded. Already she was half an hour late. She was another female he just didn't get. Thien knew his ideas were fairly conservative; he would admit he liked women to keep themselves well groomed, to grow their hair long, to wear a little but not too much makeup, to wear skirts during the week, blue jeans on the weekend: feminine but sensible. April's standards, however, were incomprehensible to him — she was self-righteous, morbid, almost trashy, weird with a capital W (laughingly she had even told him a guy she dated once described her using these words). He was concerned about her but also at times simply annoyed. She was smart, sure, but never practical, never thoughtful. In the years Thien had lived with his aunt, he'd heard this sentiment expressed often about his mother. "Why she do like that, I don't know," uncles and aunts said in regard to everything from how she cut her hair short to her lack of religion to how she'd acted (or not acted) during the conflicts between Hus and Thien that had eventually sent Thien out of the house.

When the waitress brought their food, April still had not shown. They ate unexpectantly, as if they'd not been waiting for anyone.

"Hey, where's your sister?" Mone asked after a while, in a tone of deliberate, nonchalant surprise.

"She's a chronically late person. She's sort of aimless like that," answered Thien. "She thinks she can just quit school and go hang around a movie studio and someone will give her a job. She's a total dreamer."

Shortly after he arrived home from dinner, as he was opening a letter from his insurance company, April appeared at his door.

"Hey! Let's go shopping!" was how he greeted her, surprising even himself with this surge of unguarded jubilation, holding up the claim check from his insurance company. He was pleased to see her, but it was the knowledge of the money, actually, that was making the feelings of anticipation and relief rise in him at that moment.

"All right," said April skeptically but agreeably. "Hi, Thien."

"What took you so long?" he asked, cheerfully. They hugged quickly, lightly.

"I was farther away than I thought."

She did not mind that he had already eaten, she said, to which he told her he had figured as much. It went without saying in their family that they would not go out of the way for each other — in mundane matters at least. They could take care of themselves.

She said, "I need to bring in my stuff."

Thien followed her out, slipping the check securely back into its envelope first and placing it where he wouldn't forget it, under his wallet on the hallway phone table. "How's the car?" This was something he always asked when he saw her.

"Okay. It started overheating a few times and I had to pull over, though. I was going like thirty-five up even the smallest hills." They laughed about this, though it was the kind of thing Thien wouldn't have thought was funny if he'd been there when it was actually happening. But it was true there was a hilarity to it, the picture of the ancient orange car struggling. Because it was so obvious it must. They began to joke in the way they usually did about the Saab, in their deep-voice imitations of Hus:

"That German engineering!"

Hus had always spoken in defense of the Saab, despite all of its problems. BMW, Mercedes, Braun, Bang & Olufsen, Glock, Luger. In brand names as in dog breeds Hus remained loyal to his European roots. The Saab sat in Thien's driveway, creaking with heat. Ludicrously orange, small and outmoded and urbanely European-looking. Thien noticed the inside panels of the doors were off, baring the unpainted, skeletal inner metal framework of the doors. April lifted a large black duffel bag from the backseat.

"You need to always bring along coolant," said Thien, more seriously.

"I know, I know. I brought water."

"You're not putting straight water into that radiator, are you?"

She slung her backpack over her shoulder. "I thought that's what you're supposed to do."

"No, never. Always fifty-fifty, water and coolant. Always." He walked around the car, inspecting. "And what happened here?" He pointed to the doors.

"I had to take them apart. They wouldn't open." She put her bags down at the edge of the driveway to show him. She had wrapped a rubber band around two small pieces of a mechanism inside the door because the spring was not working properly. "It happened on this door first, then it happened on that door. I was crawling in through the passenger side all the time. And it keeps happening, so it's just easier to keep the panels off, I decided."

Thien laughed. He realized, though, that they were doing what Hus would do. The few times Thien had gone home for the holidays, the first thing Hus always did was show him something: the most recently cut-down tree; a repair on the house; a new retaining wall. Hus, too, walked in a circle around Thien's car.

"I'm impressed," said Thien now, making a show of laughing at her rubber bands. She shrugged, smiled haplessly.

Once inside, she began talking about the desert. Long flat stretches of highway, black plains of sand, white plains of sand, the silhouettes of monster windmills atop distant hills, her feeling of a vast, strange awe as she drove, the beautiful bleakness of those listless, thankless desert towns; she'd loved it out there, she said, describing it to him with the kind of fervor Thien had only heard when people talked about more unlikely topics — a chance drive in one's dream vehicle, say, a Lamborghini or Porsche. Here they stood in his kitchen, the ridiculously largest room in the house he rented, with its gleaming, ruddy-textured, white linoleum floors and all its empty white cabinets, as she told him about the desert. She opened and closed his cabinet doors, looking for food, and found finally, to her satisfaction, an old box of instant oatmeal that she claimed was what she usually ate for dinner anyhow, and so she put a pot of water on the stove to boil. Thien watched her with fascination and bewilderment. He was not one to understand being drawn to the desert (or to any large, sparsely populated places at all, for that matter), for he was an advocate of the city, of the proximity of shopping centers and movie theaters and coffeeshops and beaches and other people. He was not one to understand the appeal of long flat stretches of anything or to marvel at such a thing as a "constantly receding horizon." What was a horizon anyway? It was just a line of land, out there, too far from everywhere else for his comfort.

"You should drive to Las Vegas sometime. You should see it," she was saying. "It is a totally awful place."

"And why would I want to go to some place that's awful, April?" retorted Thien.

April had taken several small metal film canisters, flat and circular like pizza pans, out of her black duffel bag and was now placing them in his refrigerator. He wanted to ask if she planned to eat those tins later, or make some kind of joke about it, but she had already shown him her camera, a boxy black plastic-and-metal apparatus that seemed too rectangular to record motion (had been Thien's first thought at the sight of it — the lens was short and placed asymmetrically above two smaller lenses that looked like mini-eyes), and his sister handled it with such serious, casual dexterity that he felt wary, now, trying to mock her.

This is only the Bolex, she had said.

And what did her *only* imply? That there was better technology than what she was showing him and she was familiar with it already, unfazed by such special equipment? Yet she could still show up in their stepfather's sputtering joke of a car without even the common sense to keep coolant in it. Thien, watching her, thought she had become something else lately, something worse than what he last remembered. She spoke about the camera and its specifics in some sort of specialized lingo on purpose, it seemed, as if to make a point of excluding him. Her clothes (tight-fitting black leotard shirt, paint-spattered orange cut-off sweats, cowboy boots) all had edges that had been cut or altered and were fraying. She seemed to Thien unhealthy, composed of too many disparate elements thrown together. Nothing matched, this flurrying mess under and over her skin. It was that San Francisco thing, he conjectured. Everyone up there looked mal-nourished, troubled, artsy. It seemed to be a matter of principle, to dress as badly as you felt.

"Irony," she was answering his question about Las Vegas, "it's called irony. It's so awful it's beautiful. Some things are just like that — beautiful and terrible."

The water on the stove was boiling. She poured some over the dry oatmeal. She stirred with a spoon, pressing her hip into the counter.

Shortly after this the call came. Mone with an uncharacteristic tremor in his voice. "I saw your car," he told Thien.

The relationship with Valerie is over now. For months. It was a back and forth ending, alternately reluctant and determined, on Thien's part, mostly. He is sure now, though, it was for the best. She finally found a way to be angry with him, citing his wavering as cruel. She began to blame him. It became easier, then, for Thien to close his own book on her; his compassion for her finally dissolved. And now, when he thinks back to his time with her, he views it (he finds he must) as a period of self-weakness, or self-punishment, for all the years of his life up to this point of having felt: undeserving. They'd had nothing truly in common; he was selling himself short with her. He had not loved her. He had only partially respected her. (He thinks of Tammy, the bru-nette in the red bikini, but knows she wouldn't have been right, either, was also of another world; weren't they all, really?) He has come to believe that even if he'd gotten the things he wanted — the right girl, certain opportunities — he still wouldn't have been able to accept them, would've found some means of sabotage. He'd been just too scared of everything then.

This is where he is now, able to see this much, without con-tempt; with mercy. *Self*-mercy. And what pushed him to move in this direction?

The night he stole back his car.

It was like slamming doors and meaning it, it was like tying a firm knot, it was like standing in the light. What that action gave him was more than his vehicle or an adventure. It secured for him the *defiant* fact of ownership — that he could and would take a stand. (And, now, seven or eight months after the fact is when Thien can sit in his living room and view himself as a grainy black-and-white image on his own TV screen — from a videotape sent to him by April — breaking back into his vehicle by the stark glare of a single flashlight beam. He is surprised at his own image, for he never dreamed he could appear so stylishly angular, shadowed, that a black-and-white representation could convey, so coolly and dauntingly, these facts about himself that he will from now on own with confidence: that he has good cheekbones and well-accentuated eyes; that he is lean and vigilant and good with cars.)

The body of his car had been stripped of all its adornments — silverplate rims, bumper lights, chrome-edged mudflaps, rear-view mirrors, the leather car bra; it looked naked. Mone had recognized it by the pencil-thin pink tubing of light that ran the length of the car's body; he had recognized this detail, in fact, on another car at a gas station in another part of town and had asked the driver where he got the light. The driver had said he didn't know, it wasn't his car. But Mone figured it was a stolen part and had followed that car into another neighborhood, where he had soon spotted Thien's car parked in front of a body shop. A lot of tank-top clad, mostly Mexican boys were working under and around several vehicles in various stages of disassembly. Some kind of Spanish or Latin-American pop music played from a stereo atop the hood of one of the cars. Thien's car had sat by the sidewalk, intact but stripped of most of its extras.

And later that night, Mone, Thien, and April had come back for the car.

Thien has noted some other changes in himself since the stealing and his breakup with Valerie. One, he has become interested in dating only other people of color. When he meets a woman he likes now, he is struck by an almost familial recognition — a gentle, grace-filled acknowledgment, a small door opening inside of him, giving ever so slightly. Thien realizes he was missing this before, missing out on it entirely, was walking sidewalks as if they were nothing more than sidewalks; he was unaware of the subterranean network of energies linking and testing and shooting messages among people as they pass. Now he notices the subtle nods, the movements of eyelids, the burdens of history that are transferrable in the passing sullen looks of long-haired, brown men in front of bus depots, in the wary strides of certain unkempt black men he previously regarded with suspicion. He is aware of degrees of detachment between himself and white customers dropping off their cars, and he assesses these whites according to how they do or don't respond to the flow of the question he sends out beneath his feet at every moment now. He has come to recognize a perpetual and deep sense of — waiting. Waiting for what? An understanding perhaps? A promise?

Thien also feels in the world around him lately a sensation of reverberation. The flow of traffic, the floods of faces lined up at supermarkets, the quick dazzle and din of sound bites on the radio, billboards on the freeway — all this crazy merging and diverging at last *makes sense*. He is willing to watch and wait and not search every day. (He has locked up his guns.) Sometimes, driving along the seaside in a stream of traffic at sunset, he will glimpse the rooftops of houses stretching row upon row over the coastal hills, all their matching peaks turning orange in the setting light, and, with the thin clouds curling in, and the smell of salt and mist from the sea, suddenly he will be awed by the number of lives being conducted inside this panorama. An intensely euphoric feeling will grip him and turn him almost emotional as he stares at the gold sparkles on the water.

And only seldom does a reminder of Valerie creep back in, some small hint of a forgotten shame.

That night they waited down the street in Mone's car. April was hunched in the space behind the two front seats, winding her camera steadily, her hands and the camera and the film all in a black vinyl bag across her lap.

The garage had been long closed. Lights flickered on and off behind curtained windows and several groups of revelers exited houses to loiter on driveways or the curb, then piled into their vehicles and drove off. The three waited. Initially, Thien had wanted to call the police but Mone had persuaded him not to. The biggest problem Thien foresaw now was with the camera, which needed light. April had brought along a very bright flashlight for this purpose. Thien had tried to dissuade her from coming at all, but she'd insisted, her argument being that you had to take chances and Thien never did. Thien had thought she was being juvenile and impetuous, until Mone had taken her side.

When the neighborhood finally fell quiet, Thien and April got out of Mone's car and walked quietly up the dark sidewalk with their jackets zipped and their heads down, because this was how it seemed to them they should walk. Thien could hear their footsteps and the whir of the camera, could see their shadows cast long in the oblong patch of light April was shining straight at the back of his head. Thirty seconds was a long time on film, she had said, and she would film their walking for only thirty seconds; she had promised him she would use the light as little as possible. They startled once at the sight of a trash can, and giggled despite themselves. April cut the camera and they continued in silence. It occurred to Thien the filming was silly but his adrenaline was high, and soon there was no more room in his head for opinions, only motion. April had already taken what she called her establishing shots: street, exterior view of Mone's car, interior views of their faces waiting inside Mone's car, frivolous details such as the gearstick, the radio glow, a hand, a knee, fingers on the steering wheel. She had asked them to repeat certain actions with their hands wider apart or closer together to fit into the frame; she even asked Thien to hold his cigarette in a way he never would, to make the ash fall at a particular angle. Thien had thought this was stupid (though now, as he watches the tape she has sent, he sees what it was she was trying to get).

On screen, his fingers loom in closeup and the ash flakes off the tip of his cigarette in fine gray detail, then disappears out of the frame.

Then he is walking shakily to the car. His black-gloved hands are graceful and quick, sliding the long silver tool under the window frame. The door opens without a sound. It's a silent film; her camera didn't record sound, and this soundlessness lends his actions a fluid, diminishing quality even though the camera shakes and jars, and the images slip in and out of focus. The camera pans up: his profile close, the sharp shadow under his cheekbone, the dark arch of his eyebrow, the big white of his eye. He is in the driver's seat and the inside of the car is abruptly lit with a bright white light, his head and torso blasted away for a moment, but then the light changes, dims, the picture is darker but clear once again. His hair, which was shorter then, makes a square, spiky helmet above his forehead as he bends over the steering wheel. Then comes the jumbled moment, the surprise. The picture jumps up and down and turns dizzying, moves quickly, sloppily backward, not coming clear again until a gun is already pointed.

Instinctively he had reached under the seat, groped for it, found it, stood. But when he looked at it, he saw it was not his gun. It was smaller, lighter, made of cheaper materials. And he felt then as if he were watching someone else's hand pull it up and point it at the person coming toward him. A man not much younger than himself, and all he actually saw of this person at the time was his color. Brown. The aura of a scavenger more than a predator, and now the TV image reveals exactly how little this man was, the same size as Thien, with a wan black moustache, barefoot and shirtless and shocked-looking. Mexican or Filipino or otherwise Asian or Indian, even. Like two animals in a spotlight they stood beside the car, Thien backed into its open door. This moment — he remembers it all, of course, in very slow motion (and he is a little sickened, now, somewhere low in his gut; he will not watch this tape again) — he had felt it gratefully as an agreement between them, he and this other man, this stranger, an agreement about the manner of contact they could make with one another. They could push or relent or try to stand one another down. Thien had felt energized, sinister, strong.

This is mine — mine, you know.

All right. That's fine. But that gun's mine.

Where is the one that was in here?

It was sold, man, it was sold.

Somewhere in the middle of this Thien had remembered his insurance claim check, and that was when his urgency lessened (that he had enough money to buy a new gun if he wanted to slightly quenched his indignation toward the other man). More words exchanged. Here, the picture flashes, white bands cutting vertically across the frame, Thien lowering his gun as the camera stops.

He remembers the rest. He and April got in the car and drove it away and threw the gun out onto the sidewalk for the man to retrieve at the corner.

And there were other things: where the other pieces of his car had gone and who or what was driving around with them as decoration now; his sister following at his heels with her bright flashlight and that metal box pressed firmly to her eye (how could he warn her — *open the other eye, sis* — without sounding futile, naive, rote?). And: climbing over a fence into a field with some idea of a deer's leg in mind, looking for traces of blood in the late-summer grass, what had they ever hoped, really, to recover, to rectify?

5

LETTERS

(August 10 and August 14, 1975)

Dear Ms. Tran Anh Trinh:

Your story in The Sacramento Bee *touched me and caused reflections on what I also had to adjust to some years ago as an immigrant from another part of the world.*

Like yourself I came from a structured society with an entrenched national and historical identity. You must give this up, though, if you want to realize what it truly means to be an "American" — a participant in a society so elastic it can afford permanent outsiders. This is where I feel I should advise you, from the very start, not to think of yourself as an outsider. In this country you may have all the opportunities you want, but only as long as you understand it is necessary to confidently step forward to claim them.

War is a calamity and can do ruinous things to children's spirits. My own father was a Socialist (the purer form of what has gone awry in your and certain other parts of the world, as you know) at a time and in a climate when any such unconventional thought was misconstrued as being in line with Nazi sympathies. My father was also a writer like you, well known and politically affiliated — and our whole family suffered the consequences of his unpopularity during and following the war in which I was a child. Thus, my sympathies go out to all children of war who had no choice. Tell your son I, too, know what it is like to wish to forget, to have had not much of a boyhood to recall without fear or anger; your young daughter's memories will likely be different, hopefully fewer. Though I believe they have equal chances, here and now, as do you.

I will refer now to the oft-admired American custom, the direct question; from your writing and the photo, you seem an intelligent and attractive woman. Why are you still in the camp?

I am a 44-year-old bachelor, an Architect, 6' feet with light blond hair and green eyes, speak with a slight Scandinavian accent, love animals and the outdoors, swimming, snow skiing, bicycle riding, good books, and classical music. Though I am a private person, I do like and enjoy people. It is with respect that I offer my hand to help you and the children along however I can.

Dear Mr. Hus Madsen,

I should address to you in more friendly way after reading your warm letter as well as ask you just call me by my given name, Tran. I received several letters from my American readers, but yours is the first I respond to with enthusiasm, not because you offered help, but because you mention many things interest to me, especially about your own experience which I thought show a very intellectual person who has known failures as well as successes, and tasted bitterness and loneliness, too. I must say thanks for sending me such a sincere and honest letter.

So you are an architect. I love architecture . . .

6

THE THIRD FORM OF WAR

It is true I was born on the fringes of several wars. It is true no bullets grazed me, no mortar blast stunned me, no tear gas blinded me, and no mother was actually taken from me; nevertheless, I hold images.

I was a morbid teenager. A part of me was attracted to the apocalyptic. Is it the lackadaisical, capricious weather of California that breeds this? Is it television? Or is it the simple, not unusual, adolescent urge to flirt with nihilism? I was a science fiction junkie; I entertained scenarios of nuclear holocaust and imagined who might survive it with me; I fantasized about terrorists infiltrating our high school pep rallies. In short, I enjoyed imagining the familiar routine of the world overcome — violently disrupted, evaporated — and the possible ensuing freedom of chaos, of annihilation. I exalted the romance of desolation. In my mind I held clearly an image of a ruined city, rubble and bricks and splintered wood and dilapidated buildings under a cloudy purple-black sky, with no people in sight: some place of necessary primal living I was trying to get to or back to. (These images of disinhabited cities are very real to me, I have almost a feeling of nostalgia toward them.) In '92, when the race riots broke out, I wanted to go looting; and as a film student in college I was one of those who thought it a prize to capture on celluloid the vision of a burning car on the side of the freeway, or a decrepit homeless person — life at its most dismantled moments.

But in this was in fact a wish to see people come together. I was not truly callous. I just wanted to meet with others on vital ground, in a more urgent context than day-to-day life seemed to allow: to share with someone even just a millisecond of an understanding of need. This, I thought, might at last break down the barriers. Even though I had my parents, I would often think of myself as an orphan. Something in me knew I did not wholly belong here, wherever here was.

My mother had told me nothing about war per se, or growing up in the time of one, but her personality (she still took interest in the inconsequential things — little pockets that my sister and I thought were cute on some shirts; our preferences for wearing our socks pushed down around our ankles instead of folded; our favorite snack foods, which she took pleasure in serving to us some days after school) revealed that even within the midst of war, people manage to find some modicum of a "normal" life; that people, no matter what the context or constraints, will at least attempt to blunder through the usual — lusts, intrigues, revelations — of life. People still manage to fall into some form of love, however scarce or violent or misconstrued or visionary it may be. I do know my mother sought men and buried bodies, alike. I could blame her, my mother, or an enemy like the Viet Cong, for passing on an obliviousness to pain, but responsibility is never as simple as that. As it is I have already blamed my mother — for not healing her own losses fast enough to present herself to us as a whole and unafraid parent. In defense I can say only that children are selfish in their helplessness; at least I was.

The way my mother's superstitious aunt put it was this: the spirit of the man who was to be my father and the spirit of my mother's unborn child (myself) had been at odds in another lifetime, and in order for the child to come into the world this time, the spirit of the man who was to be my father had to leave it. This assessment was made after my mother's first husband was killed (albeit the marriage was brief), and the superstitious aunt never knew that he wasn't my real father. But it didn't matter. My mother blamed herself. Perhaps she blamed me as well, secretly.

The first form of war is obvious. Men and artillery and lost limbs, charred houses, fires — all the visible losses. The second form, I believe, is less talked about. It is the soul's experience of war, the *contract each soul must enter into regarding what kind of contact — or impact — their bodies will make in the environment of war; a concurrence with the particular circumstances of violence must occur somewhere deep inside each person, as victim or inflictor, whether the conscious mind ever grasps it or not. I imagine an invisible thread guiding every victim to his killer or killing agent, and vice versa. The third form is ongoing; it has more to do with what remains for those who survive.*

But what do I really know of war? I know that in dream analysis you cannot take conflict for granted. You and the objects or persons you are at odds with in dreams are never separate entities. In this way your dream-enemies come not to frighten but to show you: an inner struggle, a piece of yourself you must still integrate.

This should be the proper role of anomie, I think.

I have read of archaeologists finding evidence that massive, meticulously plotted fires destroyed much of the ancient Chaco Canyon civilization's expansive architecture in the high deserts of New Mexico. And the care and intent behind the fires show some decisive collective mind at work. The Chaco Canyon people had recognized their end to be forthcoming and had proceeded to break their civilization back down to the dirt from whence it had risen.

Something about this strikes me. Whether the end of a people comes as a grand elegy or as a consequence of all they have abused, lost, and ruined, the end does come. The trick seems to be in whether we will recognize it ahead of time and bow out gracefully or not. Perhaps clues — an event such as that famous plane that exploded while taking off from Danang in 1975, in plain view of the news cameras — must be given after we have disregarded the negative conditions of a situation long enough. In whatever fashion the end comes, somehow a marked population of people (be it family or nation) must knowingly or unknowingly join together in an acceptance of the fate of: dissolution. Home — whatever that is — will be extinguished or rearranged. And what remains afterward, the survivors, eventually they are scattered, too, like seeds, or sent out like scouts but bearing messages they've forgotten by the time they land and begin to roam amid other populations of people. They set up smaller, sadder camps of the old life, always with the same sense of something shattered and undistilled behind them. It is my belief that all survivors contain within them an understanding of the true ephemeral nature of location, but it is up to each to realize this as potent, or terrifying, or meaningless.

I had a dream the other night about my sister. She was pregnant and asking if I would take the child. She could not give up men and adventures, she was saying, for the responsibility of a child. I was willing to accept it but fearful that she might have a change of heart and that I might surrender myself to loving her child in the meantime. I was trying to find some way of explaining to her the commitment she must make toward her decision.

When the Gulf War struck I was seventeen. I was still a shoplifter. I had a headful of movies, was aspiring to write screenplays. I was pining over a boy. Later this boy joined the marines and perhaps got more in tune with national concerns, while I (years off, still) would continue to conjure up — at any mention of the phrase "current events" — certain pieces of clothing I wore in the eighth grade, the designer labels of which read: Current Threads.

May you please forgive me.

GUERRILLA

April was always talking incomprehensibly about weird things. Not that I didn't see her point sometimes — she was just so desperate about it, about avoiding everything you might call "normal." I agreed sometimes but I didn't have to be dramatic about it.

For instance: I was there. She was not. She refused to participate because she thought putting on camouflage clothing was too "disturbing." While to me it was just a little extra exercise and a chance to camp out and be away from Dad for a night. Heidi Ogden and I got to laugh at the boys on outings like these and tell stories in our sleeping bags. But all right, Sensei had also made us paint our faces green and told us to pretend we were in Iran. In my mind Iran was a small, flat, sandy-brown slab of land inhabited only by men in green uniforms, every one of them sporting a thick black mustache.

The lot was small. Treeless. A clearing carved into a mountainside. The mountain's insides: gray hard rock. An old mining quarry halfway between our town and Lake Tahoe. We were at the moment pretending to look for Sadaam Hussein's boy-lackey, the strategic plans–bearer, who was hiding somewhere in the vicinity of this one lot of the quarry. This would've made Sensei our Sadaam, as he was the one in charge of hiding the plans-bearer. We looked in the windows of and underneath all the cars in the lot. We climbed over all the mud-crusted machinery, even peered into gears and lifted hoods to search inside old engines. Three piles of serpentine rocks — frosty-blue pyramids — were the only other places to search in this landscape of scraped gray ground. And a Dumpster. We leaned over and rifled with bare arms through trash. A thousand aluminum cans. Newspapers. Small rusting metal objects. We walked sinking to our ankles, our knees, in the gravelly rocks, up and down the mountains of serpentine. All this I knew April would not care she was missing.

Finally we gave up.

Sensei climbed atop the middle pile of rock. The smallest. He squatted. Lifted a Pepsi can, held it up for us to see how the bottom had been sliced off to make a funnel for air. Then he removed rocks by the handful until there was a hole. He reached down, grabbed hold, pulled. Contours of muscle slid beneath his skin like gears. Our sensei, David Ogden, was everything you might think of when you thought of perfection in California: he was six-foot-four, blond, with deep-set, electric-blue eyes in a chiseled face, and when he walked, he glided. Now, at the end of his arm, a boy rose out of the pile of rocks that fell away like a stone flower opening. Grinning, triumphant as a fool, Jeremy Todd — Sensei's star student — emerged with his hair and face caked in a fine layer of blue dust.

Sensei had a way of not speaking. He reached his hand to his own belt. He wore camouflage khaki parachute pants and a black mesh tank top. His skin was the color of wet sand, his spiky crewcut hair a shade or two lighter than his skin. He unfolded then folded closed his black-handled knife, stood. His glowing eyes swept over us with a steady, questioning look as if to be sure we'd all gotten the message, the lesson here: *leave no soda can unturned?* Or was it: *be resourceful,* or *hiding places are everywhere you don't expect them to be?* He would probably fashion another famous Japanese-Okinawan Koden-Kan karate axiom out of this for us later, in typical David Ogden style (he had taught us how to say "don't mention it" in Japanese — *doitashimasihte* — by pointing out it sounded like "don't touch my moustache"). Sensei's boots crunched against the blue rocks as he descended the pile. Jeremy yelled "Geronimo!" and leaped, crashed, down the rocks. A mini-avalanche followed. The other boys gathered around, wanting to know what it was like to be buried and breathe through a Pepsi can. Heidi and I agreed we didn't care.

Then it was time for lunch. We collected our lunch bags from Sensei's van and sat at the picnic bench above the quarry, as if we were just another class on a field trip to the old silver and gold and rock mines.

Heidi and I were practicing walking on our hands. We were back at the dojo with all the other kids late Sunday afternoon, waiting in the parking lot for our rides home. We had washed our faces, we were back in our normal clothes. Jeremy Todd was of course outwalking us both. He could walk on his hands the whole length of the parking lot, stop, turn around, *and* come back. He walked with his legs curled like a scorpion's tail, toes pointed. His body was rigid. When he needed to catch his balance he bent or unbent a knee. Slowly. He was always steady and we hated him for it.

Heidi was Sensei's oldest daughter. She was thirteen, milky-skinned, with flat brown hair, skinny. They lived at the dojo, Sensei and his three daughters, in small loft rooms built close to the rafters. The ceilings of their rooms slanted sharply. Heidi's posters all hung at a slant. They were living there now because their mom had left them six months ago and the house they'd been living in before had belonged to her family. My mom had also left about six months ago, a little more, though that was because she had died. Had passed away. However people wanted to say it. They didn't need to be gentle with me.

The other boys were practicing their Defensive Arts reactions. Toby and Jonathan Sandusky and Kenny Davis and some of the younger boys were all in a line, jerking back their heads, groaning, grimacing, doubling over and collapsing, in unison, crumbling down and sprawling themselves out on the asphalt. Then they sprang back up. Toby called out another number — "Number Eight!" — and it started all over again. Number Eight ended with a long-side thrust, and the boys would always compete to see who could fly backward the farthest in what were their wishful ways of overreacting — I thought — to that kick. Sensei had recently required us to memorize not only each Defensive Art Numbers One through Twenty but the reactions to each as well, *without* a partner. His theory was that if we could perform the reactions alone, we would also better understand the techniques involved.

Kenny Davis had flung himself backward into the path of a car pulling into the lot. The car honked and tires squealed as the mother inside slammed on her brakes.

"Oh, shit," gasped Kenny, picking himself up and scrambling aside. "Man, did I just land on my ass!" he crowed, laughing.

"Hey, now, watch your language around here," said Jeremy Todd, always trying to be Sensei, who was a righteous Christian and against cussing. Jeremy was still upside down and red-faced.

The mother stuck her head out the car window and yelled, "*Phillip! Are you crazy!*" and Kenny whipped around, pointed to himself, said, "Who, me?" There was no Phillip among us. Sometimes it felt as if the mothers didn't pay much attention to who we all were. Kenny had wispy fair blond hair and a soft face. He was the sweetest boy in class and his father was the Georgetown sheriff.

The mother, Mrs. Whalen, climbed out of her car. Her hair was red and curly and she wore tight pants. Since Sensei's divorce, it seemed a lot of mothers were coming around now in tight pants. But maybe I just thought this because I still half believed the rumors I'd heard from older students, about affairs Sensei had had with students' mothers even before his wife was out of the picture. These were just rumors, though, and we kids had been told a number of times by some mothers to stop repeating them.

"Hi, girls," said Mrs. Whalen to Heidi and me. "Are you girls showing these boys something or what?" She winked. Then she disappeared inside the dojo to look for her sons, the Whalen twins. Casey, the fat one, was ten, and only kicked high when Sensei was watching him. The other one, Robert, was thinner and shy and almost cute for a ten-year-old. Sometimes, to test our reflexes, Sensei would throw tennis balls at us at unexpected moments in the middle of class, and you were supposed to either duck or block. Casey, the fat one, was one of those always getting beaned.

But, as Sensei put it: *Pain only lasts four seconds, the rest is in your mind.*

Sensei lately was living part of the time in L.A., part of the time up here. He was trying to break into Hollywood as a martial arts action-picture actor, in hopes of making money for the dojo. The dojo needed it, now that his wife had left the business. Sensei also had plans to produce his own karate adventure movie for kids and wanted us, his own students, to star in it. This was another reason we were perfecting our reactions — to hone our acting skills. We were all crossing our fingers we'd get to do the movie. I knew well enough to be skeptical of his Hollywood stories but still couldn't help being reeled in whenever Sensei came around telling them, smiling and sure of himself, as he always was. He waltzed back into the dojo every two weeks or so in shiny new shirts, silver sunglasses, sun-bleached hair, teeth practically glowing. He was beautiful. He was awesome. He must be rich by now, we would think (though most of the parents thought otherwise of Sensei's new style and would voice their opinions — once Sensei had left again for L.A). Most recently, Sensei had gotten a bit part as a villain in a Jean-Claude Van Damme movie. He told us he could've had a bigger part, but he looked too much like Jean-Claude himself — and the producers were afraid that would confuse audiences. Sensei also did a stint as a performer in the *Miami Vice* show at the Universal Studios Theme Park, and at a party once he'd run into Don Johnson in the flesh and discovered — as if this was all the proof we needed to have the myth of Hollywood penetrated for us — that he was actually taller than Don.

Sensei had learned quite a few telling things in Hollywood, he warned us: one, that nothing wins admiration, or at least curiosity, better than self-assured indifference. He had found, for instance, that he received more call-backs when he told casting agencies he lived "up north." (I pictured him saying this, handsome and casual and exuding that laid-back mountain-man charisma, while sitting on the edge of some pretty secretary's desk.) Since going to Hollywood, Sensei had also begun to speak about God's Army — and he meant us. Everything he was doing in L.A. he was really doing for us, he said. L.A. was full of ways and people he disliked, but he would keep at it down there, he said, to keep the dojo going. Last month he bought a Camaro Z-28. My father hated Camaros. Called such vehicles white trash low-life ambition.

These were the men in my life.

Lately something was changing with me. I was finding questions now, holes in Sensei's logic and rules. I couldn't see the relevance anymore in maintaining head-hip-knee alignment, or pulling back your fists between every punch. What impact would that make on the rest of my life? I wanted to ask Sensei, but of course I never would — he would've taken it as impertinence. At practice now I often felt annoyed and unmotivated and awkward. My breasts got sore whenever I was pushed against or punched; I worried incessantly about bloodstains if I was on my period. It was unfair, I thought, that boys never had to think about these things, and Heidi didn't either, yet. My sister, meanwhile, was unsympathetic, saying I should just quit if I didn't like the dojo — it was what she had done several months back (though she'd told Sensei she wanted to devote more time to schoolwork, so she had not actually made a complete break).

But it wasn't as simple as that for me. There was another feeling I'd been having. I felt nostalgic for my youth. At the same time I knew this was absurd. I was only fourteen years old.

"Where *is* my sister?" I said suddenly, to no one listening. "I *wish* she would *get* here like before *tomorrow.*" My sister was my ride. She was seventeen. She could be ruthless; sometimes she left me waiting for hours.

"Girls," said our father over the automatic bread-maker that night, "did you remember to water the horses this evening?"

"Yes," I lied, and my sister pretended she hadn't heard him. April sat on the couch reading a book called *The Fountainhead.* "They still had water from yesterday," I said. He looked fixedly at me as if to shake me and I stared back at him, unshaken.

"Or are you two running around after boys all afternoon and neglecting the animals?"

"Beth's the one with a boyfriend, not me," said April, from the couch. She was referring to Donny Silver, my sort-of boyfriend, who hadn't called me once in the past two weeks. This didn't bother me; we'd gone through spells like this before in the six months since I'd met him. And truthfully, I wanted to break up with him. I just couldn't find the courage to say so to his face. April enjoyed antagonizing me about that.

"Hardly, April," I said, vehemently.

My father seemed not to be listening to us as he pulled the fresh loaf out of the bread-maker. He usually didn't listen if it sounded like we were arguing. The loaf steamed, whole and rubbery-looking. There used to be a time — it seemed long ago — my father baked bread for us in the real oven, back before it had broken. He still hadn't fixed it, and we used the toaster oven for everything lately. The point being, all those things he had once led us to believe we should resist, all those dubious, unnecessary modern appliances — now it seemed we owned just as many as everyone else did. I blamed the 1984 Olympics. Because that was when my father had decided being televisionless was no longer bearable, what with the Russians boycotting and Mary Lou Retton and oh, to see the strength of the swimmers. He had climbed onto the roof and begun to erect an antenna. It had to be a tall one for us to get any reception in the depths of the ravine where our house sat.

"Fresh whole wheat bread!" he announced. With his bare hands he pushed the hot loaf across the counter, muttering, "Ow! ow!" and wringing his hands. In my head I vowed not to eat a bite of it, because I was still irked at him for his comment about neglecting the animals to run around after boys. He stood the loaf on its end on the cutting board, placed his hands on his hips. "Now I let it cool," he said to no one directly. "And before I go to bed, I place a damp rag over it to keep in the moisture. Your mother never did this. She never used fresh bread when she made your sandwiches, did she?"

"My God, Dad," April groaned from the couch, "it's an *automatic* bread-maker."

"It looks good, Dad." Try as I might, I could never hold out for long against my father. I knew he was more sensitive than he acted. And in a funny way I couldn't stand to see anyone put down, even if they deserved it.

"It *is* good. Good homemade bread." Dad raised his eyebrows at the loaf. "And," he added, "it saves money."

April and I fought the next morning over her red skirt. I had asked to borrow it, but she wouldn't give me an answer and it was already six forty-five. As I said before, she can be ruthless. I put on the skirt anyway. She told me to take it off, but I wouldn't.

She narrowed her eyes at me. "I was *going* to let you wear it, but now? No." She smiled. "*No*, Beth. Now take it off."

If I backed down I thought I might literally explode, pieces of me, Beth, all over the place. So instead I told her, "You are such a jealous bitch, April. You don't want me to wear this because you know it looks better on me than it does on you. You know it looks funny on you, it makes you look bowlegged and short. No wonder Gunner Harasek doesn't like you." Cheap shots, admittedly. But I knew how to utilize her weak points. I turned around and headed downstairs.

She was crying in the upstairs room; I could hear her from the kitchen. But she could go from crying to evil, wicked, in a half second; that was how she was. I ate my oatmeal slowly. Kept my blood pressure normal, did things exactly as I would've if I were happy. We were alone in the house; my father left early for work every morning. Finally April came down the stairs, not looking at me, and walked out the door. I let her, though every muscle in my body was positively jumping, I was so mad.

All of this was nothing new between us.

The neighbor drove me to school. I was late. So was the girl whose locker was next to mine. She was the only Muslim person in our school, the only Muslim person I had ever met. She always wore a shawl over her head and long dresses or long pants, even when it was hot. I'd seen her hair, though, in the locker room. It was amazingly thick and full, and dark, dark brown. She was not pretty. But she was nice and I went out of my way to be nice back to her, because most other people wouldn't. Today she opened her locker timidly. Somebody had vandalized it. "Go Home!" it said in red spray paint, and "Sadaam-fucker!" and "I like to suck camel dick." It also said: "I drink Yuban." She gave me a sheepish, mystified look. I didn't get the Yuban part.

"They don't understand," she said. Her English was perfect. "My family," she said, and she almost laughed, "is from Pakistan."

"Well, you can use my locker if you want," I offered, swinging wide my locker door. But suddenly I was embarrassed because my locker was crammed full already. I became aware of my sister's red skirt on me like a scalding blush, a flaming stain, the evidence of petty conflict.

She smiled. "That's okay. But thank you, Beth, that's kind of you."

I could've sworn she was looking at my skirt.

At tutorial break I sat by the window in the French classroom and scanned the quad outside, everyone gathered in crooked or lopsided circles, their breath showing in puffs of gray in front of their mouths. April and her best friend, Tommy, were sitting on the benches in front of the drama room at one edge of the quad. Tommy who was so cool she didn't need to spell her name with

172

an "i." April was all in black, as usual. A black Morrissey T-shirt and her long black crinkly skirt under a far-too-big sweater that was tattered at the cuffs and neck. Her eyes peered out like a raccoon's from behind the curtain of her straight black hair. She was pretty in an exotic and trashed-looking way, with thin lips that she painted burgundy, and she was always doing this thing with her body, folding her arms and leaning all her weight on one hip, or balling her knees up against her chest if she was sitting down. It made her look smaller than she already was. I didn't think it made her look good, and that sort of unwelcoming shell couldn't help matters with boys any, either. But boys were ambling over to them now. They wore striped shirts and old army fatigue coats and clunky boots. They were occasionally shoving each other, tilting their heads, laughing, swaying on their feet — they never stood still. The boy April liked was a year younger than she was; she had been giving him rides home after school lately. He had curly dark blondish hair and wore glasses, and his boots were all beat up. Gunner Harasek. Jason Gunther Harasek, actually, but his friends had always called him Gunner; only teachers sometimes called him Jason. April and Gunner were just friends, and April would often say this was enough for her, that she was happy with just his friendship, but sometimes she got insecure about it. She wished for signs that he liked her more, but I knew she never said anything about it to him or gave these signs herself. The two of them stood over a rusty trash barrel at the edge of the quad, poking at its contents with sticks while they talked.

When I got outside, Gunner was trying to look over April's shoulder at something in the barrel. In his way of slightly slouching there was a wary ease with the way things in the world didn't always make sense: I got this. I didn't know if April did. She was in love with him, she said, because she thought he was "beautiful," and she didn't mean physically. He was actually a little awkward physically. But he was talented at art and music and read deep books and was smart to talk to — was what she said often — though I saw another side to Gunner. He was also desperately, clumsily *kind*, I thought.

He said, "Your hair's in the way," and April tucked her loose black hair behind her ear. When they looked up they were looking up together, it occurred to me.

"Hey," I said.

"Hey, Beth," said April, with the subtlest hint of a question in her tone. I gave her a cautiously sorry smile.

Gunner didn't notice anything. "What is *up*, Beth!" He grabbed for my hand, shook it, grinning. "Hey, look," he announced, pointing at an old cereal box in the trash. "'Eat right, sacrifice nothing.'" As if this was something to be taken seriously, but we knew better. Gunner had a way of saying it, though — you felt as if he was trusting you with something personal, something fragile and allusive.

"Well, I vote for abstinence myself," said April. She folded her arms in that shrinking but challenging way of hers. "Abstinence from all things impure or crude or cowardly."

My sister wanted only the rawest, purest, most honest of all possible action or thought. Even if what you had at the bottom of your consciousness was ugly and criminal — that was what she was after. She had bought into the theory that most human motivation was basically barbaric; she believed everything came down to violence or sex, yet at the same time she wished people would "rise above" all that. She was a walking contradiction, my sister. (I liked to point this out to her.) She wanted connection but was afraid of physical contact. She'd been getting into astral projection lately but as yet had not accomplished "leaving."

"I'm talking about celibacy," said April, "but figuratively."

"What I figure, April, is that *you* need to discover *sex*," interjected Tommy. She was standing up on the bench. Her hips shifted purposefully beneath her hands. She wore tight orange stretch pants and expensive-looking knee-high riding boots and a loose, loudly patterned blouse.

"That's because you're a whore, Tommy," retorted April, matter-of-factly; and Tommy shrugged. She was coy.

"If you've got it, flaunt it," she said.

And, "Ooo," went the boys, laughing, ducking their heads, glancing expectantly from girl to girl.

Tommy stuck up her middle finger. My sister shrugged, smirked.

Gunner crossed his arms, looked at April seriously. "What you're talking about is all abstract and impossible again. You're talking about the way things should be on some level that has nothing to do with, like, how ordinary life really is. It has nothing to do with me having to, like, recall the numbers of my fucking locker combination and open it up and take my books out and walk to my next stupid class twelve times a day. You're pissing me off again, April." But he said this good-naturedly, and it seemed more like honest, unserious distress — like over a math problem you couldn't solve. "Like, what do you really mean?" he said, shifting his weight back so he was standing taller. "You can't expect people to be flawless, April. And who're you anyways to say what is better for people or not? That's the kind of stuff you say you hate that your father does."

Our father. Let me interrupt here.

Was it apt that the character Sensei had in mind for my sister to play in his movie was the mysterious "Oriental" girl who didn't talk to the other kids in the group, only appeared and disappeared without explanation at certain key points in the plot and wowed the others with her out-of-left-field fighting techniques? In a way this was what April was really like. She had made kids cry. I don't mean just with karate. The baby-sitting job she once had — the parents fired her after they heard her telling the kids the Bible was propaganda, and how evil not good was what was inherent in human nature. April would claim these things she said, it was all in the name of honesty.

I thought it was more in the name of our father.

We used to watch the news on TV, and afterward he would sermonize. The rapes, the kidnappings, the killings, the fantastic crashes! One could not take a step that was not overshadowed even if only thinly by potential harm. And violence and accidents were not random — these were mishaps you could be responsible for having called upon yourself, whether through blatant carelessness or just a slight lapse of concentration. Our father prided himself on having never in his life been in a car accident. If I lost my watch, he would insist I'd done it on purpose. Our mother's illness, too. His irritable unease with it at the time had led us also, at the back of our minds, to blame her — this was what I thought now — to believe *she* had gone wrong somewhere, left a window open or something, and this was why it had happened, her sickness; or maybe it was her diet of too much white rice starch. He had said this once, for he always had to arrive at hypotheses. He was a scientist by nature. What we didn't know then was that it was normal (I read in a book a few months after her death) to resent loved ones for dying, even before they'd died. Our father simply hadn't known what to do with our mother's weakness. He hadn't known what to do in the face of helplessness. It made me think of the dogs he had had put to sleep, the ones other families would've probably let lie on the front porch till they'd made that final passage on their own sweet time. Control freaks were control freaks because they couldn't understand or accept the natural messed-up cycles of things. And this seemed to happen to parents, I'd noticed.

I understood it, though, the messed-up cycles of things. I was willing to be and let be.

But when you are eight or eleven and listening to your father's rants, the world can be made to seem a gigantic, out-of-control, debauched place. Dad talked on and on even as April cried, as if this had been what he needed to see in order to feel assured we were absorbing the caution he wished so to drum into us. I had listened but would be thinking about petting the dog. Our big brother, Thien, had kept quiet, also. Then finally our mother would exclaim, "Daddy, you're scaring the girls!" She had always called him Daddy. *That* in a way was scarier to me. It meant she could not save us, either.

Now of course April would say she feared nothing. Not love, not death, not misery. If you didn't care, you didn't get hurt; if you didn't aim to please, you didn't disappoint. Yet she still hadn't told Sensei she wanted out of karate and his movie plans for good. Or that she thought him a brainwasher of children. Let alone what she hadn't told our father.

"Well, I never said I was excluding myself," she said.

"I guess not. So what's your point?" answered Gunner.

"At least I'm not fooling myself with contrivances."

There was a moment of the two fixing glares at each other. "Well, you can't exactly not participate, April. I mean as long as you're living," said Gunner slowly, "you can't just sit in your room and stare at a wall forever exactly."

"Well, maybe I can, maybe I can," argued April feistily. (And sometimes I thought — no, I *knew* — she looked foolish; and I wondered why everyone else didn't see it, too, it seemed so plain to me she was lying to herself.) "I just don't believe in relenting to a system of beliefs I don't agree with," she said. "I just don't want to ever relent."

Over my sister's shoulder, Tommy shook her head, sighing.

"Oh yeah?" Gunner's mouth shifted, almost imperceptibly. "Well, I'd like to relent from this conversation, please."

"Fuck you, Gunner," said April, flippantly. But she was hurt and I could see it.

Gunner was laughing but not meaning it.

"Hey, did you check out my new key chain?" he said to me as he pulled his keys out from his belt. The other boys were staring off in other directions across the quad. The bell rang. Circles of people began to drift, distort, break. Gunner's keys made a zipping noise. They were on a retractable ring attached to his belt. "It's part of my janitor fantasy," he said, "because I'm a Socialist, see? I'm a worker, man." He shrugged. "I'm just not comfortable with being comfortable when other people aren't."

April stared at him with an expression of pain on her face, but I knew exactly what he meant even if I didn't know a thing about politics.

"I understand that," I said, nodding, and Gunner peered at me suddenly with earnestness and said, "Do you?"

April turned to me, rolled her eyes, and it was the first time she had addressed me since I'd walked out there. "Dad wants us home for dinner tonight."

This disturbed me — her saying it as much as what she was saying. "But there's never any real food in the house," I exclaimed, more emotionally than I meant to. Dad didn't yet have a handle on things like what to buy at the grocery store. April and I didn't have much of a handle on it, either. We'd been surviving on frozen pizzas in the afternoon in front of *Donahue*, and when Dad came home he heated up his own dinner in the microwave. The rare times he tried to coordinate our having dinner together usually turned out stressfully.

I know the way I'm telling this story so far — it is convoluted. But I was never the logical, not even the sensitive one in our family. I was the impulsive one.

"I know, I know," April agreed. But I had already forgotten about the food.

At karate practice that afternoon, I was feeling more and more detached from the other kids. I performed my Defensive Arts like a rag doll, though this was a good quality for my reactions, at least. Sometimes it could feel quite natural, pretending to get beaten up.

At our first water break, to further the feeling, Toby Sandusky rushed up behind me, put me in a headlock, and hauled me away from the fountain before I could take a drink. He hollered to his brother, "Hey, Johnny, let's pin Beth!" and no matter how I kicked and squirmed and screamed, I couldn't get loose. This was what often happened to April and me at the dojo. Heidi, too; it was the privilege of being a girl there. In a way, it was flattering. The boys cared, I realized. And manhandling us was sometimes all they had to show it with.

But when it was Toby Sandusky who was fat and too rough and held you down forever, it seemed — that I didn't need so much.

I had almost gotten to my knees when Jonathan Sandusky leaped in and tagged me in the temple with a flying side back-knuckle and even though it didn't really hurt, I started to cry. I covered my face with my hands and wailed, and immediately the boys jumped backward because now they knew they had pushed the game too far.

"Oh, my God, Beth, I'm sorry," said Jonathan. He knelt beside me and put his arm around my shoulder. His arm was light and surprised me with its comfort. It also made me nervous; I was used to responding to Jonathan only in a retaliatory way. "Hey, take your hand away from your face. Let me see. C'mon, take your hand away," he said.

I let him lower my hands.

Sensei was there, too, kneeling behind Jonathan. They were all looking at me, all the others, too, as one by one they took their drinks at the water fountain. I spotted Kenny Davis looking sympathetic and Jeremy Todd looking stupid, his eyes lit with that kind of brightness people got on their faces when they were re-calling a near disaster or something else they were proud about having escaped.

Sensei took me aside and sat me down in the weight room, on the bench under the lat bar. *Laterals are muscles,* I was thinking.

"Now, Beth," he said, "I know you've been kicked harder than that before and not even blinked an eye. Is there something else going on that's upsetting you, hon? You can talk to me if you need to, you know." I pressed my hands against my knees and looked down at them. He smelled musky and sweaty close up. I felt embarrassed for noticing. I wished he would move over, though I did not want him to move too far. He nudged my side with his elbow. "Is it boys?" he said with a wink in his voice. "You can tell me about that, you know."

"No."

"Is everything all right at home?" His voice was lower. "I know you girls don't always agree with your father. April's told me."

"No, it's fine." I was about to cry again, but this time I held it in.

"Beth, let me ask you. I am sensing you need direction. Have you spoken to God lately? Because what I'm sensing from you, what I think, is you are in a very crucial space right now. Sweet-heart." He was trying to get me to look at him, but I hated it when adults, especially men, called me "honey" or "sweetheart." My father never did this. He never sat us down for talks of this kind, either. He always just said what he had to say, point blank, and this made me suspicious of Sensei's gentleness. "What have I told you about the fence? Do you remember my rule about fences?"

I remembered, but I wasn't going to say it out loud. *Gray is a shade, not a value. You can't stand in the middle of a fence: it's either one side or the other, buddy. Black or white. Especially if the fence is barbed wire.*

"You know you can talk to me, don't you, Beth?" he said. "I love both you girls a whole lot. I love you like you're my own — all you kids." Then he laid his hand on my shoulder. This and the "love" stuff were another thing my father never did; it made me edgy because I knew there was a way I should respond, but I could not make myself do it. I could not make myself say "I love you" back, or look at him and smile, at least, to let him know he had reached me. I just kept sitting there, tense. "Do you still love me?" he asked then.

I stared at my toes until he asked again, his tone a little teasing. "C'mon, now. Do you still love me, Beth?"

"Yes," I muttered finally. And wondered if in a circumstance like this we were still supposed to say "sir" as well.

"That's my girl. You're my toughest girl, Beth. If there's ever anything you need to talk about, I want you to know you can come to me, okay?" He slid off the bench and squatted on his heels in front of me. "Let's just have a hug now," he said, and I fell into his arms. I admit. He was big and warm and strong and I would be lying if I said that didn't help, that I didn't want that.

He stood. "You tell that sister of yours, she keeps slacking and not showing up for class like she's been lately, no matter how smart she's getting in school" — he raised his eyebrows conspiratorially — "I just might have to give you her part in my movie." He winked.

What he promised and the conviction with which he promised were two separate things. He could've been offering Cracker Jacks, for all I cared.

At the end of class we stood and faced the flag on the wall and recited the Student Creed, hands clasped behind our backs. *For God and the good of the community. Right makes might.* "And strength and courage to those boys over there in I-ran," Sensei added, and the way he said it sounded like the way some people say *Ah-men*.

Gunner Harasek was standing in the doorway, watching with my sister. He watched with his arms calmly folded across his chest, his shoulder leaning on the doorframe, a smirk lighting his face.

"That was the weirdest thing I ever saw," he said afterward, in the car.

And April wouldn't shut up about it later, Gunner's insight, his *right*ness.

She didn't know it, but sometimes I read her diary. I looked through her letters, her notebooks. I didn't consider it snooping exactly, since she told me most everything anyhow. But in doing this I had learned from her. I had learned how there was a difference in how people tell something to others and how they tell it to themselves. I had learned what to allow, what not to allow, into my own mind: I had learned the cost of *thinking* too much.

What she did tell, when I asked why she liked Gunner, was about that book he'd lent her. "It's like six hundred pages long and really deep. I don't know if you'd get it, Beth." She didn't consider me as book-smart as herself.

What she didn't say was that the book itself was as much gesture as it was message. It was what she hoped with all her heart existed between them: a world of singular yet shareable ideas. She was a total romantic. But she was also a huge skeptic. She couldn't leave anything unworried about. She wondered, was there someone else he'd considered lending this book to? Was there a difference, his lending her this book and not another? Did it mean something, his lending her this book so soon after he'd read it himself? *Did it mean something?* This was the question that followed each item she wrote about him, and she had written down everything — I could've told you every outfit he wore for the last 126 days of school, at least. *I feel like I am always reaching, I will always be reaching,* she wrote.

The book, she told me, was about architecture. Men building things.

Thrilling.

Our father, have I mentioned, was an architect for the government, and built our family's house? The house had poor water pressure, thin walls, no heat, and no windows on the entire south-facing side. In this way we kept our costs down.

"Beth, do you ever believe in God?" April asked me that night. It was a question she had asked a number of times in our childhood, usually late at night or after we'd seen or heard about something scary.

We were lying in the dark, me in blankets on her floor, next to her bed. It was too cold in my room; hers had the better heater. Whenever I slept in her room, I woke in the mornings to the distant yet warm feel of her preening. She'd be listening to The Smiths, sitting small and cross-legged on her stool, applying her black eyeliner, black lipliner, burgundy lipstick. Her mask. Sometimes I liked the smallness of my sister, I *appreciated* it. I wanted the whole world to see it, her true smallness, beneath the obvious blackness. Our mother had been small, too, like a doll. Like a tiny, round-cheeked porcelain doll. Girls at school used to tell me, "Your mother is cute." It was only partially a compliment, though. I knew they were also saying something else — something patronizing — about our Asianness, about her harmless, little, peculiar hands and face and feet. Those mornings I woke slowly, savoring something I wasn't sure we'd ever had or had even now — but maybe soon. Maybe I would find it.

"I believe in trees," I answered. There was no reason behind this. Not even a thought.

I could see her trembling; the heat had risen, leaving us cold below. One floor down, in the master bedroom, slept our father, and it was probably even colder in that room. "On windy days you should watch where you walk," said April. Occasionally our fears were the same, my sister's and mine.

Donny Silver called the next afternoon, just after school. The first half of our first conversation in more than two weeks he spent telling me about the Metallica concert he'd gone to the night before. Donny had been kicked out of his parents' house last summer. He'd been living from friend's house to friend's house — some of them were older and had their own apartments — and could go anywhere he pleased even on weeknights. He had since dropped out of Independence, which wasn't even regular high school.

"So, Beth, what've you been up to?" he asked after he was done talking about the concert. He talked painfully slow.

"Not much."

"So, you wanna hang out or something today?"

"I don't know. If you want to," I said.

There was a pause at the other end of the line. Then, in an almost injured tone, "Don't say that."

"Well, was there something specific you had in mind?"

"Well, was there something specific *you* had in mind?"

"No." I hated it when he did this.

"Are you mad at me or something?"

"No." But I said it in a deliberately concealing way. I wanted him to notice my indifference and get uncomfortable. I wanted him to ask questions, to have to coax it out of me. Though of course I would never admit this was what I wanted.

Instead he said, "You know something, Beth, I had a chance to get laid last night. Laid, get it? But usually when I have a girlfriend, I'm faithful." This surprised me for two reasons: one, that any boy was actually referring to me as his girlfriend; and two, that Donny Silver of all people cared about fidelity. His voice was full of spite.

"Well, I wouldn't have minded," I said. Slowly, so it was clear. And as I said it I realized it was true — and it felt liberating, like a weight lifted from me and placed upon him.

"Are you high?" said Donny, incredulously.

"Of course not. Maybe I just have the ability to be detached about a thing like sex." But this, as I said it, did not feel true.

"What's *that* supposed to mean?" said Donny. "Look, Beth, it's simple. If I'm gonna have sex and I have a girlfriend, I think I'd like my girlfriend to be the girl I have sex with." His voice became petulant. "I mean, that is probably *why* that girl — who I'd like someday to have sex with — *is* my girlfriend and not another one, don't you think? That's part of what having a girlfriend is for, you know. Part, I said, not all."

"I have to go now," I said, and I hung up the phone, feeling a strange flash of adrenaline shoot through my body just as I did this.

"Was that Donny?" April was lying stretched out on the couch, listening.

"Yes. I don't care, though," I said. "I don't care about anything."

"You're just scared."

"No, I'm not."

She stared at the ceiling. "Well, you should be," she said, and I thought there must be ice in her mouth. Or marbles. The way she said it.

I looked at her.

My sister, who had never had sex before, either, would claim she didn't "need" it. It was just one more of those things that caused people to act dishonestly and foolishly, in her opinion. And, she would say, it was motivated by the barbaric side of our nature, again, much like those impulses that bring about killing and war. But the world was what it was: there were wars.

Gunner, on the other hand, didn't even notice girls "in that way," according to April. This was another reason she liked him. She believed he had only higher concerns, that he was an "innocent." He didn't need romantic relationships, either. They were of another genus, those two. Her love for him, she claimed often, had nothing to do with sex or looks or his reciprocity, even. That she had felt what she had felt — that was proof enough. She had told me this countless times and had told me never to repeat it to anyone.

I had told it to Donny, though, in December, several weeks earlier. His response was "No way, Beth. No guy is 'above' sex. If it seems like he's not looking, he's just hiding it, like, really, good. Your sister must be blind." Donny had been serious and heated and adamant about this point, as if it was a right of his being infringed upon. I'd thought his attitude was amusing, but I also thought maybe he wasn't wrong. To be honest, I had felt Gunner's eyes on me before — evasive, curious, almost vulnerable. Once, sitting with my sister and her friends in the grass on the quad, I had felt him staring at my hair. I had been sure of it. But I never looked up. I never said anything.

To get back at me for telling Donny her theory on Gunner (Donny had had to remark about it to her afterward), my sister had informed Donny that I was a virgin. We were in April's car, eating our McDonald's; I was right there in the backseat. It was Christmas Day. "She told me to tell you she's not, but she is," April had said.

Donny had looked at me, crushed. He had taken my hand. "But why would you try to lie to me, Beth?" he said, his eyes dark and emotional.

And that's when I decided: *I will show her.* If a war broke out in the Persian Gulf (because that was the topic in the news every day), then I would have sex with Donny Silver. In this way I would connect my fate to the fate of current events. It would be out of my hands and my conscience. It wouldn't be a question of love or persuasion or lust — it would be based rather on the decision of the president. A large and distant man.

The phone was ringing again. I knew it was Donny, calling back to prompt our, as usual, diffident amends.

April sat up on the couch and looked at me as I reached for the receiver. "Donny's just too much of a wastoid for you, Beth," she said, in a loud whisper. "When're you gonna put him out of his misery?"

Zane Harris opened the door for us, a shiny black guitar dangling from his neck like a medal. Zane was blond and blue-eyed and good-looking with the kind of lean, graceful body that had just the right amount of muscle, and the way he moved in it, as if he took it all for granted, made you think life must be easy for him. He was one of those boys who glowed.

We were at Gunner's house to watch the boys' band practice. There were three boys in Gunner's bedroom, a giant mirrored closet, a drum set, guitars, coils of black cable all over the carpet. A cat was perched atop one of the boy's amps, purring.

"She's into the vibrations," said Zane, meaning the cat.

"Sweet girl," said April. The boys watched as she walked over and started petting the cat, who didn't react. This seemed awkward, but nobody said anything.

Gunner sat at the edge of the bed with his feet askew and a thick purple bass guitar across his lap. His mouth hung a little open, something our father said was an affliction teenagehood brought upon boys. It went along with the one about where they kept their brains. The third boy, Tom Hocks, was sitting behind the drums, also with his mouth a little open. He had slow eyes and straggly brown hair and looked as if he had just crawled out of bed.

April introduced Donny to the other boys. Donny was now "catching a ride" with us, as he called it. This was how we spent what time we spent together.

Donny stood awkwardly against the wall just inside the door, his arms crossed and his head tilted. His eyes were half closed. I knew him well enough to know he was trying to look tough.

"It's a pleasure," he said, in a sardonic, drawn-out tone. He wore combat boots and a black T-shirt with the sides slit open, and his wavy brown hair was half shaved but long on top. He had a scar that ran down the side of his nose. When he was ten, he swung too high on the swings, jumped off, and landed on his face. His face had been so bloody, his mother hadn't recognized him when she drove up and found him lying on the driveway.

"Have a seat on that chair," invited Gunner, pointing to a chair in the corner. My sister had sat next to him on the bed.

The boys went back to playing their music and we watched. All the boys around here wanted to be rock stars or they were

juvenile delinquents like Donny Silver or both. I didn't judge
Donny for not wanting to stay in school, but I did think sometimes he made his problems bigger than they needed to be. I
would admit, his problems were part of why I began hanging out
with him in the first place — I'd thought I could *do* something to
help him. But I didn't think that anymore.

The boys were playing their instruments with steady expert
expressions and staring into one another's eyes in a way that ex-
cluded everything else in the world, in a way they could not have
done if they hadn't each been holding instruments as safe barriers between their bodies. But the *potential* this showed — you
couldn't help wishing they'd find a reason to look at you that
way, too, regardless of where their mouths or brains occasionally
fell to.

Zane faced Gunner, and they were watching each other's guitars.

"Change now," said Zane, "and change *now*. Right." They were
reading fingers, I realized.

"Aces." Gunner grinned a tiny, satisfied grin. There was something in the stillness of his eyes, the sureness of his lips, curled
only at the corners, all in that second frozen and wise and alive
on his face. The room was filling with envy and some kind of
electricity.

But Donny was bored — he made this plain in the look he
gave me — and said he was going to go walk around outside. I
knew he hated U2, and the boys were playing a U2 song. It occurred to me I should follow Donny out, but I happened to like
this song.

Donny Silver would tell you his father walked out years ago,
over a song. Donny was seven; his mother had a record player
and would play certain songs over and over. One time his parents were fighting and his father declared, "If you put that song
on one more time, I'm out that door," and just to spite him,
Donny's mother had put it on again. That was how Donny remembered it. Though I suspected it might've been a little more
complicated than that.

There was a magnetic hum in the air when the boys stopped playing.

"Let's play it again," said Zane.

In the kitchen, Mrs. Harasek was sitting by herself at the counter, watching the news on the TV set that was on the kitchen counter. The kitchen looked out on to the living room, and all the furniture in the living room was brown and cozy. A fire blazed in the fireplace. The noise of the boys, from out here, was dull and muffled and distant. Steam rose from a pot on the stove.

"Hi," I said, "I'm Beth."

She smiled at me. "You must be April's sister. What're you looking for, honey? The boy in the black shirt? He just went out that door." She nodded across the room. She was a slightly plump woman with short brown hair. Her son looked nothing like her.

I asked for a glass of water and she told me to help myself. As I stood over the faucet, her attention returned to the TV.

"Those poor people. Those poor innocent people. Those Iraqis — they are just an immoral race," she said softly, shaking her head at the screen. "That Muslim religion, can you imagine? People are killing people over it."

I looked around the kitchen and saw on the side of the refrigerator a photo of a Christmas tree, next to a baby in glasses, completely open-mouthed, in a frame made of painted macaroni. "Is that Gunner?" I nodded toward the photo.

Mrs. Harasek smiled again. "He was the sweetest baby." She turned slightly on her stool, looking closely at me for the first time. "Where're you girls from? I mean, your heritage. You have such an interesting color, and features, both of you."

"Our father is Danish," I said. "He grew up in World War II. In Denmark. He says growing up in a war makes you grow up faster." I felt I had to say something substantial about current events. I leaned on the sink. "Which is part of the problem with the youth in America right now, he says. Our lives have been too easy, we don't know how to take anything seriously. We're sheltered." I twisted the cup in my hands.

"Does your father support going to war?"

"No. He thinks George Bush is a baboon."

"Is that what your father thinks?" She was starting to smile.

His actual word had been "buffoon," I remembered, but I didn't correct it. I didn't know what a buffoon was, actually. Instead I said, "We wouldn't be over there except for the oil. It's a war for profit and power." I realized I was wanting her to think me remarkably smart for a fourteen-year-old when she responded as I'd been half expecting she would: "Well, I'm glad to see my son has found some impressive young ladies to associate himself with." With a tiny, warm, distracted smile.

It was like a switch had flipped inside of me — suddenly I wanted to win Gunner's mother's favor. In my mind I saw my sister sitting on Gunner's bed, contented and smug among the boys, her book on her knees. Next year, I knew, after my sister went off to college, it would be just me, my father, and the automatically made bread. A few ornery cats, the disappointingly fat dog, the ache of silence. One woman less in the house, once more. It seemed to me people were always defecting to one side or another, and I was the only one staying put, right in the middle. I didn't blame her, though, my sister. I didn't blame anyone.

"My father had a hard life in the old country," I said, "that's why he came here."

"But your mother isn't Danish also?"

"No," I replied. She was waiting, so I added, "I'm mixed."

She asked what with and I told her. About that other war. 1973? 1975. The first one he rescued us from. I didn't mention anything else about my mother; usually people already knew. Maybe a year from now it would be easier to drop into conversation with new people, *she died when I was . . .* , when it would've been long enough ago for them not to react too dramatically, I thought.

"My father says what we need in this society nowadays is a good war but this one will hardly do. It's a false war."

"Your father is a man of many opinions, isn't he?" Now she was looking at me in a peculiar, gentle way. She smiled vaguely. "What an interesting family background you girls have." She set her forearms on the countertop. We watched the news for another minute together, not saying anything else. At the commercial break she turned toward me. "Will you tell me something honestly, Beth. You seem like a smart girl," she said, as an ad for toothpaste (people with sparkling teeth) danced on the other side of her like a backdrop to her face, which was so earnest now I was almost embarrassed for her. "Do you believe they can actually go anywhere with it?" She nodded down the hall, in the direction of the bedroom. Where the muffled thudding of the boys' dreaming was trying to force its rhythm through the walls. "Do you think they're good enough?"

"I guess they're good. April thinks Gunner is really talented," I said, trying to be reassuring; and I hated that I, the child here, was the one doing the reassuring.

She sat back, her face worried. "I'd just hate to find out later that those boys were spending all this time for nothing."

"Was my mom trying to talk to you?" Gunner asked, when I returned to the room. Practice was done. The clutter of instruments was now just ordinary mess; chaos, in fact. Scattered toys.

"She was talking about the war," I replied.

"Waar!" boys bellowed in each other's faces as they passed in the halls.

This morning was the morning of the headlines. U.S. AT WAR and WAR, SAYS BUSH and ("the best one," as my sister had put it) WAR!! were a few of them.

A tiny ray of sun cast long, thin shadows over the dewy lawns as I walked through the halls, shivering and half awake, dazed with the idea that now I was walking about in a world at war. But I was even more dazed by the lack of change war had brought about. I passed Gunner and his friends, stomping on each other's shadows in front of Madame "La" Jefferson's first-period French. They were doubling over in mock pain and clutching the parts of their bodies the shadow-parts of which were being stomped on, and they were laughing about it — because somehow it *was* funny, it had to be, to pretend pain could be transferred like this from your shadow to your body. This was the type of activity I passed the boys engaging in quite often. To ward off the cold. To fortify themselves with enough amusement for the day ahead. And I realized, as I sat through the rest of the day's classes, that it would always be as it was yesterday, war or not, at least for us, at least in America. The traffic lights would never stop, and if they did they would never be irreparable, and lunch would always come after fourth-period algebra for some fourteen-year-old girl, and I was beginning to feel ill. I wished for explosions, fantastic crashes, vanishings — anything to mark it. I wanted to see the news here, now; I was tired of distant feeds, third-hand information.

But the only thing out of the ordinary that happened was: before sixth-period English Dusty Thomas, the football player, pulled his jacket up over his head and zipped his face inside it. Then class started. He tried to unzip himself, but the zipper was stuck. Everyone saw and laughed. Even the teacher, old Mrs. Fremont. Even me. "I hope you've accomplished what you needed to in there, Mr. Thomas, because it's time for our spelling test now," said Mrs. Fremont. They were guilty as well, the adults — they, too, perpetuated this rhythm of nothing stopping for anything else.

"This 'state of war' is just a technicality, you know," my sister had said the previous afternoon, when the news first reached us (Mrs. Harasek knocking on Gunner's door, poking in her head, and saying, "Gunner, you and your friends might like to come see this"). "We still have to go to school tomorrow morning."

And gravely, shaking his head, Zane Harris had said, "I wish people would stop talking about the war, because it fucking bores me." He was radiant and sulky and devious all at once, his elbows hooked on his guitar, black guitar shining, ankles crossed in the center of the room. I couldn't help but stare.

"That's because you're a moron, Zane," said Gunner.

"Fuck you, Harasek!" Zane yelled. Then stomped over and, bending down, grabbed Gunner by the sleeves and shook him. "I'm always at war, man. I am always at war. My soul is in turmoil."

Gunner fell back on his bed, laughing, beside my sister, who was reading her book again.

From the corner, Tom said, entirely sincerely, "There is no war." (He hadn't gone to the kitchen with the rest of us and heard the news. And there was no TV in the bedroom, where he'd stayed to look out the window, to twiddle with his drums.)

Zane continued to yell. "Shut up about the fucking war! I don't wanna hear another fucking word about the fucked-up fucking war!" Then he straightened, began to shrug, madly, out of his guitar strap. Threw down the instrument.

Boys are stupid.

Our violence is aimless.

Tommy's mother was away, so I spent the night with April there. Donny also came. The rich, sprawling, suburban-style house at the end of Thomasina Jones's long, beautiful, landscaped driveway. We were ten days into the war. Tommy's mother was cool; Tommy showed us all her old Carole King records. Her mother's current boyfriend was a lawyer, younger than she. He flirted with Tommy, too, Tommy told us as she stood in the kitchen, pouring tea.

"He's not handsome," said Tommy, "but I can tell he has a big dick."

"Must you always judge a man by what is in his pants," said April derisively.

"Get off your high horse, April," Tommy told her. And slammed the milk carton down in front of her. "Help me," she ordered. April got up and began to pour the milk.

"I don't want milk in mine," I said, covering my cup with my hand.

Donny, seated at the yellow-tiled kitchen table, looked like a tornado blown into Tommy's house and rendered meek, pathetic. "Is this what girls talk about together?" He was rapt. "This is cool."

Tommy was slender and wore clothes that draped and made her shoulders appear attractively frail. She was the only girl in school who dyed her hair something other than black, ritually.

The same color, burnt umber, each time. Because she understood her color wheel. "I'm a winter-complected person," she
had explained. What was umber? I didn't even know.

"You want in Gunner's pants, just face it," said Tommy to
April.

"I don't want in his pants," argued April, "what the fuck is
wrong with you? I want in his *soul*. Is what I want." She glared
into her tea cup.

Donny's eyes roved the ceilings. "Do you mind if I look
around your house?" he asked, and Tommy replied, as if it was a
tired subject: "Knock yourself out."

Donny and I sat in front of the TV in the living room, holding
hands on and off, while my sister and Tommy made phone calls
and then announced they were going out. They went into the
bathroom to get ready and came out a few times in different
outfits, asking for our opinions. Donny got up after a while and
wandered off. After Tommy and April had left, I walked through
the house until I found Donny in Tommy's mother's bedroom,
sprawled on his stomach across the bed.

Tonight, had been my plan, tonight it would happen.

I sat down beside him and Donny asked me to scratch his
back. Then he turned over and I scratched his stomach, too. He
stretched like a cat showing me his stomach. The sight of his
body startled me a little. He had taken off his shirt, and I could
see his ribs under his skin and the flatness of his chest. The overhead lamp was glaring. The only other times I'd seen him shirtless were when we'd been outside swimming (he was always in
motion then) or under much dimmer lights. He closed his eyes.
He was tired, he said, he hadn't had a full night's sleep in a week.
Then he turned over again, placed his face in Tommy's mother's
pillows, and slept like a baby. And that was as close to sex as we
got that night. It was my own fault, I supposed, for not having
informed him of my plan — but I had expected he would just try.
He had done as much at other times. I felt almost rejected. I sat
contemplating a pair of scissors on the nightstand. That, and the
distance between my hands and the back of his neck. It occurred

to me what was possible. The scissors were of a heavy, durable quality, and sharp. I picked them up and held them in my hands as I wandered around the room, looking at Tommy's mother's things. There was a look to adult dressers, adult bathroom countertops, a look that was a little mysterious. The accoutrements of adulthood; the secrets of self-care, you would remember them: a bowl of dried twigs and flower petals, slim tubes of mascara, dainty underpants, even a few crinkly plastic condom packages under the underwear. A plush red velvet cushion on a stool in front of the makeup mirror. Things our own mother never, never displayed. There was a lot to learn, a lot of items to acquire in order to be a "normal" or "total" woman, I thought. Every object in the room exuded an air of feminine guile. In my head I made a list — things a sexually confident woman should own. Fuzzy slippers. Thick, creased paperbacks on the nightstand. A pink vinyl shower cap on the doorknob of the bathroom door. I felt coarse and ugly, uninformed.

I sat on the bed and looked at Donny again. I looked at the texture of his scalp, the unflattering angle of his jaw and neck, his unclean ears, his vulnerability as he slept — this was all knowledge I didn't know what to do with at fourteen, images they didn't sell in popular representations of closeness, of people coming together. I tried to ignore it, but a feeling of revulsion toward Donny had risen in me. It wasn't fair, of course. I looked at myself in the mirror. My face was calm, showing nothing of the questions, the revulsion, the coldness in me. I was still holding the scissors in my other hand as I traced my fingers up and down Donny's back in an attempt to feel love, to mean love. *The way a woman should,* I thought. But it all required acting. Was what I had discovered.

I put the scissors back on the nightstand. I didn't want to grow up.

Late, Tommy and April returned from wherever they had been. They had met some older guys, they said, who invited them back to their motel room where they all watched TV. Who were they?

Who knows, they said. Questions were sometimes the only answers, they said, toying with me.

"Where's your lover boy?" Tommy asked me.

"He's asleep," I replied.

"Well, I hope he took a shower." She tossed her coat across the
kitchen counter, flung herself over a stool, sank her face into her
arms.

April climbed up and sat cross-legged on the counter. She was
moony. "He is so incredible," she said. "He is so beautiful, it just
makes me want to cry." She was talking about Gunner, of course.
"The way he said that. 'It all sounds like Communism to me.' He
is so smart."

"He's a *boy*, April." Tommy was yelling into her own arms. "A
little *boy*."

"You just don't get it."

Tommy raised her head, stuck out her hand, grabbed hold
of April's ankle. "Why're we friends, April? Why? Because we
are the two most different-from-other-people people we know."
Tommy was an actress, a Drama Queen. She was certain to become famous, she said often, because there was nowhere else in
the world someone like her belonged but on a screen, on a stage.
Everyone at school was frightened of her. But as far as she was
concerned she was already *There*. No when, if, or in the future
about it. *There* was where she had always been. "We are both talented and beautiful," she said, "so why are you forever torturing
yourself?"

And somehow April was now crying. She was saying a lot of
things, but all I could understand was "I hate nighttime sometimes. Nighttime makes things so weird sometimes and then
everyone always forgets about it in the morning, even if they
agreed with you at night." Tommy crawled up beside my sister
and they talked for a long while, whispering intricacies back and
forth, deliberating over "your idea" of this and "well, your idea"
of that.

I didn't know what else to do, so I ransacked the freezer and
found ice cream. In the living room I curled up on the couch and

turned on the TV, and at three in the morning the news was on. I waited to see scenes from the war, but there were just talking heads with an occasional switch to some live coverage of a desert compound or a desert aerial-view map where nothing, honestly, was happening. I tried to listen, but the truth was I didn't understand most of what they meant; I couldn't string the facts, the lingo, together.

"Do they never sleep, those camera people?" remarked my sister when she and Tommy at last drifted in, their previous conversation already dismissed, forgotten.

(Yet there *had* been something in the air that afternoon. Me and my sister with a backseat full of boys. Years later and still I feel it. How we drove around town after the news first broke in a feeling of crazy unity, how even stopping to get gas was a sincere group effort. We had to scrape up pennies. We all joined in — we were digging them off the carpet under the seats and out of the lint in our pockets. Then April strode boldly inside to pay while the rest of us lingered outside. I bought a soda and sat on the curb beside Gunner and offered him some, but he said he would not drink from a straw, could not see the point of straws, as if it were a matter of principle, and I laughed. Suddenly I was laughing a lot.

"You better watch it," said Gunner, as he took the cup from my hands and pried off the lid and straw and drank right from the lip of the cup.

And I watched Donny and those other boys next to a black pickup truck across the lot, in their cut-off black tees or muscle shirts, wiry-bodied and shaggy-haired, their hands rubbing their own long, flat stomachs. They were going to war soon, some of them. Donny would come back and tell us this, just then I'd known it. And I'd wanted to say so to Gunner. I'd wanted to capitalize on the moment, my intuition, my secret sureness.

Instead I said, "What do you think of my sister?"

He seemed ready to enter immediately into what I was asking. "April's funny," he said, "I don't think she always means what she says. I mean, I think war is stupid, too, and I think people are stupid, but I don't want to see proof of it necessarily. I don't want the world to blow up." He handed me my soda and pulled his hands up into his sleeves. Something about that gesture — I knew at that moment, absolutely, that there were things about him I was going to learn that my sister never would. It had to do with being willing to wait. She would leave soon, had always been impatient to do so. But I had no such aspirations. And she had projections about Gunner; I did not. "Sometimes I feel like there's something else she wants to say to me, but she won't say it," he said.

She won't say she's crazy about you was what I could've offered, but I did not. I refrained. I was protecting her when I said to him, "A war is what brought her here with my mom. It's like she doesn't even think of that."

"Well, a war brought you here, too," said Gunner. He had a diplomatic way of reprimanding; his tone was hesitant.

"What do you think of Donny?"

"He just seems kind of sad to me," replied Gunner. And I felt then like a coward, because I saw that what I'd been expecting — wanting — to hear was a confirmation of my own doubts about Donny's character, as I had about my sister's. But my cowardice was redeemable — I was told in the next second — as Gunner held his hand out, above mine, with something pinched between his fingertips. I glanced sideways at him, and he was smiling his frozen little smile. I opened my palm, and he handed over whatever it was he'd been fidgeting with inside his sleeves. A tiny ball of lint. And I closed my fingers around it.

The first time Donny Silver ever handed something to me was on the night we met, a summer earlier, at the County Fair. We'd been introduced by Kenny Davis, who knew Donny from grade school, and Kenny had told me Donny Silver was on drugs but a nice guy underneath it all — "he just needs a girlfriend." Why me, I didn't know, but I had liked being trusted and I had trusted Kenny. Through the game booths, between The Gravitron and The Hammer, with neon pink and green lights spinning in the still black sky above us, we walked. Donny was toting his skateboard, sucking the ice cubes out of his soda cup, when a little girl ran in front of us, dropping her fluorescent-orange plastic brace-let in the flat grass at our feet. But wait. I've misremembered — it was not me. Donny stooped down and picked it up and handed it back to *her* without a word.

We sat on a picnic bench on a hill behind the lights and rides. Me with my hands between my knees the first time we kissed, the second, maybe third kiss I'd ever had. Soon I would learn to stop counting, that it was like counting pennies, kisses, they came and went so easily after a while. The summer night air was warm. I had been just looking for proof of compassion. It didn't matter whom toward.)

So at last I told Donny that I had intended to have sex with him because a war had broken out. I told him I didn't feel that way anymore (the idea had lost its significance; the war was already over), but had he tried in the past few weeks, I might've been willing. I knew this was the last intimate conversation we would have, Donny Silver and I. We were sitting on a park bench by the city pool, which was closed for winter. He scooted away from me in disgust. I was looking at his hands, brown and dirty against his dirty black jeans.

He said, "You are one sick tease."

What he was missing, though: it was all theoretical for me. The fact is, I never let or made anything happen. I never stopped thinking about it long enough to actually allow my body to act, and I probably never intended to.

The path was marked by tiny ribbons of torn yellow cotton tied to the lowest branches of bushes, roots, some trees. We followed the yellow. The hill was covered by hard, chunky red dirt. The bushes were dry and crackly-looking. The pine trees were sparse because this area had been logged frequently.

We were in camouflage again. Sensei had bought a whole box of surplus army gear from the thrift store on Main Street. I had borrowed my brother's old Civil Air Patrol jacket. I was partners with Heidi. The other team hid in the trees along the path at various ambush points. Heidi and I traveled back to back. We had already decided that she would take care of head and stomach, I the legs. I would take them out at the knees, if need be.

"It's Kenny!" she shrieked suddenly and crashed into my back.

Kenny Davis had dropped out of a tree and landed behind us. He wore twigs in his hair and looked more like a youthful Greek forest god, I thought, than a camouflaged fighter. "I got you! I got you!" he was exclaiming. We were supposed to determine if someone was out of the game by judging our own skills fairly. We weren't supposed to make actual contact: we pulled our kicks and punches, went through our fake reactions. But if you didn't react in time or block adequately and you knew it, you had to be honest enough to admit you were dead. These were Sensei's rules.

I didn't care, though. I was just waiting to die today. We had been doing training exercises all weekend and I was tired of them.

"Beth, you're not even trying!" said Kenny.

"Yes, I am," I said. "Kill me, kill me."

"Legs, his legs!" Heidi reminded me from the ground where she was doubled over. "I'm still alive, I'm just injured. You can still save me," she mock-groaned.

Kenny scowled. "You can't do that." He came at me with another punch. I did Defensive Art Number 2, the only one I could do spontaneously because the first move it required — the first action — was to step back. Was to go where the strike had wanted you to go in the first place but before it put you there itself. It was an entirely subversive Defensive Art. Because what followed was low kicks. To the groin, the knee — they buckled — then you swept out the leg. It was all about undermining your opponent's tactics.

But it was *my* ground, my ground always, that was the real problem, it felt like it was forever slipping away. I was the one shaking here.

We were into the next exercise now, and I had been finding it increasingly hard to stay alert. I had already been kicked in the gut once during this new exercise but was trying not to show it.

Sensei had us performing long sparring sessions with no gloves, in a dirt clearing with piles of branches prickly with needles and huge, stacked pine trunks, a logging site at the base of a mountainside. Turkey vultures reeled high above us, and our voices resounded crisply in the dusky pink air. Every now and then Sensei would replace one of the fighters who'd been going awhile with a new one, pitting the former against a fresh opponent. To test our endurance, he told us. "It's important to know what we're capable of when it comes down to — *the wire*," said Sensei, melodramatically.

He had kept me in the "bullring" for three rounds. Now he stepped between Kenny and me, took the prop weapon out of Kenny's hands, and unbuckled the leather case on his own belt. I shook the sweat out of my eyes.

He said to Kenny, "That's real American steel in your hands now, son," and grinned at me. "Beth. My tough girl." Sensei stepped aside — taking with him the rubber knife we usually used in practice — and Kenny and I were facing off again. He nodded at us to resume sparring. From the sidelines the others were watching. I think pain sometimes registers like a noise you're not sure you've heard — faint then suddenly so apparent you can't fathom how you had missed it. I had failed to block. When I realized this, then I heard the music in the trees: the chattering birds and swishing needles drawing my attention almost completely away. I saw a preternatural light I'd never seen before flash in Kenny's baby-blue eyes.

On top of a stack of logs the boys were ducking and running and pretending to shoot each other and jumping off. From where I lay, a few yards away at the edge of the clearing, I heard them scrambling up the logs, and the thud of their feet and bodies as they hit the ground, and for a moment I imagined it, gray fallen rubble, broken stone-and-straw villages, blackened walls, streets full of wailing. A sea on fire. A river aflame. The desert awash in mercury-gray fluid. The flat brown flood coming at me was a flood of faces. Bobbing, jagged, brown faces: they were running. The placid, permissive heat — tropical — I had never actually felt, only been told of through TV coverage of places where these unending battles occurred: places of frequent catastrophes. Monsoons, bombs, unnamed deadly winds.

But really — it was only this: the boys had caught a snake. The Sandusky brothers were beating it with sticks. When I sat up, I saw what they were doing. The snake was supple and black and thick like a beautiful piece of steel cable. It thrashed and thrashed with an insane will to live. I felt pity not for its death but for the earnestness of its fight.

The Whalen twins' mother doctored me with a cotton swab and rubbing alcohol and small beige strips of adhesive.

"Hold still, Beth," she told me. Her presence was soft and pleasing. Her fingers were cool. "I'm just making a little butterfly now."

My sister picked me up, and on the drive home she told me that while we were gone this weekend, Dad did something I would not believe. He bought two hundred dollars' worth of groceries — it hadn't been his idea alone, other parents had pitched in, too — then he and a couple of other fathers drove to the dojo to sneak the groceries into Sensei's family's cupboards and shelves and refrigerator. They sent Jacob, the youngest Sandusky, in through the bathroom window. Then he went around to open the front door. He let in our father, the other fathers, the bags of groceries, all, into Sensei's home. *They filled his kitchen with food, Beth.* So that he and his daughters would come home and find their shelves stocked and they would feel grateful, relieved. I listened to this, confused. It had never occurred to me there was a shortage of food in Sensei's home.

"That man," our father had said bitterly afterward, "that man can't even feed his own family."

"And what he really means," said April, "is 'see how well I've done? See?'" She told me how she had refused to help. It was too weird for her. "'Feed *us,*' I told him, 'Feed *us,* why don't you?' Something more than TV dinners, frozen beans, you know? He's no different than Sensei when you really think about it. They are both force-feeding someone else's kids. I was telling Gunner about it. I finished that book he lent me. There's this part about love, it's really beautiful and true, we were talking about it. '*Love is the upward glance,*' it goes —" She looked over at me. Only then did she notice.

"What happened to your eye?" she asked.

Our father asked, too, once we were home. "Hi, hi Beth." He appeared to be in good spirits. He was knocking his pipe out on the deck railing. He frowned at the sight of me. "What happened to your eye, skunk?"

"Forget it, Dad," said April. "She won't even tell me." *Butterfly,* I was thinking, *is a beautiful way of saying "bandaged."*

"She got hit or something," said April.

"I got hurt," I said.

7

THIS IS WHAT HAPPENED UPON MY RETURN

My cousin and I were sitting on a bench facing the Saigon River when she told me that sadness is actually the main current of life. To feel sadness is evidence of the true texture of experience. Sadness, it seemed she was telling me, is also an inherent characteristic of the Vietnamese culture. They have staked their claim to it. They are certain they are among those in the world who have had the most of it — and how can you say they are wrong? They use the word "sentiment" to describe it, though. "We are people very sentiment," or "This is a nation of heavy sentiment, life always hard here," they will say, and having no grammatical structure for the past tense in their language seems to confirm that this must be an ongoing situation. I, meanwhile, was thinking about the negative connotations of the word — in America many of us would define "sentimentality" as a sinister thing, a thing not to be trusted — or, at the least, an embarrassing thing. A weakness of character, an indication of insincerity buried beneath the overt show of emotion. And where does this idea stem from? Does it have to do with the northern Europeans (I want to blame them), the stoicism of those emigrants from colder climates? My father has his theories about hot and cold climates. Why is it, he says, that colder climates for the most part have produced the more socially progressive, more technologically advanced societies of the world? The cold requires people to think more sharply because a lack of proper awareness in the cold might mean death, is his theory, and thus these people have been conditioned to exercise their mental faculties. While in hotter climates barbaric conflicts have prevailed for thousands of years without change, as well as an indulgence in life's baser elements (they came up with the "siesta" after all). It must be that the heat dissolves the brain's capacity for rational thought, he will actually say, or for an understanding of systems. By systems he means things like Time and Government and Mathematics and Science. I don't argue against such views. Arguing is another thing that requires systematic thinking.

I went back to Vietnam for the first time in 1996, expecting as I always do to feel underwhelmed, and instead I felt everything. My body felt awake — abler, thinner. My skin felt at home for the first time anywhere, unfettered, natural. I recognized things I shared, like my relatives' gestures, the shapes of people's faces, their body types, their smiles and tired expressions. I cried freely there, felt — equally — purged and chaotic. I had dreams of myself drawing objects up from underwater, or of standing over an unconscious girl in a dark cave — I had to fight to wake from these dreams. Occasionally I felt a deep sense of retrieval. But I never felt as if I belonged there, no.

There is nothing insincere about true, honest-to-God sufferers. There is nothing sinister in the sharing of one's own sorrows. I, too, am willing to admit I don't always know what I'm talking about and that often I feel defeated, but I've not mastered the tact of Third World candor. You will see it in the way they are so good-natured, able to laugh at their own heartfelt dramatics; they will, in irony, make sweeping gestures with their arms in the middle of a love song that in private they might usually take very seriously. They will admit, charmingly, that in private they usually take this song very seriously. They will dance with true abandon. You must know how to laugh among these people. Or their laughter will seem to you almost annoying, quite mysterious, and perhaps that is why I was to find myself weeping on the sidelines of their dance floor, on my second night there, and my cousin had to take me outside to the bench beside the black water of the river, where I probably more appropriately belonged.

Conversely (to the remarks above about embracing sadness), for I was reading Joseph Campbell on the plane, there is also the rule of mythology that says all extremes — evil and good, birth and death, suffering and wealth — are born of the same primordial matter. And that is why we must also be joyful in life. I am sure. I am not so sure.

PASSENGER

When you are flying west, the sun rises for seven hours: a perpetual morning. There is no such thing as rest.

June 19:
They come at you from all sides here. Humans, dogs, cyclos, bicycles, motorcycles, produce trucks, squawking chicken-trucks. All these wheels. Bent old ladies carrying baskets of rice on bamboo sticks across their shoulders. Pretty girls herding piglets. To cross the traffic these people must engender absolute trust in the mad drivers; arms close to their sides, they inch forward, keeping their gazes fixed and blank on the oncoming traffic — and the traffic swerves easily, indifferently, round them. The noise of all the scooter engines is like a sick cat purring, punctuated by growls and grunts and choke-ups, an inconsistent but continuous grinding. Men squat barefoot in dim doorways, arms resting on knees to smoke cigarettes. Women glare out from metal-latticed windows. Half-naked children run up and down the sidewalks.

I was born here. I have never quite grasped this.

I show the address to the taxi driver and he takes me to Aunt Long's house. The widow of Mom's older brother, who died in the war. Her house has two rooms with a single faucet in the side alley outside, on a narrow rutted street where all the houses are low and small and built very close together. Father, I am loath to tell you this because I suspect you will interpret it as their failure to develop intelligence, or something. They store water in large plastic tubs and hang their clothes to dry on a line at the back of the alley; there are two cots in the second room, where everyone sleeps together, a few of them on the floor. The bathroom has no plumbing and no roof; it is open to the sky.

I am stared at and told over and over how much I look like Mom. Each one has to hug me, and do you know how many cousins that is? I was surprised you suggested I come here, to be honest, and I'm still confused as to what you expect I'll discover here. Maybe you thought I needed the culture shock? It's 1996. I'm twenty-three years old, twenty-one years past the last time some of these people leaned down and spoke to me in a language I can't remember I ever knew. It just doesn't seem like you to say these connections still matter.

Sorry. I will try to start again more gently.

I sat on the wooden bench just inside their door for a while after I first arrived, and they asked at least ten times if I was hungry. I said no, thank you, again and again. Then there was confusion over the water. I was afraid of getting sick, so I took the glass but didn't drink from it, and they kept asking about it and finally gave me a Pepsi instead. Though I didn't mean for them to do that, either.

Ha, the one cousin who speaks English (her daughter speaks a little, too), knelt on the floor in front of me. She had a very happy, affectionate expression on her face, and said, "It is very good to see you, you do not know." And put her hand on my leg.

You do not know. Well, I guess I don't. But I have to take a break now because they're telling me it's time for bed.

June 20:
Morning. They wake early (six A.M.) and it's hot by eight-thirty. They dress in shorts or loose, thin pants and sleeveless tops, like the outfits Mom used to sew that I always said looked like pajamas. All the women wear them here. It's too hot to wear much else. It's too hot to even bare your skin, and tans are unfashionable. Women here want rather to look delicate and fair.

Seven cousins (all much older than I am) live in this house with their mother. Three have kids of their own. Ha's daughter, Thi, is the closest to my age. She's eighteen, and beautiful.

Round, high cheekbones. Elegant and childlike both. She and the boys — who are all ten or twelve years old — are taking English language classes at school. English is the language to learn here now.

I know it's rude, but I can't remember everybody's names.

I want to finish telling you what happened yesterday. I was sitting with the cousins when they heard Aunt Long's footsteps on the stoop outside and they all jumped up, exclaiming. I heard my name — my other one. *Thuy.* The way I can't pronounce it myself, a noise rising up from the bottoms of their throats (though I tried to tell them I'm more an April now than a Thuy). It is what they at least have never forgotten or questioned about me, though, I realized — so I didn't insist. Aunt Long stepped down into the house. She has gray hair and looks a lot older than Mom ever did. She saw me and grabbed my hands tightly and her face crumpled and she started to cry. She said a bunch of words I couldn't understand. I didn't know what to do but stand there.

"She say it very long time since she see you," said Ha. "When she see you before, you only very little baby." My aunt spoke and patted my face. "She say you very pretty," said Ha, "like your mom. We all love your mom so much. When she here, she give advice to all the girls and we listen. She say, be strong, you be smart, no let man think he so important. She like big sister to me."

The boys were crouched against the far wall with their knees in their armpits, poking at the concrete floor with their fingers and glancing up at me only every now and then. The women kept speaking on top of one another, nodding and nodding at me. I didn't know where to look. They asked a lot of questions: "How old you are now? Do you like the Vietnamese food? Do you still love the tomato?" This one they laughed about a lot. "You love to eat the tomato when you little baby," Ha explained, "and then you want to hold her hand" — she pointed to one of the cousins — "but she no want to hold your hand no more because they are sticky!"

Another asked, "Why your father no here too?"

I answered, "He thought I should go alone." (Which is better than the other answer I give about you sometimes, which is "He's a hermit. He won't go anywhere.")

Ha studied me for a long moment. Her face softened and she smiled and patted my leg as if to comfort me, which irritated me slightly, since I didn't think I needed it. "When you here now, I take care of you," she said, "like when you a baby here, I always protect you."

"I can take care of myself," I said. I tried to explain this further, and again Ha said that she would protect me.

Then another cousin asked, "You have boyfriend?" When I said no, they looked at each other and giggled. Ha spoke in an eager tone to Aunt Long and they laughed more.

I wanted to know what they were saying.

"We are just make funny." Ha patted my leg again. "Joke. Okay?" Even the boys looked up and covered their mouths. I didn't say anything, but Ha must've noticed my face. "Why you look so sad?"

"I'm not *sad*," I said.

There was something almost critical in her gaze, or was it hurt? Her large, bright eyes turn down at the corners even when she smiles. She wears her black hair in a loose bun. "It so long since I speak English. I am sorry," she said. "More than fifteen year since I speak English." She tilted her head away for a second, searching. "Why your mom no teach you your language?"

And that's the only question they've asked so far about Mom. And you know the answer to that.

"Well, my father's American" is what I said.

I asked if they knew who my birth father was. They showed me pictures of another man, in military uniform, the one who died shortly after I was born, but who I know for a fact was not my father, because Mom said my real father wasn't in the military. He worked for a newspaper. I didn't press, though — I may know his story but I've never known his name. Besides, I'd like to think I already know who my father is. (I mean you.)

I am just joking around.

Do you know, sometimes back home when I meet people for the first time and they ask "What are you?" (the question I hate), I tell them, "My father is American," or "My father is white," or, if I want to be more specific, "My father is from Denmark." It's not a lie, because you are the father who raised me. It's a test for me, in a way, to see if I feel strongly enough about a person to go the extra distance and clarify. And often I simply don't.

But really. What kind of answer do you expect from a question like that, *What are you?* Not a straight one, surely. What are *you?*

June 21:

This afternoon they have taken me to a karaoke bar in what seems to be somebody's living room. I can't tell what is a home or what is a store here. I could hear voices from other rooms, though, and the sounds of cooking. There's an open window with bars on it behind the sweltering vinyl couch. The walls are cracked and dirty. The floor, bare concrete. Other things to note: a large-screen TV (if you want to talk about lack of modern technology, you'll be glad to see they've not missed out on what matters); a couple of plastic sitting stools, kid-size; a disco ball hanging from a hook on the ceiling in the corner.

I didn't want to go but Ha insisted. "We do many things together, we make the good memories for you when you to go away." She says, "In Vietnam, the man, they are addict. To karaoke. Like when you no want to stop drink the beer? But here, no go home to wife — sing, sing, sing instead!" And she laughs.

The images on the screen are of men and women walking together under palm trees; a man singing with a pained expression and clenching his fist in front of his chest; silhouettes against a backdrop of the ocean. The verses of the song are in Vietnamese, but the chorus is in English. "Thank you, America, no more do we roam, thank you, Democracy, for our new home," or something crazy like that. This music was recorded by Vietnamese singers in Canada or France or the States, then imported back into Vietnam.

"They want to make present for you," says Ha.

The youngest boy kneels on the floor, wailing off-key into the microphone. He keeps glancing toward me and cracking up, and so do the others. I'm not sure if they're laughing at me for some reason or at themselves for trying to imitate the singer on TV, so I just keep politely smiling. The music makes the room seem bigger than it is. They hold the microphone out to me. I say I don't want to. They keep insisting and I keep refusing.

"We just try to have good time, make funny," says Ha.

"I can't sing."

Thi places her hand on my leg. "It is easy," she says in a soft, careful voice.

"I don't like this music," I say.

Another song comes on and Thi reaches for the microphone.

"This is the song she give to her father for when he is away." Ha sits back against the couch, tired. "Her father, ten year ago, he go away to America." The melody is familiar, though the words running across the screen are Vietnamese. I realize then: it is an American song re-done by a Vietnamese singer. I have to laugh.

"Why you laugh?" Ha asks, surprised.

"In America," I try to explain, "Richard Marx, this singer? He's bad. This is a bad song." I don't know how else to say it.

Ha looks confused.

"Not good," I say. But I want to explain more clearly what I mean by "bad." I want to tell her how sometimes someone might say a thing that's meant to be sincere and true, but they say it in such a generic way the truth is taken out of it. I want to explain to her about both the irony and pain of this, how it's a distressing fact of commercial society, how it is both so upsetting and so ridiculous, how my even trying to explain it is also ridiculous and demeaning and untrustworthy of whatever the truth of the experience is, and how sometimes all you can do about that finally is — laugh. That is all I mean. Really.

Ha doesn't quite get it, of course. She says, "He is not good?" and shakes her head. "Wow." But it's me she's looking at in disbelief.

On screen a pretty woman walks along a white beach. The water sparkles. The wind blows her hair off her shoulders as she hugs herself and gazes out over the sea with glossy eyes. Then her face is superimposed onto the sky. (Dear Father: it is *your* stoicism I've inherited.) But I became ashamed at that moment. Here was Thi, sitting on her stool singing her heart out, and there was my aunt crying when she first saw me, and then I thought of Mom, and I looked at Ha, who was watching her daughter sing, and Ha's eyes, black and worried as they are. Sorrow is what is infectious here. I wish I could take back what I said about that song, but I can't.

Here are the Vietnamese lyrics:

Em ở đâu, em làm gì,
Thi anh cũng đợi em về nơi đây.
Tim anh thương nhớ vưi đầy,
Thi anh vẫn ở nơi này chờ em.

Even though I've never liked the song, the American version, it's one I've heard a thousand times. In English the refrain goes: no matter this, no matter that, "I will be right here waiting for you," or "I will be always waiting for you," or something like that. It's pretty corny but as you can see, it makes sense.

And there's a story about Ha's husband I'd forgotten until just now. Mom told it to me, the year she died.

Ha's husband's family had applied to go to America back before Ha and her husband were married, and it took some years for the application to be approved, as those things do. When it came through, after Ha and Cuong had married, Cuong's family forced him to divorce Ha so he could leave with them. That is the family ethic here. Cuong went with his parents and brothers, and they settled in San Francisco. Six months later, he committed suicide by jumping off the Bay Bridge. Did Mom tell you this? I hadn't really thought about it much when she told me. Just another sad story and there were plenty of them. But now I think I see how it must've been incomprehensible, to go from here to there, to be suddenly in a place where all you had previously known no longer counts and you know you cannot go back.

They haven't asked me anything about Mom's death. Maybe because there is nothing I can tell them about loss they don't already know. For all I think I understand here, I take another step and the ground collapses yet again. It's better not to believe too strongly in anything, it seems. Mom was not the last or only person to leave my cousins here.

And when *you* left home all those years ago, Dad, I mean Denmark, I mean your *first* home, how did you prepare yourself? At what point did you know you would not return? Did you believe from the start that the past doesn't matter? Or did you adopt that belief later, along the way, because it became necessary to do so?

A late lunch. Aunt Long lays out dishes on the floor in the back room where all the beds are. We each have our own bowl of rice. They hand me a fork at first because they believe I won't know how to use chopsticks, but I do know that much at least. They seem pleased.

One of the boys, the one who sang for me, has gone now to stand in the doorway with his back to the outside. He is leaning his shoulder against the door frame, his limbs are loose and thin. His yellow T-shirt has a faded pony decal on it. I think he is watching me; I'm writing about him, this very moment. The sunlight touches the top of his head and the rest of him is under the shade of the house, so that it is like the whole dusty white-hot brightness outside is emanating from the back of his head. His face is calm and brown and shady. He turns a piece of fruit, a lychee, in his hands. I can hear the buzz of scooter engines and a dog barking and voices on the street behind him.

The lychee is golf ball–size and covered with a skin of red-orange prickles that look like giant spider legs. The boy laughs when he holds it out to me. I shrug. He shows me: he sticks his fingers through the prickles, pushes his thumbnails into the ruddy skin — it splits into two perfect halves. The fruit inside is wet-looking and pulpy and translucent white. He pops the fruit into his mouth and sucks on it. Then he spits a small, black pit into his palm. He holds it up between his thumb and forefinger.

"That is everything," he says, grinning, then tosses it outside over his shoulder through the open doorway. He hands me the two pieces of prickly skin left over.

June 22:
Last night we went to a Saigon nightclub. Girls there wore red lipstick and long sleeveless evening dresses. They were all very slim, with their black hair swept on top of their heads to show off skinny necks and arms and tiny shoulder blades. I felt certain I was bigger. The band was playing a Beatles song. *Let it be, let it be,* in heavy accents, making the statement sound absurd and far too heartfelt. But I *am* trying, is what I thought.

(Some of these girls, my cousins told me after we'd been there a little while, are actually escort girls or prostitutes; they dance with businessmen and foreigners and in some places there're back rooms for them to go into. Not in this place, though, they assured me: "Only dance here." My cousins spoke about this with an odd mixture of spite and plain admiration. Clearly, these girls make more money than any of my cousins do, and they are better looking and far better dressed. This is what my cousins seemed to think. "But you pretty like them," they said to me. "You probably make many, many money if you go dance with some old men." This soon became a joke, with them pointing to certain men, the fat ones, the uncontestably ugly ones, the old ones, and asking me, "How you like dance with him? Or him?" And they would laugh when I gave the appropriately firm refusal.)

Along with Thi, Ha's daughter, were two more girls and three boys, all around my age or a few years younger. When I first sat down, the boys kept looking at me and nudging each other.

"They no believe you Vietnamese," Thi told me. "They say if you Vietnamese, why no speak Vietnam? All Vietnamese speak Vietnam."

They asked me to dance several times, but I didn't feel like it and kept saying no. Except once. I'll get to that, though.

When our drinks came, Thi's boyfriend, Minh, paid even though Ha protested. When they moved onto the floor to dance, Ha told me Minh's family is poor, like hers, and she is worried about Thi leaving her to marry Minh. "He have no money, she have no money, and I have no daughter then. I say, why?" They were all dancing in a circle and sort of swaying side to side. None of them were very good dancers.

"Minh seems nice, though," I said.

Ha frowned. "Vietnam men no good." Mom used to say this was why she married a Westerner.

Ha and I sat drinking our 333 beers.

Ha raised her can. "I am too old to dance," she declared.

"No, you're not," I told her, and we smiled at each other.

Later, the band played a tango and people began dancing in couples, ballroom style. Girls danced with girls and younger kids danced with older cousins or sisters or brothers. A disco ball spun red and green patterns of light over the floor. Mom loved the tango; she used to call it "mysterious." I began to feel sad, but awake, and everything I looked at now appeared hyperreal, magnified. People moved in slow motion, and they all seemed to me very, very beautiful. Especially those sleek thin girls at the other end of the floor in their fancy dresses, their red lips, their plate-like faces. I felt all at once grateful and jealous and intoxicated. I felt as if a gift was being handed me — or maybe it was just the alcohol — but this sight, these thoughts, crystallized into one benevolent moment. Then I saw a woman in a brown fur coat. She had pale skin and a smooth, fine-featured face, and she was walking in a regal, sultry manner, in a way women do not walk (unless they know they're being watched, I think) along the edge of the dance floor, several paces in front of a man following her. She stopped, her chin up. Then she removed her coat and for one moment in the dark it looked as if there was nothing beneath that fur coat but a small, black empty space. Then I saw her leg showing through the slit in her black gown.

One of the boys returned to the table and gestured for me to dance with him. This time I said yes. He didn't speak a word the entire time we danced, but when we looked at each other, he smiled. He was tall and took long steps. I guess he didn't talk because he didn't speak any English. He had a beautiful smile though, warm.

When everyone was sitting again, he sat leaning back in his chair with his arms crossed, ankle on his knee, and I noticed he didn't talk as much as the others. His lips were sort of square and permanently set in a slight smile as if he had a secret. His eyes were brown and lazy with heavy eyelids that blinked very slowly, and he smoked his cigarette in a calm, efficient way I found attractive. Through Ha, he said it was nice to meet me. His name was Vu. I said it was nice to meet him, too. He said something else and Ha translated, "He has brother in Los Angeles. Maybe one day he go to Los Angeles also."

"Does he want to go to Los Angeles?" I asked.

Ha asked him. "He say no," she told me.

June 23:

Tonight I sat up with Ha and she was a little drunk and ended up taking out photos her husband's family had sent her.

"At the airport." She showed me pictures of her and her husband, her husband and their daughter, her husband and his family.

"You look very sad," I said, repeating what they say to me constantly, thinking it would be appropriate.

"Naturally, naturally," Ha responded. She turned the page. "His first day in America." A picture of the family walking down a sidewalk on a street of houses. "Where he live in America." The husband kneeling next to a stereo and television set, posing with his hand on his leg, the carpet under his shoes white and thick. "In the first month he send to me three hundred dollars, I don't know how," she said with awe.

I said, "Well, that's not too much money in America."

"My husband at his job. He wash the dishes in China restaurant." He is a skinny, lanky man wearing a white apron and his eyes are red because the photo was taken with a flash.

"Look," she said, and turned to the photos from the funeral. "This one," she said, "my favorite." It was an open casket service, and she pointed to a photo of the man's face. His eyes were closed and his thin lips smiling, but the picture was out of focus because the photographer had leaned too close. "My husband's family, when they return to Vietnam they bring me the ashes," said Ha. "They bring many paper, too, but I don't know, they are in English." She brought these out to show me — a removal permit for the ashes and a photocopy of the death certificate. Under cause of death was a stamp which read "pending investigation." I tried to explain.

"Oh," said Ha. "Why do they give me these."

"I don't know." I tried to say it hopefully.

"There was another man on the bridge," said Ha, "and he hear my husband, he hear him call."

"What did he say?"

"I do not know . . ." Ha looked at me, confused.

"What did he call?"

"You are thirsty?" She held up her 333 beer can.

No, no, I waved my hands no.

Ha tipped her head to drink the beer. She peered curiously at the can. "I drink the beer, I smoke the cigarette, you not know, here in Vietnam in my life now days, I live like the man. In Vietnam, Vietnam woman trap. So I live like the man. But Vietnam man no good."

I nodded.

"You know, I wish to tell your mom, she like big sister to me, you know — if ever I see her — I am sorry. I cannot do like she tell to us. Be strong, no let man be so important. I try, but no good for me now, here, in Vietnam now days."

I started to say, "She would've understood —"

"My husband, he jump. Like fish." Ha cupped her hand around her mouth. "He call, help."

"Yes."

"But he already jump. Why he call help? I never to understand." She shrugged, reached for another beer. She said, "Maybe I am just stupid drunkard."

I can't sleep.

I have heard — it is possible — water can become concrete. And that a body descending far enough through the air will at some point reach terminal velocity. And go no faster. Need go no faster. And still shatter all of its bones on the surface of what is at that moment, for him, rock-hard water.

If this is true (I fear) it must mean the substance of things need not be consistent with any fixed reality but is determined by other factors, such as where and how fast we enter a new environment. In the dark here with my flashlight I am writing to you, beside these shaded walls and my sleeping cousins, the boys all jumbled up like puppies, everyone touching. I feel an awful dread, as if I may not make it to tomorrow, or I might live but have no one to share my life with and no place to feel I belong to, and each continued affection for any person who passes in or out of my life will bring with it only the challenge of new pain, while the hollow in my stomach repeats, *I dare you to live here,* over and over.

There is a piece of night sky peeking through a corner where the wall doesn't meet the ceiling. It is a very soft glowing dark blue and there are actually a few faint stars visible. If it could be as simple as saying right or wrong, what Ha's husband did — but it never is.

June 24:
I went into the bathroom last night because I couldn't sleep. I squatted and peed over the toilet hole, then put my hands in the water tub. The water was cool and ripply, reflecting the sky because of the roofless bathroom. I looked past my reflection to the bottom of the tub, where there was a painted scene of two ducks floating down a river beneath some Chinese characters. My hands in the water made crisp, splashing noises.

I woke again because of the mosquitoes. I sat up and cussed and slapped at my legs. One of my cousins woke and shook my aunt awake, and they set up the mosquito net around me. I didn't say thank you, even though I felt bad about it. I just crawled under the net and closed my eyes and wished I could understand things better here.

▪ ▪ ▪

June 26:

I've been writing in two notebooks, one for myself and these pages to you. This is why I didn't write you yesterday.

Today Vu came to Aunt Long's when Minh came to visit Thi. Ha cooked lunch for everyone, and afterward Aunt Long sat cross-legged on the floor, one knee up, and cut fruit with a big kitchen knife. She peels apples and oranges so the skin comes off in one long spiral, just like Mom used to. Funny, now I know where Mom got it from.

The oranges here are not actually orange, they are green — something to do with having no frost.

After lunch, I sat on the stoop outside to read. I've been reading *The Asian Journal of Thomas Merton,* one of the only books in English at the used book store, left behind by some other passing-through American, I suppose. While I was reading, Vu came and sat beside me. He said a few things in Vietnamese, I guess hoping I knew at least a little. I was truly sorry I didn't.

He pointed to my book and in English asked, "What is?"

I showed it to him. He held it in his hands and stared at it as if looking hard enough would tell him what it was about. He has nice hands. (Am I really writing this to you? Should I move to my other notebook now? But you should know these things, too, about your daughters, I think.) His hands are square with long, slightly knuckly fingers; the lines of his palms are deep, coarse. His fingernails were dirty. I thought of his hands touching me; I couldn't help wondering. They looked as if they would be gentle and probably naive but in that naivete not exactly generous, not exactly unselfish — but that isn't the real point. The real point is that I was trying to picture in my mind a union. Maybe you thought you saw something like this, too, in her? Before the two of you had speech, a common language, to divide you?

He handed the book back and I had an idea. I got out my traveler's phrasebook. Unfortunately, it only has travel-related questions such as: *Where is the bathroom? train station? a room with air-conditioning? How do I get to (this place)? I would like to go to (that place).* And lists of foods and numbers. There were a few questions in the greetings section, though. He pointed to:

How old are you?
I pointed to: *Twenty-three.* Then I asked him.
Twenty-four.
What is your religion?
I had to search for it. *Not religious.*
He looked surprised. "No," he said, with disbelief but smiling, shaking his head.
I shrugged.
He pointed to *Buddhism.* "Number one," he said. "The best."
He went back to the phrasebook. *What are your hobbies?*
I read the list. There weren't any specific or interesting enough to really explain much, so I chose: *Reading. Music. Hiking.* He laughed a little and shook his head. He flipped to the glossary in the back and pointed to the word *plant.*
"You grow?" I said.
His eyes got this wonderful glow. His whole face did, as if he was smiling though his mouth was still. He motioned with his hands as if digging and putting something into the ground. I nodded. I can't tell you

Not a thought to be finished, I guess. I am content just to sit. We are under a bridge, by the river.

June 27:
I saw a Scandinavian couple today. I could tell by their accent. They were in the market, the clothes vendors pressing the woman to buy shirts and skirts which would've never fit, and the woman was irritated, repeating "I don't want, no no!" as if she were scolding a dog. Inconsideration on both sides. The Scandinavians were sweating — it's very hot here — their faces red, their T-shirts sticking to them. The woman was wearing baggy jungle-print pants that made me think she must've bought them with a certain idea of Vietnam in mind. The man was handsome and blond. He was yelling, "Bao nhieu, bao nhieu?" to none of the vendors in particular and laughing, as if it meant "hello" rather than "how much." *How much? How much for everything?* he seemed to be saying. And I thought of you, Dad. Of you leaving

Denmark, even younger than I am now, and what kind of traveler you might've been then. I thought you must have traveled with much more at stake than this couple, Scandinavian though you all may be. You must've appeared *leaner*, less obvious, warier of yourself and where you called home. There must've been something dissatisfied in you to drive you to live for years as you did, migrating steadily from one foreign place to the next. Unwilling to depend upon anyone but yourself, for you were refusing to partake in the world as you had so far found it — unjust. I wonder, did you walk among people and places and not speak a word, or did you talk all the time, freely, as you do now to us and have for as far back as I can remember? And did you know, then, that the farther you went, the more ruined the air would become between you and those left behind? For quite plainly, to them, you were *refusing* them — you were not returning *by choice.*

As obviously this was not so for us.

I picture you: your angular Aryan blondness (both natural and worthless to you), your collar turned up against the cold in some gray city at dawn, your prideful reserve, your restlessness, your injured eyes. I wish I could have known you then. I would've asked you questions, dealt you the future.

I feel an attachment as deep as my resistance to you as I think these thoughts.

From *The Asian Journal of Thomas Merton:*

> Calcutta is shocking because it is all of a sudden a totally different kind of madness, the reverse of that other madness, the mad rationality of affluence and overpopulation. America seems to make sense, and is hung up in its madness, now really exploding. Calcutta has the lucidity of despair, of absolute confusion, of vitality hopeless to cope with itself. Yet undefeatable, expanding without and beyond reason but with nowhere to go. An infinite crowd of men and women camping everywhere as if waiting for

someone to lead them in an ultimate exodus into reason-
ableness, into a world that works, yet knowing already beyond contradiction that in the end nothing really works,
and that life is all anicca, dukkha, anatta, that each self is
the denial of the desires of all the others — and yet somehow a sign to others of some inscrutable hope.

June 28:
Tonight an old friend of Mom's who heard I was in Saigon took
me to dinner. Mom's friend was the wife, My-Kim. She and her
husband are in the jewelry export-import business, they seemed
proud to say.

They picked me up in their shiny black Hyundai and we drove
down the narrow street away from my cousins' house. They had
invited only me, none of my cousins, and that made me feel awkward. I sat in the backseat with their fifteen-year-old daughter,
Trang. The street was too narrow for a car and so crowded with
people and bicycles that we had to go two miles an hour with
My-Kim's husband leaning on the horn. That is how they drive
here. We had all the windows rolled up, air-conditioner on, and a
tape of the Eagles playing loud. The Eagles are big in Vietnam
right now.

We pulled onto a bigger street. Several large trucks with bun-
dled loads rumbled by, but ours was the only passenger-size vehicle on the road trying to merge with the scooters and cyclos
and bicycles and pedestrians. Occasionally scooter passengers or
cyclists reached out and pressed their hands against our windows for balance, never even glancing in at us behind the tinted
glass. And we couldn't hear any of the clamor outside because we
had the Eagles turned up so loud, plumbing our senses. The first
time I ever heard "Hotel California," I can remember, I was seven
years old and it terrified me. I didn't understand it. All that
stuff about a place you can never leave and not being able to remember and dancing to forget, and that image of something,
they never say what it is, rising up through the air — all of that

spooked me when I was seven. I would plug my ears whenever that song came on the radio. (I know it's all the same to you, you won't even call it music, just noise.) Now, in Saigon, they are slow-dancing to it.

Trang was looking out the window, mouthing the words. And I understood what she was probably feeling right then, seeing everything on the other side of the glass go by so quietly and smoothly, those sights enhanced by the music. She turned to me and began practicing her English.

"Do you go to school?" she asked me.

"Not anymore. I just graduated from college," I said, carefully and slowly.

"Ah" — making a show of searching for her words — "have you like this school?"

"Sometimes I did," I said.

She smiled. "Yes, me, too. Sometimes I like. But most I want to travel. Like you."

"Where would you like to travel?"

"Out from Vietnam," she replied. "When I travel, I want to travel for my life."

A car gave her that, I thought: *a car and a song.*

They took me to their apartment. My-Kim's husband had some business to finish, they said, and also, I think they just wanted to show me the place. This is how the other half lives, I guess. It was small but new. Upholstered furniture, tile on the floor, full-size kitchen range, flush toilet, two upstairs bedrooms — they showed it all to me. Then I sat on the couch and they poured me a Pepsi even though I said I wasn't thirsty.

My-Kim's husband went upstairs to use the phone. My-Kim sat on the other end of the couch with her legs crossed and her face turned toward me. Trang sat on a chair across from us. "My mother ask, you like our home, yes?"

"It's very nice." I couldn't say what I really thought.

My-Kim spoke more and laughed, swinging her foot slightly. Trang translated, "My mother, she say she very good friend with your mother once. They both like to eat at nice restaurant and go see American movies with American boyfriend. My mother, she have very much sad but good memory of your mother."

"Did your mother know my real father?" I had to try.

My-Kim's reply was brief. "She not know him herself, but she hear he is good man. He die in the war, he is good soldier. Your mother have many boyfriend before she marry. Like all the pretty Saigon girl."

My-Kim's husband came down the stairs, announcing something to My-Kim and Trang. Trang smiled at me and nodded. "We ready go now. We go to very nice restaurant. You will like, my father think."

We got back in the car and drove through the now dark streets. Scooters made herds of bobbing headlights. We drove into the Cholon district, the Chinatown of Saigon, where we passed several high-rise hotels. We stopped in front of one with lights along even the edges of its wide gold-brick steps. A gaudy monster. But just across the street — you'd think it was a canyon, so vast the leap — the usual city tent-shops, and half-naked cyclo drivers loitering on the curbs, and dusty stalls where men sat at rickety card tables, drinking beer and talking loudly.

We got out and stood on the hotel steps while My-Kim's husband went to park the car. And this is when it happened.

I spotted a dirty little orange kitten in the middle of the sidewalk, meowing. I couldn't hear it, could just see its mouth opening and closing. It was tiny and its ribs were showing and suddenly I had no appetite. Yes, perhaps my sympathies were mislaid but the feeling was still real, I mean it was a physical, palpable nausea.

"This song, I hate this song." Trang tilted her head to listen to the karaoke music wafting out from one of the tents. It took me a second to realize she wasn't talking about the kitten. "It is story of two lovers, but she is to go away and she promise she return if he wait for her at this bridge. And he go, and he wait, and he still wait at end of song." She rolled her eyes. "It is like many song, how you say, very common. Very popular music with the, do you know, country people."

I was still upset by the time we got to the table. (I had lingered to pet the kitten but they had called me on — "Thuy! We go eat now!" — Trang translating for her parents. And in the elevator up to the restaurant I had held back tears and stared at my feet with the worst, trapped feeling.) On the menu Pepsi was spelled "Pessi." When it came time to order, I smiled and said, "I'll have a Pessi." I wanted to do something irreverent, I guess, but nobody noticed, since that is how they all pronounce Pepsi themselves. So the joke — like many — was on me and for me alone.

I decided to order the most expensive meal on the menu and eat only two bites of it. Cowardly righteousness, I admit. But in the end I ordered only the second-most expensive item: the "biffsteak." Eight U.S. dollars. That is the cost of a piece of luxury here. And to come all this way to eat steak, imagine. My hands would not stop shaking. I was envisioning myself running, meat in hands, out of the restaurant, down the stairs, out the hotel door, and feeding it to the skinny kitten on the sidewalk.

But when the steak came, I ate it. Half of it.

"You are not hungry?" Trang looked surprised when I stopped eating.

"Eat," urged My-Kim, one of the few words she could say.

"I can't eat any more," I said.

My-Kim took the rest of my steak and cut it into small pieces and wrapped it up in a napkin. She and her husband began exchanging words in an argumentative tone. The grease was leaking through the napkin, so she had to use a few more. She slipped the whole mess into her purse. I felt terrible after that. I felt awful for every reason.

We drove past buildings with water- and grime-stained facades. We drove over the river, brown and bobbing with bits of trash and rusty barrels. Shanties on the far bank with fallen-in Popsicle-stick roofs. People everywhere. On rooftops, under them, moving in every direction up and down the streets. Standing barefoot on a bridge railing. Little shirtless boys with hair in their eyes, mouths open in soundless yells as we went by. I was looking out the window, too, yes.

▪ ▪ ▪

June 29:

I don't know what my name is anymore.

Last night after dinner they dropped me off at Aunt Long's. Everyone was still awake and Vu was there with Minh again. I was glad to see him but didn't feel as if I could be very good company, so I took my notebook and went and sat outside on the stoop, facing the street. The houses were quiet and mostly dark. A few men walked by, and pairs of children holding hands; they glanced at me without any real acknowledgment. Way down at the end of the lane, I could just glimpse the bigger street from where a low hum of traffic and activity still came.

Vu came out and sat beside me and offered me a piece of gum. I smiled and put it in my pocket. He sat squatting with his arms outstretched over his knees, fingers brushing the dirt. We sat for a few minutes like that. Then he looked sideways at me and put his hand on my shoulder and sort of gently shoved it. And he smiled; warm, dopey.

He pointed to the cover of my notebook, where I'd been practicing writing my Vietnamese name. "Is you?"

I nodded.

"Thuy," he said, pronouncing it the way they do. He shook his head, laughing slightly. He took my notebook and held it up. "Like here, no," he said, taking the pen out of the spine. He pointed to each letter of my name: T-H-U-Y. "Is no word like here," he said. Then he wrote it again with an accent over it so it looked like: *Thúy.*

"Yes," he said, smiling, and handed it back to me.

I looked at it and blinked and something unfolded inside me, the oddest, loneliest sensation. I could feel the strain of my hair in its ponytail like a headache. I could feel everything. Suddenly Vu was looking dumbfounded at me and trying to pat me on the back, then he jumped up and ran inside calling to the rest of them (so much for our mutual comprehension), and Ha came out and sat down and tried to comfort me.

She said, "My English not so good, but I listen, I try, yes? Maybe I no understand all the word but I feel, yes, what you want talk about?" And she gestured between us.

But all I could do was apologize and cry and feel guilty for confusing them. She kept asking, did I miss my mother or father, and I kept saying no, that wasn't it, but she didn't seem to believe me and kept asking me again. I said, "I don't understand." Her eyes were so concerned, I don't think I have ever seen a person so genuinely worried. *"Toi khong hieu,"* I said carefully. And watched her face cloud some more. *"Toi khong biet."* *I don't understand. I don't know.* The few words I have learned here.

Then she got me up. "Sometimes, when I am sad also, I no like sleep, I like to ride, all around the city."

We found a cyclo driver and rode around in the cyclo for the next half hour, Ha with her arm around me the whole time. There was less traffic at night but still it was busy. Voices called back and forth between houses, kids ran back and forth, voices echoed. Saigon at night is warm and humid. I saw men leaning back in their chairs at a café, cigarettes in mouths and shirts open, exposed chests oily-looking in the lamplight. Out a window of one house a whole crowd of children was leaning, laughing and squealing and handing down something to the woman on the patio below. I saw yellow lizards dart down dusty gutters.

We stopped at a food vendor's cart on one corner and Ha bought me a sandwich, insisted really, because I'd said I wasn't hungry. She pointed to my necklace and told me to cover it up. "It is late," she said. "You no want they rob, the boys." She would worry about me as long as I was here, I realized.

We drove around some more and I ate the sandwich. It turned out I was hungry after all.

I checked the dictionary. *Thuy* is a word usually paired with another to mean something. For instance:

    thùy = boundary, border

with the example:

    ngủời linh chiên trân ngòai biên-thùy

which means:

    the soldier stands guard way out by the distant border

And there is:

    thủy = water

which can make:

　　thủy-dịch = aqueous humor
　　thủy-tai = disaster caused by water, e.g., flood
　　thủy-táng = burial at sea
　　thủy-ách = drowning
　　thủy-bọ = amphibious

But there're only two that match the accent Vu wrote for me:

　　thúy-uyên = abyss

And as a single word:

　　thúy = a kind of bird

I know which name Vu gave me, but I don't know which Mom was thinking of when she named me. Do you? I would assume not.

A dog is passing by with a chicken in its mouth. I am sitting on the stoop, facing the street. The dog is keeping his eye on me as if he's afraid I want to steal his chicken.

June 30:

I have these questions. What did the streets of Southeast Asia, of Saigon, mean to you? Did you pity them? Did you ever love them? Did the heavy air in that single, brief time you were in this part of the world make you breathe differently? Or did the sights of sallow-faced men and women crouching under grass roofs and the unfamiliar animals pulling wooden carts and the crumbling buildings scare you? In 1975 when you sat on your sofa in front of that television set or in your cubicle at work, and watched us in the news, and it began to evolve inside you that there was some key role for you to play in this unfolding drama — whom, or what, truly did you mean to rescue?

Now that I'm here, I guess I want to know why you took *this* from us.

I look around me and see how the traffic, though it appears hectic, regulates itself moment by moment in its own fashion, and how the boys hang out of the bus windows and doors, yelling freely, how accustomed to the thickness and sadness of mobility the drivers here have all grown.

And though I may not be able to remember the facts of leaving, I realize leaving has nevertheless made me what it makes people: dissatisfied. And I think of you, my *adoptive*, who left his own home years ago and won't return (the old country, you always called it), and I think it must be tenfold in you. Or something.

I don't know if I can actually send this to you anymore.

June 31:
In the morning, Ha took me to the park which used to be the cemetery where she said my father was buried. She meant the one who was in the military. I didn't have the heart to tell her the man she meant was not my real father. I listened to the stories she told about this man, though. She even said I look like him. He was a good man, a good soldier. I guess he might as well've been my father. He was more father to me than the man — to be crude but precise — who actually planted the seed, as you have been more father to me than he.

We sat on the park bench and I took a picture of Ha. She seemed not to understand why I would want to take a picture of her and gave me a doubtful look instead of smiling.

From a drink vendor we bought Pepsis. Pessis. (If it were not so difficult for me to laugh sometimes, I guess I would laugh now.) The bottles here are smaller than in America; the label reads "Made in Thailand."

They are not even real Pepsis.

We walked around the park some more. There was a zoo nearby, attached to the park, Ha told me. She was offering out of obligation, I realized, out of the thought that this was the kind of thing a visitor might want to see. I shrugged. I didn't have the energy. She put her hand on my arm. "The zoo here," she said frowning, "is bad." She pointed to her own ribs. "The animals no eat." I understood then that what she meant by "bad" was the same as "sad."

"I don't want to see it," I said.

We have traveled worlds. Father, would you admit? Do you re-member? *Once you wanted me to be a stewardess.*

August 1 (on the plane):
They are kind, thoughtful, tactful. They are distributing pillows and blankets, coming round now to close the shades, for we are traveling too fast for the light to change at its natural pace any-more.

Afterword

THE SHADOW-SELLER

The old woman under the tree is propositioning any male passersby who appear to be foreign or Viet-Kieu and in the company of local women. All morning I have observed these exchanges from the café across the street. A local girl cannot walk down the street alongside a Viet-Kieu cousin or brother without the old woman beckoning to them — it will be assumed that the girl is a prostitute, walking alone with a nonlocal man. In fact, a local girl walking alone with any man is ill regarded. I fall into that harder-to-ascertain category of being Viet-Kieu (though often enough I'm mistaken for just another foreigner, Japanese or Mexican or Italian even, go figure) and female besides. Being a female of Asian appearance in itself makes me dubious, in their eyes, and places me in an incongruous position: I may not be expected to uphold traditional virtues, but I am not exempt — as a white female would be — from judgment, either.

A Swede or a Hollander, a big man anyway, with a mustache and something gallant and soft to his appearance beneath his big muscles, approaches my table and invites me on a boat ride. He has already rented the boat, just happens to be traveling alone, thought he would ask, would I like to join him?

I decline.

Would we get past the old woman? No. Besides, I have my reasons.

The old woman is ancient and crooked, like a crone in a mythology, with one corner of her mouth perpetually grinning, one staring pallid blue eye. The deformed here, they are deformed as only they could be in a story. She is stooped, in black peasant rags, standing barefoot in the dirt beneath her tree. It is not even a large tree; I don't know what kind it is. Maybe it bears fruit; there're some buds and long, weepy-thin branches. She is indicating the shade of her tree to the current passing couple. They stop, a little taken aback. What is she offering them? Relief from the heat? An old woman's concerned advice? If she is selling something they don't understand right away, for there is no blanket or basket of goods laid out. "Five dollar," she's saying, "five dollar." (I know this because I've heard it, have already passed by close enough to hear it.) And she is looking only at the man, an obvious visitor, the one who must be the spender here. "Five dollar," she says, "more cheap than hotel. Very private. No police, no police."

It's true it's the only tree in sight. It's true it's sheltered by a building and set around the corner off the street, a very strategic location. It's true its shade, though patchy, is tempting, inviting in this blasted heat. And did the old woman plant it there herself, years ago, I wonder, with such foresight as this when once she was still beautiful enough to earn a decent living in this manner, under trees?

The local girl is shaking her head vigorously, covering her face, innocently horrified, while her Viet-Kieu companion speaks a harsh string of Vietnamese words at the old woman — he's not so Americanized as I am, can retaliate competently in the mother tongue. He puts his hand protectively on the local girl's shoulder, to draw her away, and the old woman spits at their feet.

"No, you are wrong," I imagine the young man will tell his parents and elder relatives when he returns to America (for they are probably all former dissidents too afraid to revisit the motherland themselves). "It's not a Communist economy over there anymore. No, actually, it is quite capitalist now."